Lammastide

Abigaile Maydon

MOONRAKER

First published in Great Britain by ignotus press 2004
BCM-Writer, London WC1N 3XX
© Abigaile Maydon 2004

All rights reserved. The book is sold subject to the conditions that it shall not, by way of trade or otherwise, be re-lent, re-sold, hired out or otherwise circulated without the publisher's prior consent in any form of binding or cover other than that in which it is published and without a similar condition including this condition being imposed on the subsequent purchaser. No part of this publication may be reproduced, stored in a retrieval system, or transmitted in any form or by any means, electronic, mechanical, photocopying, recording or otherwise, without prior permission of the publishers and copyright holders.

British Library Cataloguing in Publication Data
ISBN: 1 903768 17 9

Printed in Great Britain by A2 Reprographics
Set in Baskerville Old Face 11pt

Cover photograph: Abigaile Maydon

This book is dedicated to my mother and grandmother who taught me to listen in the stillness ... to Jim for all his love and support ... to Suzanne Ruthven who believed in me ... and to the Ancestors, everywhere.

Lammastide

5

JAKE

August 1999

The valley was lit up by the sinking sun, soon to set on the other side of the hill. Some had doubtless thought it an ancient burial mound, and as I drove by I mused on the warrior it might have held. These thoughts kept me on the straight and narrow for a while, postponing the inevitable slide to shame, to a pain I knew was coming. And so I focused on the great shadows of green thrown up on the face of the hill, the clumps of oaks eerily clinging to the rocks, their own long shadows tracing the bulge of the contours.

My journey was nearly complete. I had made it countless times only to turn back once I saw the gate leading to your house. But now my hands – mottled by time – gripped harder on the steering wheel, forcing me onwards. Time would not grace me with many more opportunities.

The old wooden gate blocking the path was almost consumed with green moss, so that the crumbling structure beneath left a powdery residue on my hands. It swung round with a loud creak cushioned on a clump of nettles. From behind the grey ash trees, an old black billy-goat eyed me satanically, watching my progress along the path.

As I closed the gate, I paused for a brief moment and surveyed the narrowing driveway for the first time. The track had been almost devoured by elder and brambles. Obviously it had few visitors. The pathway, now only just discernable between potholes, narrowed into the deeper shadow of over-hanging branches. Gnarled boughs of old apple trees hung low with pendulous fruit. Some apples had cracked and come away under the weight of their load, discarded like broken toys on the grass below. Through the corridor of shadow, the house seemed to glow with the last golden rays of twilight.

It stood on the edge of a great wood that crowded so closely behind, that it seemed almost poised to devour the sunken terraces and steeply pitched roof. The darkness of the trees casting the Elizabethan gables into sharp relief. Only the decaying ironstone chimneystacks rose defiantly into the grey blue of the evening horizon beyond.

I walked over the dusty remains of a gravelled driveway to a large studded oak door. Gruesome distorted faces were carved in the corbels above, as if to ward off casual visitors. A female gargoyle was spreading herself shamelessly over a water pipe. There was no doorbell, and so I knocked for a while, perversely relieved because there was no answer.

Through one of the murky ground floor window panes I could make out the pattern of a dark flag-stoned corridor, and through others, the dark heavy proportions of country oak furniture. The rooms had heavy curtains and oak panelling and were so dark that I could not what the heavy ornate frames on the walls contained. Becoming bolder in the silence I pushed on further, walking around the yellow crumbling house, past clumps of still blooming hollyhocks until I saw a sunken garden at the back of the house, over which the trees towered.

I saw you there at the end of a stone pergola, framed by cascading boughs of dying roses and jasmine. You were reading in a Victorian summerhouse, and on either side, the crenulated arms of the stone walkways craned to embrace the scene. As a young girl you would have jumped from a columned walkway like this, flinging yourself cat-like onto an imaginary broomstick, convinced you could fly. You had known even then. I recalled with a shudder that still surprised me, the fairytale looks of your youth, the unearthly beauty that swept you along, unaware of the dangers, before it was too late.

I tried to make out your features, sadistically trying to match an old lady's face to my own memories of you, but you kept your head bowed in the shadows, absorbed in the large book you were holding. You were just a beautifully-shaped silhouette of light blue, a cipher symbolising everything to me. The long blue-grey dress covered even your feet.

It was as if time lay suspended between us, as if you knew I was there, but were controlling that impenetrable force that existed between us still. *It was so simple*, this distance of mere yards between us. I just had to cross the sunken lawn to find you, but my heart suddenly felt so heavily constricted that I could hardly breathe. A large black raven glided ominously overhead, and its flight-path crossed the final stage of the journey I should have made - from where I stood - to your side. It reached you in seconds and perched on the windowsill of the summerhouse by your shoulder, as if it were protecting you.

You didn't seem to belong to this house with its rows of blank windows bleakly staring out over the herbaceous borders, which I had imagined often caught your sweeping cloak on misty mornings. Now the evening was drawing in, the sunken lawns were veiled in a fine vaporous blanket, which slowly rose up to devour a tantalising glimpse of what had been. In the half-light, a barn owl skimmed over the surface of the cloud, searching silently for its prey. It seemed so ironic, to witness such a graceful and carefree flight over this mounting tension between us. A wood pigeon sang a sad lament in one of the oaks and all the time you kept on reading, as if obsessed by that book. It seemed as though you dare not lift your eyes in case the haunting memories resumed life once more, and so resolutely you kept your head bowed.

Angrily I kicked the heavy autumnal heads of the fallen flowers in my path, scuffing the dusty gravel of the driveway as I retraced my steps. Suddenly, I was unsure of where this could leave me: this pointless plan I had had of seeing you again after so many years.

Words and memories now seemed too flimsy and unconnected to the stark reality of what had happened to us all those years ago. I now retreated like a coward, convincing myself that the past was best left as a beautiful dream which couldn't be added to, or altered in any way.

Inhaling the safe, strong, practical smell of the car, I breathed a sigh of relief now that the panic I had unexpectedly felt was over. It was still amazing that despite my age, you could make me feel so foolish and vulnerable. Angrily I revved the engine and sped out of the gathering darkness as fast as I could, leaving a whirlwind of dust that veiled the diminishing house in the wing mirrors.

I hoped that I was wrong, that you hadn't seen me behind the strands of hollyhocks. I had felt the shame and frustration of the changes that had slyly crept over me in my old age, and particularly all those wasted years.

Although, on reflection I was sure you *must* have sensed me because you had bristled like an animal sensing the change in the wind, and raised those great pools of light up towards the end of the pergola where I stood transfixed, as I had forty years earlier in another spot. And even though you were now old and weathered you shone out and arrested my breath until I let out a sigh more like a moan. Because my soul was stricken by the beauty that I remembered was in you, as you stared out through long tendrils of white hair that was once golden, and which you still wore in defiant wild waves as you had always done. Your eyes were still as forceful in lighting up that sad face, and the world it contained. I still loved what I had known of you. And even as my soul was breaking for that lament of time - I had felt sure you of all people would escape its grip and I could not bear to see the lines etched over your girl-beauty - you carried on with your book unaware of anything else. Least of all me. I was as unable to enter that sacred world of yours as I ever had been and so I left you, in the isolation in which you have always surrounded yourself.

9

LYDIA

I had been reading the first of my adolescent diaries since that early afternoon and in no time at all, it seemed the cold damp of the evening was setting in. Autumn embracing the dying summer. I had always hated the cutting of the last sheaf of corn, and the dying of the long summers seemed to run on and on forever in my youth.

It was only when I sensed you standing there that I became aware of the lapse of time. Although I knew from my dreams you would come in the end, I hadn't expected it to be now — after all the expanse of time that lay between us, and so I sat paralysed with the shock and the realisation that you *had* come, but too late to conclude anything.

And so I gripped the old battered book, Georgia, my favoured school friend had given me when we were twelve, in which to write my first musings. I fixated on the bright Russian sleigh she had painted on the cover, harnessed by a team of beautiful galloping ponies flying through the night sky. It encapsulated our young dreams and ambitions, and I can still smell those scents of school that cling defiantly to the withering pages. Each time I touch them, I inhale mournfully for those lost days of promise.

I thought back to how we schoolgirls had looked upon the paunchy headmistress, sternly directing assembly from her podium, with revulsion. We vowed never to get a big paunch like she had, or a double chin, or such a weak husband. We wanted to make something of our lives, and we both believed we had the power to live life spectacularly and in our own way. I had my own first thoughts of immortality there in the wizened pew of the chapel. Under the brow of a summer straw hat, crowned with the bright hope of youth, I vainly imagined how playwrights and poets would dramatise my early life, before fame cast its wondrous golden glow upon me. The magenta rays pouring throughout the stained glass window bloodied the feathers of the bronzed eagle on the lectern and I imagined them to be a sign of my metamorphosis.

Rows of school-girls' heads marshalled before us, expanded the flight of fancy and we would imagine how we would become famous actresses, or authors, and the lovers of heroes. The ideal was, to one day be loved, and love beyond measure. Reality quickly snapped us back with the familiar ease of English hymns, lulling us all into a dreamlike euphoria of easy tradition.

Turning the pages of that book I was aware of the razor sharp contrast between what I had planned for myself and what had come to pass. I had envisaged being entwined with my love for life, being amongst children and grandchildren, and your presence sealed my realisation that it had not, and could never have been like that for me. And yet, who would have such a love as this: this love I had felt for you. It still gripped me forcibly so that my laboured breath was caught up with the sigh of the trees around us, as I tried to keep my body still.

And the thought that perhaps you too were filled with this sad reflection, made me unable to look at you when I became aware of your presence - standing there at the end of the pergola. But there was also a more shallow reason, a remnant of my youthful pride that paralysed me. I would have risen and laid my heart open at your feet, even after all these years, if I had not been as vain as a silly young girl. I could not bear the thought of registering the shock of dismay on your face as you beheld all the changes in me; the predictable comparison that I imagined would be inevitable in your mind's eye, which would struggle to comprehend the old lady before you and a beautiful girl from so long ago. Surely my great sadness had etched more than a century of grief and ugliness onto my face: more than you would have expected to find.

For so many years I had strained to find you, to have you here, and now it had come at the wrong moment. You had caught me unawares and drowning in hours of sad recollections. The crescendo was the overwhelming tide of grief I felt as I saw you and it prevented me from moving or speaking.

I was paralysed by the fear that over the past fifty years, I had merely dreamed it had all been so beautiful. My memories were safer left untouched than risking them all for the reality we had left. My legs were aching to walk that short distance, but my heart stopped me all but breathing, and I knew that we were both transfixed on the magnificent bird that passed above both of us on its course.

You deserved some gnostic knowledge of me. But then a *grande mall*, descended over me just as it had when I was young; as it had to the detriment of both of us, and to the others I had showered with it's terrifying catalepsy. I sensed your sadness and isolation over there by the roses, and I charged the closing mist with power so you should not cross it and break the spell.

For my life's theory was triumphant and, nearing its end, I knew if we spoke of it the power would lessen. For as you stood there silent and alone I knew that despite everything, we would die in love with each other, with our untainted pure memories of youth, when we shone brilliantly with pure emotion. Reminiscing in old age would dull all of that, soil its nobility by bringing it to the here and now.

All my life they had tried to tell me it didn't exist, that love was just a metaphor for life and, like a shapeshifter, it changed and adapted according to the weather. My seasons were all rooted in the same eternal source and always returned to it as the circle turned and the winds carried us all helplessly along.

When I heard your car roar so suddenly out of the drive I felt a great relief that you could leave with your memories of me, and mine of you, intact. Yet I baulked at the fact you had left me once more in this vacuum where I could only reach you in my dreams and visions.

.

CHAPTER ONE

July 1941

Lydia and her mother, Isobel, followed the rusty red tractor up the drive to the farmhouse. It was planted neatly on either side with young horse chestnut trees and the summer sun glinted on their billowing leaves. The dusty track swept them past a flinted cattle shed and suddenly, the house was visible, amid the undulating pasture land.

First impressions were difficult because so much of it was hidden behind a wall of voracious ivy and old gnarled thorny rose trees. The red brick, where it was visible, shone out against the endless blue sky. There were three stories to the house and pretty Dutch gable ends to the roof. It had been built in 1760 as the Home Farm for the large estate surrounding Eddleton Hall, whose grounds were being designed by Capability Brown at the time.

The dark green door – painted in the estate's signature colour - swung open easily, to the satisfaction of Billy, the decrepit manager of Eddleton's vast holdings. Lady Eddleton was running the estate with an iron rod in her husband's absence, organising armies of land-girls and Red Cross functions. Her stately home was now overrun with refugees from London, her fields were tended by Italian prisoners-of-war, and hunting was restricted to once a week because the hounds had insufficient meat to maintain stamina. Now that she was reduced to just one maid servant, she had leapt upon the chance to let out

13

Home Farm to her daughter's friend, who was moving from the Midlands to the deepest of rural Norfolk with her own daughter.

The click of the latch echoed over the red stone flags inside and the midday sun immediately thrust the tomblike shadows into brightness once more. Possessive spiders grudgingly scuttled into their crevices. There had been no human occupants here for eight years.

As the door swung slowly to illuminate the dark interior, a crow with reddened eyes lurched out into the sunlight, angrily squawking its disgust at the intrusion. Lydia peered up at Billy's red and veined face, grimly weathered by a life of rain and winds that had originated in Siberia before lashing their fury on the North Norfolk coastline. The skin had slackened around his nose and mouth, his eyes were pinched, and his hooked nose gave him a birdlike look of shifty malevolence. Slicked back iron-grey hair completed the picture of somebody whom the twelve-year-old already in her own mind had turned into a character not to be trusted.

"You'll get lost in 'ere. I suppose you're not used to such a big 'ouse," he shouted after her as she ran to explore the stony passageways. *How dare he?* What did he know of their life before?

"My last house was a lot bigger than this, so I doubt it," she shouted out insolently, challenging him to judge them. Isobel nearly crumpled with embarrassment, but it was funny *and* true. At rare times like this, children could be usefully rude when even she found it difficult to formulate a reply against that kind of indefinable insult.

"Does it have any ghosts?" the child demanded.

"Not that I know of, unless of course ol' Mr Graham comes back. He died of a heart attack in the hall way over there. He'd just come in from seeing to the cows and as he was taking his boots off, he was gone, eva' su sudden. An' thas been empty ever since."

Isobel stifled a laugh. This had conjured visions of human combustion and smoke issuing from a pair of Wellington boots. Death lost all dignity in rubber wellies. How could she shake off this ridiculous scene every time she walked past the door?

He carried on in that dry matter-of-fact Norfolk way. "Shame really, ol' Mr Graham hed jus cured the whole herd from a virus, saved all them little calves and off he went hi'self to the Good Maker. Probably

14

only time the old bastard went to church when he turned up for 'is own fooneral. You mark my words, you'll not see a more godless lot of people as around these parts. They'll only turn up to church once when a vicar comes as' once when he goos, which is about once ev'rey tooo years. S'pose they ken' take it, preaching to just that ol' MacEnzie woman oos'e mad as a goose anyways. You jus' watch out for them ones with the dark ways, them with their flames and fire paradin' round abouts. Don' you hev anything to do with them."

Isobel couldn't imagine what Billy was referring to and certainly couldn't really picture Billy kneeling to anyone, even his Maker

"Mum, the bath's got cement in it!" Lydia yelled down.

Rounding on Billy for an explanation, Isobel found him sloping off towards the door mumbling "Well you wanted isolation and now you hev' it. Most people would be glad for such a 'ouse."

The wave of annoyance passed and she let him go. As he revved up the engine of his tractor, Isobel felt quite alone but also strangely elated after everything that had happened. Somebody had left a card and half a dozen eggs by the old range in the kitchen. It said 'Welcome Home' and it was like a homecoming at last.

The past year had been a terrible shock. Isobel's mother had died suddenly of stomach cancer. As she watched her mother slowly dying, she had felt so helpless and humbled by the extraordinary depths to which the human body can be pushed before giving in. Until the end, they went every day to see this frail shadow of a woman who had been such a stalwart. Her kitchen, once a cosy cave where stockings full of fruit for jam were suspended like stalagmites, was empty and still. And yet she carried on, eyes like dark saucers becoming larger in their sockets. Until one day, nothing. With disbelief they had filed out of the church, and the old charm of the house they had once shared was lost. The memories bubbled up everywhere as a reminder until Isobel could bear it no more, and decided it was time to make a new start.

"Lydia is special," her mother had told Isobel and now she was dead it was becoming more obvious. Lydia now chatted openly about the shadowlands that the old lady sometimes used to talk of, the realms of heaven where the soul would grow or prepare to be reborn, to repeat or learn from the last life's mistakes. Her birthday had been on All Hallows, the day when the world between this and that had been thinnest. The last time she had sat with her grandmother, Lydia remembered the old lady's sense of unease as she described the strange dog howling beneath her bedroom window. Later it seemed as if she knew death was upon her. She only spoke to Lydia of these things because the rest of the family would have laughed, but she knew her granddaughter had inherited the 'eye', and encouraged her to speak of her visions and seeings. And so the girl often fancied she saw fairies tumbling from the ceiling, hoards of beautiful fairy folk launching themselves on to the bed; goblins with black lips in wood thickets; auras of rose pink and spiky blue around the people's heads; and those dreams of flying way above the houses and woods with her grandmother. All these had endured and made up the unearthly nature of her.

Arthur, her father had always been intolerant of this abnormality. He owned a silk factory in Coventry and was unceasingly practical, raging at her to lose her "nonsense and imagination". He called it attention seeking. "Get in the real world child or you'll be no good. I'd like to see you come out to work with me, that'll cheer you up. By God you've been spoilt. If I'd have had a son, *he* would have been different."

Lydia learnt to bury her insights, but when the unexpected telegram came announcing his death she mourned him greatly. After her grandmother's death, only to her mother could she open up and divulge what she heard or saw. Isobel realised what this was doing to her daughter - living on a knifepoint the whole time, appearing one thing to others and never being able to be herself among strangers. As a result, Lydia's skin flared up in angry red wheals of eczema.

There *had* been a beautiful house in Warwickshire with panelled rooms and formal gardens, but it had been the setting of misery for all of them, with Arthur's frequent rages and his obsession with tidiness and order. And when his death came, the realisation that they would never have to feel scared again, seemed to nullify the importance of being left with nothing but debts after the factory had been obliterated in the heavy bombing.

16

It had all been a sham - the sad, safe little life he had carved out for them, but it was also a relief to leave behind even the smallest piece of furniture that might have reminded them of all the oppression. Although they had nothing but each other, there were no more rules and now there was a blank canvas on which to shape their future however they wanted it to be. Isobel's friend, Lily, had come to the rescue and offered them Home Farm for a peppercorn rent. Although she had described it as a 'cold barn of a place', it did have character, and was in the most glorious setting they could have imagined.

Isobel slowly patrolled the endless, draft-blasted corridors of the farmhouse trying to come to terms with both the loss, and the new life, that had suddenly been thrust upon them. Each room echoed with a ghostly bustle of former life and activity. One hallway led from the kitchen to a narrow passage, and finally a walled-up door to the east. Another ran off to a wing facing north, which held a library and a walled-up back staircase. Another going off in the opposite direction led past cellar steps, under a great Gothic arch that opened up into a grand front hall overlooked the overgrown lawn and the wilderness beyond they called 'the garden'. Glancing up at the ceilings Isobel detected each nook and cranny had become home to an assortment of spiders who, in turn, surveyed the new inhabitants who were to share their lair.

Rows of servant's bells lay empty and echo-less against one wall, choked with years of dust. The stairs curved sharply and unexpectedly for a house of that size, before they creakingly arrived at the first landing where a dozen or more doorways led off from the square corridor. The doors were all heavy oak, unevenly carved into panels, framed with painted iron. Many of the bedrooms, linked by secret doorways, ran the length of the house, some sealed up, others locked by forgotten keys. Despite its ghosts the house had a happy feel about it, Isobel felt. They were going to be all right.

Lydia had chosen the room above the library, which was graced with two small windows overlooking the farmyard in one direction and the Old Forge across an ancient meadow, in the other. The Old Forge lay to the east and so the sun would fill the room at dawn, its tired tendrils of light coming through the other window in the evening.

The faded rose wallpaper, a relic from the Edwardian era, now clung tenuously to the damp walls, which were so thick that they had retained the chill of many winters. Part of the ceiling hung in the balance and it was so cold you could probably see your breath at night, but the room was redeemed by a massive fireplace, so large that on either side you could almost carve out two separate rooms.

One finely panelled door fronted a 'secret' room or passage that led on to the next bedroom and so Lydia felt at liberty to take on the small room for herself. The 'box room' was a curious island in the centre of what should have been a larger, grander landing. It was like a surreal joke, surrounded by windows eyeing other windows, that seemed to overlook life beyond the house. From it she felt as though she were enclosed a vacuum from where she could observe the comings and goings of mice, or the rarer human walking to and fro. Lydia decided she would paint it black and, safe at last in the womb of this room (which was at the very heart of the strange house), she would decorate it with newspaper cuttings of every image that fascinated her.

Before it grew dark, they climbed up into the attic, a forgotten floor of nothingness. The flickering oil lamp illuminated no inner walls or doors, just an expanse of bare pine floors as far as the eye could see. House martins ravaged noisily in the roof, above deserted rusty iron beds that once cradled young serving girls. The windows were festooned with cobwebs.

"Mind Lydia, don't walk over there, the floor's not safe. I can't pay for it to be mended if you fall through. Let's go down and make some supper." Isobel couldn't imagine what they were going to eat, as she hadn't remembered to ask for firewood or coal, and Billy had gone before she could ask him when they might have it. Still, at least it was July.

"I wonder who lived up here Mummy. You could imagine it, servants in the eighteenth century, the 1820s, the Great War, Waterloo! Do you think they might have kept prisoners up here?"

"I'll keep you up here if you don't come down now and help me scrub down the kitchen and unpack the trunks. I want to unpack as much as possible before it gets dark." Isobel didn't want to admit yet that she suspected she had forgotten to pack their pots and pans.

Lammastide

18

The darkness somehow suited the house. It was as if it was their compromise not to disturb it too suddenly after all these years of slumber had won the day. That night Lydia slept restlessly in the cold room. It was as if the dark air was charged with a great presence, or another's gaze, and so fitfully she lay there, daring herself to leave the great heavy room and go to her mother, who seemed a world away. It was all she could do to keep breathing, not daring to even peep above the bedclothes for fear of what lay outside. Something she sensed was watchful, cold and menacing.

Sleep, when it finally came, brought with it a striking dream so vivid it would remain with her always. Outside, a crowd had gathered, and it had sounded restless. They had come over the meadow, over the hill even, brandishing pitchforks and flaming torches. Angry bushwhacking men shouted, with screaming hysterical women. "Get out of the house or we'll burn you in it." They were all faceless, but with the same malevolent eyes.

"Witchcraft!"

"We know what you are now. We'll carry you out of there, we'll pull you from the windows if we have to. The village don't want you here, get out!"

It was then the burning had started, ancient rafters burning one by one until thick black lethal smoke poured its way stealthily through the key holes and under the doors. Part of the roof came crashing in. Billy was the ringleader, with a maniac's grin, egging on the crowd. They had her mother outside already, tied to a stake on a mound. Petrol doused, she screamed until they lit the fire. Lydia contemplated jumping out to the crowd and the red sky. Instead she ran to the window overlooking the Old Forge. With one leap she was out, onto the cold meadow and running towards the Forge, to safety as she heard them calling for her from under the bedroom eaves.

"Lydia, Lydia ...." Her mother stood there with a familiar mug of tea. "It's half past nine. I think you've been dreaming. It's okay love, just a strange bed that's all."

But the unease would never really go away: it permeated the damp walls in the house, reached out to you even as you entered the driveway. Despite the beauty of the open fields and the wildness of the countryside, Lydia felt there was something ominous about the house, perhaps an echo of sad events and people who had lived there before.

Grudgingly she padded downstairs, her hair wild and unbrushed, as it was to stay for many years after. That was the mood that overtook you there. The hallway and passages to the kitchen were freezing, and there was still the smell of the crypt that all old houses share, having been unlived in for great periods of time. The morning sun had not even brightened the windows of the house and so escaping the icy blast of the hallway, she tentatively lifted the ancient latch to the kitchen, behind which she could hear the animated talk of women.

At least the temperature in this part has risen slightly, now the stove was working and it even looked homely. The crooked kitchen table was laden with a freshly baked loaf and some home-made jam. When she lifted her eyes from this feast, she encountered a middle aged, stocky Norfolk woman in one of the chairs. They seemed to have stared at each other for a good ten seconds until Isobel strode into the room.

"Betty, meet my daughter Lydia." Lydia wanted to ask, not *who* Betty was, but why this woman was seated in the middle of the kitchen on her own.

"Betty's my first customer. I'm hairdressing so you'll have to get your breakfast around us."

While eating her toast, Lydia watched transfixed as her mother poured something resembling creosote on the woman's head. It looked pretty deadly. She wondered if her mother really had lost her senses and knew what was what. Maybe it *was* creosote. How could you suddenly 'become' a hairdresser? Even she wouldn't let her mother loose on her hair. How were they going to survive? Still, it was too early in the morning to argue or point that out. So, she listened abstractly to the comforting lilt of womanly gossip, soothing, like hot piles of steaming ironing, a bringer of normality.

"Betty was the housekeeper when Mr and Mrs Graham lived here before us, weren't you Betty?"

So were they the culprits responsible for the brown paint everywhere and the walled up fireplaces, she wanted to ask. Her mother had always told her that farmers always had a tendency to destroy what was beautiful and preserve what was ugly. Betty was undoubtedly a farmer's wife. She was an Amazon, a huge woman. Lydia watched her massive sausage fingers holding her cup of tea and wondered what terror they might wield with a brush in her hands.

Betty was unstoppable, like a river in full flood, once the subject of the Grahams' had been raised. She now had a double audience.

Isobel darted around her with birdlike movements. It was amazing where all this force and energy came from, in such a small woman. Her nose was slightly arched and aristocratic, but it shone out of a thin finely chiselled face with huge green eyes which were usually grinning with some joke or other at somebody else's expense.

Dramatically she raised her eyes at every sentence and once she had tucked Betty safely under the drier, she nodded enthusiastically over each new revelation. Lydia thought the exaggerated nods bordered on the ridiculous. It was a bit like a pantomime, she thought with a smirk. Betty was egged on further by this receptive audience and resumed her tales at top pitch and speed, although she was deafened under the dryer.

"As I said, Mr and Mrs Graham were the best of people, you should have seen 'ow they 'ad this house. Every room a credit, sparkling it was. Helen had your room Lydia, and she *was* talented, the most talented, lovely little girl you ever saw. One Easter that little girl made an Easter tree all out of a dead piece of wood and silver foil leaves. It were beautiful, well, me and Mrs Graham wept we did. We kept it there in that corner for over nine months. She's grown up now.

"And Billy, the boy, well he was a terror used to sail across the pond to the island in the middle, like a pirate, he did. They had every breed of duck there was, and this 'ouse, they 'ad it lovely. Not like it is now," she quickly added as an afterthought, and then she proceeded to tell them about Billy.

Finally, she emerged triumphant, face beaming. Her hair rode her head like a giant glossy black helmet. *Does her husband really like her like that?* Lydia thought. And then she remembered her husband Mick, who was a great bear of a man and ran the Home Guard for the neighbouring three villages, so it probably would be all right after all. Maybe her mother would get one of those glamorous salons one day and become organised with a big black appointments book. Betty's face, hard as February, glared down at Lydia, dishevelled and smirking still.

"What do you want to do when you grow up, then? You'll have to get a job up city I expect (The 'city' to locals of these parts was Norwich)."

"I never want a job, jobs are boring." There, that would have the desired effect of shocking her.

It *had* the desired result. Betty's look was thunderous, bearing down on her, and she darted behind her mother for safety from the judgment that would have to come now. "Well Miss Lydia, I think that's a wicked thing to say. Your mother will need you to help her now she's on her own."

"Lydia, go for a walk or something. Leave us alone."

"One day you'll have a kiddie of your own, Miss Lydia."

"Not if I can help it. If it's anything like me, it will be awful."

"Yes, Betty, I'm afraid *that's* true, she can be little uncontrollable, always has been, but she's great fun. I've sort of given up."

Betty just raised her eyes to the sky as if in silent prayer, missing the look of recognition that had passed between mother and daughter acknowledging their new happiness and freedom. Despite Betty's hair being a touch too strikingly black and unnatural (Isobel noticed with alarm as they went out into the sunshine), she made another appointment, and Isobel's kitchen-career started to flourish out of dire financial necessity. The clientele swelled from those more eager to share in a morning's gossip than a set and perm. A wayward daughter was the least of her problems now. Life had suddenly thrown them both in this refuge after losing everything. Thank god for friends.

Lydia strode out into the bright spring morning, a new beginning, out from the shadows of the house. The red roof of the farm bulged and dipped precariously defying reason or gravity. Directly beyond the back door was a dilapidated wooden fence, dipping wildly around what had once been a kitchen garden, but now there was only a wild patch of nettles and weeds, standing out in glorious defiance. Rusty posts and wires trailed towards the a single dark yew in one corner of the garden.

Nothing could have been further removed from her grandmother's immaculate garden, where children idled away in swinging hammocks under soft rows of blossomed apple trees in the golden orchard strewn with daisies, roses and orderly rows of caged fruit. This was no-man's land where roses were replaced by hemlock, yew and wild grasses over-running the borders, where trees were home to the Old Gods. Even the centuries of Christian pilgrims tramping by on The Peddar's way to Walsingham, had failed to dent the lawless wildness and power of the place.

CHAPTER TWO

Autumn 1999

It wasn't until he had driven for over an hour that Jake's hands ceased shaking, or so it seemed. Frustrated at the outcome, he banged abjectly on the steering wheel with his fist. *What had he expected?* He felt such a fool. It had been ridiculous to expect to re-capture fifty lost years in an instant, when not one word had been exchanged in all that time. And still there were all those unspoken words bottled up inside him ... unexpressed; the emotions were still surging through him but lost now ... impotent.

Torrential rain began to hammer the car, smudging the vehicles in front into a muddy haze. The windscreen wipers were hypnotising, pulling him further into his thoughts as the rain beat mercilessly down, obscuring his vision. For nearly the whole of his adult life he had loved this woman. And what good had it done him to bear this great love, so laboriously nurtured all these years? There were no children, no wife, not even a sign of recognition from her even now; no strength left within him to tell her how he still worshipped her *after all this time*. It felt like he was drowning under the downpour, a wash of emotion that was so great that it sealed all expression within an airtight bubble.

A thunderous hoot from a juggernaut jolted his sensibilities back to concentrate on the road and the journey. He needed a rest, his senses were frayed. Happily he noted the sign for a trucker's café up ahead. For some strange reason, he always found something comforting about these roadside cafés on rainy days, offering a refuge from the busy traffic and miles of mindless roads.

Finding a place by the steaming windows, he grabbed a newspaper to read while he drank his coffee. Surveying the depressing scene of normality for a while, he noted a young couple communicating in monosyllabic grunts in between stuffing chips into their baby's mouth to keep it quiet. An elderly couple were staring out like zombies at the rain-soaked car park. The mundane and banal had always held an appalling fascination for him, but at least it was having a grounding effect that prevented his body floating back to where he had been ... with her and the memories. A radio somewhere signalled the time: it was seven o' clock. He could be home by nine-thirty if he pushed it. The soothing jingle of *The Archer's* lilted through the warm, safe little café and he began feeling energised and optimistic again.

It was just at this moment of reassurance and comfort that he looked up to notice a man to his left reading a paper, chubby arms outstretched above the remains of his burger. The large banner headline of *The News of the World* shocked him. "*SATANIC VICE RING UNCOVERED WITHIN LOCAL COUNCIL.*"

The words jolted him back immediately into those otherworldly ponderings that he had tried to shake off. It seemed that the past was pushing him to delve deeper and deeper with an urgency he couldn't ignore. Against the hypnotic drumming of the rain tapping against the windows, the headline forced him to re-live the almost identical circumstances of forty-seven years before.

He was cast back to his youth with a jolt. He was twenty-seven, living in London and had been sent by *The Evening Standard* to report on a Norfolk group of "black occultists". It was 1952, the year after the repeal of the Witchcraft Act, which had bought personalities like Gerald Gardner out of the broom closet. Since then, media and public interest in the occult had exploded. Half a century later, armed with the knowledge he had acquired then, he could muse upon this current news item with detached cynicism, marvelling on how the media was still able to misinform and titillate the public with half-truths and lies, and how, for their part, the public were still greedy for sensation, absurd fantasy and speculation to escape the tedium of their own day to day existence. As he stared into the weak mug of coffee, he recalled with shame how his own news story had been hatched to feed this absurd demand.

At the time, he had believed he could manipulate the story into something more concrete. "BLACK MAGIC DEVIL WORSHIPPERS BURN DOWN LOCAL FARMHOUSE OF VICE," or "HOUSE OF EVIL BURNT BY BAND OF LOCALS". It was, of course untrue, but it was just the kind of thing the readers would love. It had appealed to his sense of humour, but he was also a little curious and apprehensive about the lead he had been given. Little did he realise how his cynical hunt for titillation would end. His life would never be the same again ...

The alarm went off at 5.30am. Already lorries and taxicabs were droning noisily below the bedroom window along the King's Road and dawn cast a dismal glow on the dank room. His typewriter lay abandoned in the corner, parked on a rickety pine chair. There was an empty bottle of Scotch on the desk. As usual, the evening had turned into oblivion. They had ended up at some club in Soho.

Clarissa began to stir next to him. "What are you doing it's only 5.30? You didn't say anything about leaving early."

"I've got a job in Norfolk. It's quite a long way, I might stay overnight."

"Bloody great, Jake, it's my sodding birthday. I knew you'd forget."

Her eyes were smudged with black mascara, and seeing her without her white-blonde chignon was quite unsettling. She could look stunning when she was made up and beneath the dim evening lights but now, in the first rays of the morning sunlight, she looked haggard and grey — like the surroundings. When they had first met, she had been working as a dancer and he'd found her quite sophisticated after University.

For her part, Clarissa had been attracted to what she considered to be a 'good prospect' believing Jake to be a good catch; a Cambridge graduate with his own small flat in Chelsea, and the prospect of a good career ahead of him. She'd had enough of just getting by on her own.

Pulling himself out of the hot bath, Jake studied his own face in the mirror: fractious and hung over. Clarrie came into the bathroom as he was shaving and sat on the edge of the bath, considering him with narrowed eyes. Her face still smeared with the remains of last night's make up.

"Why don't you come back to bed and make it up to me. Wish me Happy Birthday properly ... please ..."

As she smiled he noticed for the first time that her teeth were starting to stain yellow from her chain-smoking and suddenly the flat seemed dirty, clammy. He had to get out for some fresh air.

"I'm sorry, I have to go, I can't be late. This job's important to me," he said. In truth, nothing seemed important then, only the endless rounds of parties and late night drinking with friends. He felt as if he had lost his way. Sometimes he allowed himself to admit that he would have been far happier cloistered in a library. Perhaps he should have stayed on to become a history Don because there was nothing inspiring about his job on the *Standard*, no integrity to it. Even London had lost much of its glamour.

As he walked back into the bedroom to dress, Clarrie dived into bed. Suddenly, she was all peaches and cream, whispers and writhing, under the covers. "Please come back to bed darling, you don't need to go yet". He made no motion towards her and instead concentrated on slicking back his blond hair in the mirror. He saw her eyes narrow into slits in the reflection and braced himself for a scene. "I *knew* you'd forget my birthday, you bastard. I don't know what's got into you recently, but you'd better snap out of it. Why don't you get your priorities right? I'll go out with someone else tonight, just forget the whole bloody thing."

He suddenly felt ashamed. She was right, and he really didn't have the energy to argue. "Please try and understand, I really don't have the time, I'm late already. Do you have any idea how long it will take to drive to Norfolk from here? Look, I'll make it up to you tonight. Would you like to go to Josh and Imogen's party? Then we could go out for a meal or something, just the two of us?"

She lit a cigarette, weighing him up with pursed lips feeling vulnerable in her dishevelled state as he towered over her, looking clean and pristine in his suit with his blond good looks. Even she felt devoured by the shabby room and could sense that his initial lust for her had waned. She could not perceive how choked he felt by *her*, the flat, his job and his life, that he had somehow let himself drift into, with no passion or direction. Neither did she know that he had already resolved to somehow remove himself from the meaningless conveyor belt he had unwittingly put himself on.

Trampling over the morning's post, he slammed the front door and flakes of sludge green paint fell from the window frames. A rubbish bin was upturned in the street, and he tried to avoid stepping in the unidentifiable contents as he climbed into his car. The engine purred throatily out of the road and eventually passed the bombed-out gaps still punctuating the East End. As the horizon opened up, he felt he could at least breathe again as he shed off the claustrophobia he had felt earlier.

Despite the sense of freedom, the road to Norwich seemed endless, past the mysterious and ancient crooked trees that bent to the force of the wind. Rows of them lined the road to Grimes Graves and the dark cover of Thetford Chase. It all seemed so silent and desolate. There were few road signs to chart the way on the unending and wearisome road, and eventually he came to a small village with a café serving all day breakfasts.

Munching on a crispy bacon roll, he ran his journalist's eye over the solitary truck drivers, farmers and families dotted around the room. It seemed so silent and desolate. Some looked disillusioned and bored with life, others just oblivious. Couples sat opposite each other, ordered, ate and left without a single word to each other. Fathers shouted at their children, mothers looking on in speechless despair. Grandparents seemed to savour every second that provided them with a reprieve from daily monotony. He reflected how all of these people needed the escapism his articles provided and it lifted his spirits, vindicating his purpose of exaggerating the story of the fire to heroic proportions. The modern world seemed to thrive on the ridiculous, the extraordinary. Yet the life of the individual grew more mundane by contrast. The great lethargy that had hung over him seemed to lift with his hangover, although ultimately he knew radical changes were still necessary.

Lazily he pulled himself up and paid the girl at the counter. She was pretty and as she shifted along to the till, he noticed that she had a clubfoot. It was with shock that he found that this didn't even inspire any sense of pity. Even his emotions seemed dead. In the midst of this inner turmoil he really didn't relish a day with mad eccentrics from Norfolk with a grudge, still less evil black magicians. He left the girl at the counter a generous tip and continued the final phase of the journey.

The map turned out to be irrelevant. The locals took great delight in turning round or removing the signposts, following an ancient East Anglian tradition of thwarting unwanted incomers — from marauding Vikings and Saxons to the Third Reich. There was no distinction between their treatment of invaders and general tourists, whom they still regarded as 'foreigners'. Villages were replaced by leafy lanes and as the roads became narrower by the mile, the sea suddenly appeared over the horizon along the long coast road, snaking around discarded pill-boxes. Slowly, unconsciously, the beauty in the trees and the rising summer sun lifted his spirits. The hedgerows were lush with cow parsley and wild flowers. It was beginning to seem more like an adventure as the car snaked its way deeper into the country. How would he find the old woman he was supposed to interview?

Fortunately for him, Mrs Nelson lived in a village near the Saracen's Head which seemed to be the local social Mecca, and so at the village of Eadenhoe (reached by negotiation with the locals rather than by map reading), he enquired where he might find Mill Cottage. The room was cloaked with cigarette smoke under heavy ancient oak beams. Even though the sun shone brightly outside it was as dark as a cave. Only the clatter of glasses bought abruptly onto tables pierced the silence as he entered.

A group of men sitting at one of the long rough tables turned to stare at his strange city clothes. He was obviously a stranger. Twice he repeated the mumbling question to the old man behind the bar, who carried on wiping the glass with a dirty old tea-towel, holding his gaze as if in deep thought. "Mother Nelson you say?"

"Yes. Have you heard of her? I've been told she lives at Mill Cottage. If you could tell me where that is I would be very grateful." A peel of laughter echoed from every recess.

"Well, the ol' lady may *say* she lives there, but we know diff'rent see."

Jake's heart sunk. He didn't have time to deal with jokers and he was starting to feel impatient. Perhaps he had been given a wrong lead by the paper, and it wouldn't be the first time. A man with a thick black beard started to shake with laughter. He was being played with. Anger now welled up in him. After the hellish drive, his tiredness, and the fact that he really didn't want to be here. Suddenly the huddle of men solemnly rose to their feet and parted to reveal a seated elderly lady, smoking an old fashioned clay pipe.

She chuckled and took a slow swig of her beer. The room was too dark to make her out well, but he could feel her eyes boring into him. He wanted to be out in the sunshine. The thick ribbon of smoke which was snaking its way towards him was making him nauseous. It suddenly dawned on him that this must be Mrs Nelson. Quite a different apparition from the quiet sweet old lady that he had expected.

"And who are you then?" she demanded. "That boy from London, I expect?"

Furthermore her voice was neutral, educated; again shaking the narrow assumptions he had made about her before this meeting.

"Yes I'm Jake Hammond from the *Standard*." He said as casually as possible, trying to impose some presence and authority over the situation.

"Don't say anything boys, he'll have it all noted down!" She was mocking him. "Come, we'll go to the cottage. We'll have some privacy there."

He could sense the disappointment of the men as they left. The old man shouted after them as they were leaving. "What about settling up first, Nel?"

Without looking back she shouted "Put it on my tab, Michael."

"But you don't have one."

"Do now." She shouted before the door shut out any reply.

Steadily she walked towards the village, eyes focused straight ahead. She wasn't looking or even walking with him and he had the sense he was just a huge inconvenience to her, even though it was she who had telephoned the paper with information about the fire. They still didn't speak as they climbed the gentle hill to the cottage. Most of Eadenhoe was nestled in a valley and her cottage was set apart, on the brow of a small hill hidden by trees and a large hawthorn bush. He had an unmistaken sense of being watched as they walked through the absurdly named 'Regent Street', which was the epicentre of the tiny village.

There were some eight or nine flint and brick cottages painted in the uniform racing green of the Eddleton estate. He could almost feel the curtains twitch as he felt the eyes watching their progress. They passed a group of three women, standing by the millstream, and he thought it was rather odd that Mrs Nelson did not acknowledge them, being as the village was so small. They, on their part thrust their gaze into the water below as if hell bent on avoiding her eyes. He could have sworn that they looked almost scared of her, but then on reflection why would they be scared of an old lady, he thought?

Mill Cottage was a typical red-bricked Norfolk dwelling; or at least it looked that way from the outside. Behind a large elder, heavily laden with pungent white flowers, the garden was a jungle of wild cottage flowers, herbs and roses. Because of its wildness, he could only just make out that the plot had been sown in a circle, the focus of which was a high bank of camomile lawn and herbs. Its middle was made up of a sunken garden containing a stone seat or table carved with what looked like griffins or sea monsters. A fat tabby cat eyed him lazily from underneath.

Mother Nel watched the journalist taking in her home, summing up her life around his first impressions. She brought him back to his senses with a start. "Do you want to come in, or are you going to gawp out here all day?" she said witheringly.

When he turned to look at her, he saw a smile flicker at the corners of her mouth. As her expression softened, he was struck by the realisation that it was one of the most extraordinary faces he had ever seen. Bathed in light, he didn't notice the wisps of grey thinning hair, the weathered hands, or folds of wrinkles. He just felt naked and exposed under the gaze of those immensely powerful eyes, which were of the brightest emerald green he had ever seen, hooded by heavy brows. He wanted to look away but found himself unable to move. She didn't exactly glow, but there was a great lightness about her, or perhaps the sun gave the illusion of her whole face being lit up like that. He supposed that anybody who lived in such beautiful surroundings like this *should* glow. No wonder he looked and felt grey by comparison.

Obediently, he followed her into the cottage. The light, or lack of it, reminded him of the pub. No wonder she liked it there, he thought grimly, it was home from home. He wondered if there was a Mr Nelson, but eyeing the chipped and broken glasses, the rafters covered in drying herbs, the cats eating freely from the saucepan on the rusty old Belling cooker, he soon came to the conclusion that it was unlikely. She pointed to a rickety chair and he sat precariously at the scrubbed table where a much thumbed book on gathering mushrooms lay open. Some of them looked pretty deadly and he wondered how she had managed to pick her way through the legions of lethal ones and still survive after all these years. Other old books were balanced dangerously on the flimsy shelves above and threatened to fall on his head at any moment.

He hoped that she wouldn't be moved to offer him a slice of whatever it was on the table. It looked as though it had once been a fruitcake, but now the edges were covered in a dusty grey mould where mice, or the cats, had nibbled at the jagged corners.

"I didn't agree to you coming here for money you know," she announced, perhaps reading his mind. He sat there as if he were a chastised school boy and was at a loss to know what to say next. "After friends of mine were contacted about the fire, I thought it provident to contact the paper, to give the *correct* version of things. I can only tell you what I know, and it might not be as glamorous as *your* interpretation, but it's the truth and that ought to count for something."

"We were told that you were a local ... um ..." the words seemed ridiculous, they wouldn't come out. "... occult leader, witch?" He felt a fool saying the words. "That some occultists had set fire to the farmhouse in the next village as some kind of vendetta. Wasn't it some kind of black magic revenge attack? Our photographer was shown a dead cockerel that had been nailed to the church door and other things relating to the fire ... I think the fire took place two days ago, and it was a full moon, was it not? Tell me, are there lots of occultists in the area? Are there really still witch covens in these parts?" he asked hungrily, now getting to the points he wanted to raise.

She whistled in the air and rolled her eyes theatrically. "Well Mr Hammond, or Jake is it? You mean to tell me that's what's going on in my *own* back garden? Human sacrifices? Satanic rites?"

"No, I mean, yes. There are stories of a cult around here and there *was* some anger surrounding the fire, because we've had locals calling the paper." He was beginning to feel stupid again. Even he thought it sounded incredulous. "Not that I believe it myself."

She looked at him for a long while before replying. "I can believe that, young man. You don't believe in anything much do you? Just want to fuel the twisted minds of the public, fuel the other misconceptions to keep yourself in a job. Is that it?" She was as straightforward as a man. No wonder she held court at the Saracen' Head. He felt hemmed in now she had cut so swiftly to the core of his thinking. "Think we know all about life do we? And how old are we? Twenty seven years young?" she quipped as she poured the tea, having turned the tables on him completely.

His feet wanted to turn and leave, but for some perverse reason, despite her rudeness, he instinctively liked her. She wasn't meaning to grab control for herself. She wasn't even purposely rude. She was just being honest, which was a refreshing change from either the overblown exaggerations he was used to, or the sleazy lies the newspaper encouraged.

The chimes from a large clock broke the silence as she studied him, its rhythm as hypnotically soothing, as a heartbeat. A large grey wolfhound, awoken from its slumber, padded over the grubby flagstones to greet them.

"Would you like milk in your tea?"

"Yes, that would be great, thank you."

The great brown ring of grime around the milk jug was the least of his worries at that moment. She munched on the cake, oblivious to its condition. The clock seemed to demand silence and for some reason he no longer had the words for what he should be asking her.

"So why are you doing this interview, Mrs Nelson, if you don't mind me asking?" he said finally.

"Good boy, now we're getting somewhere," she chuckled. "To set the record straight, to stop some other local ignoramuses getting it all wrong. To stop this hysteria."

He thought back to all the mayhem surrounding the repeal of the Witchcraft Act, to the fuss around the fraudulent mediums, and the strange character named Gerald Gardener, who had recently divulged that witch covens still existed in Britain. The public had been genuinely amazed. It was as if they had forgotten that anything like that had ever existed for their ancestors, and the appetite for tantalising detail was insatiable. For his part, he only knew what he'd read.

"All right, I'll listen. Just tell me the truth as you know it." He had a nasty feeling it wasn't what he was expecting. "How far is the house from here?"

"About two miles as the crow flies."

"And you know the occupants?"

"Like family, well Lydia is."

"Who's Lydia?"

"The daughter, a bit younger than you. She's in London working at the moment."

"I understand that the house was deliberately set alight by about twenty villagers carrying torches. I checked the archive and found there was record of similar events in the same village. We reported on it a couple of years ago. I also discovered that Mathew Hopkins, the 17th-century Witch-finder General, searched out two witches in the village, who were later hung in Norwich on the Castle mound."

"You *have* been busy!" she chuckled deeply. "Alright, I'll stop teasing you because I like you. There *is* a coven in these parts and witchcraft, as you call it, *is* thriving, but it has nothing to do with show business, like this man Gardner may have led you to believe." He strained forward, pleased that they were making some progress. "But as far as the fire goes, forget it. We were not involved. I think you'll find it was nothing more than a local dispute of the worst kind, i.e.

Lammastide

two grown men, Lydia's stepfather and a local farmer. It's a personal matter, I should imagine, involving male pride and that's the way it will stay. He's an outsider, see?

"Neither will you get a squeak of sense out of any of the fools in the village. Someone has scared them all to death with these ideas and, as a result, much of the village is divided. Doubtless the story was made up to blacken Lydia's stepfather. You should put the record straight, if there's anything about you at all, if you value your own integrity. Understand and write about what *traditional* witches are really about after centuries of mis-understanding.

"Find out what our old laws stand for first, and then decide. We're nothing new. We have always been at the edge of every village since the beginning of time. You've all just forgotten us in the interim, simply because we have had to be silent and canny since the Burning Times. Devil worship doesn't come into it. How can it if witches don't believe in Christ?"

He felt like a child again. She was making it sound so sensible and mundane, like it was the most natural thing in the world. She placed a hand on his shoulder kindly. "Do you know how long we have had to hide, and how much longer too, if stories like this are allowed to continue, even though they have changed the laws? It will take more than that for us to lose the stigma of people's opinions. It is like bearing some great shame for no reason. They weren't against using those with the sight in the war, mind you. Not only for the secret occult war – but then that's another story – but to contact all those loved ones who had died. The comfort it gave them is probably all but forgotten now." She sounded weary. "Come with me."

Leading him out of the cottage, they walked along the high grass verges by the roadside until they reached a rusty iron gate. It led to a disused pathway meandering into a churchyard. Rows of beautifully kept graves nestled around the base of the crude Norman flint tower. Some gravestones leaning with age, casting dark shadows. Summer was in the air, freshly mown grass and leaves in their final flourish of green. He was mystified as she strode past the weathered gravestones until it appeared that they would walk through the hedge surrounding the graveyard into the field beyond. A wind-clipped oak marked the

Lammastide

boundary but he could not fathom the reason for her sudden standstill amid the wild grasses blowing thigh high in the gentle breeze. Then she looked fondly over to the old tree. Among its roots was a mouldy wooden cross that looked so fallible and lost, a pentagram was roughly carved on it with the name, 'Morgan'.

"Who was she? Why is it so far from all the other graves?"

"She was two years old when the accident happened. A tractor ploughed into her and her mother when they were driving about a mile from here, over the crest of that hill. Her mother was part of what you would call our 'group'. We worship the seasons, heal the sick and rejoice in nature. That is all. Her mother was paralysed at the time. Although she can walk now, after all these years, she doesn't like to come here. I don't blame her, look what the Christians; *your* church has done to this innocent little girl. The family carried the little girl here themselves in an orange box, that day they buried her. They had no help or sympathy from the locals, or even the church.

"Fifty of us came to say our prayers in our way and we weren't allowed to bury her in consecrated ground. When they cut the grass for the others, they still leave this spot out of spite. Perhaps they thought she deserved to die with parents like that. Evil. That is what they think of us ... until someone needs healing, or someone asks for a curse to be lifted. They are surprised when we refuse to lay curses to serve their own petty gain and squabbles. We scythe the grass when we can. Ignorance. That's the kind of thing you can blame your fire on. Not us. *They* call it evil, but there was more love for that child than anyone could have given her, and more grief since her death than a whole congregation of this church could have mustered."

He had to admit, there seemed more dignity somehow about an orange box than the fake veneer of a coffin. With harshness in her voice she suddenly raised her voice to an unnatural pitch. "Remember this! What goes around, comes around. What ever you sow, you *will* reap, as sure as the seasons turn."

With that she spun on her heel and he was left shivering in the sudden breeze that shook the small wooden cross, as it swept over from the fields beyond. He was so moved by this tenuous memorial to a small girl, frail and over-shadowed by the roots of the tree, stuck out apart from the cosy inhabitants of the safely mown churchyard. He couldn't imagine Mrs Nelson summoning up the devil, when she had just shown so much emotion, all that grief and understanding for the little girl. But he *had* been awed into silence by a sense of some great power, whatever it was. He was humbled, ashamed now of the dirty task he had been sent to do.

He turned, running down the lane to catch up with her. At the cottage they sat for an hour or more after he had begged her to explain more of their ways, now out of genuine interest after the unexpected shock of the isolated grave. Without being aware of the sudden shift in his mind, he determined that he would write the truth and give some justice back to her people - at least what he could understand of it. It was the least he felt he could do after being privy to such a close personal tragedy that he felt masked another secret.

"It's gratifying to meet someone with an open mind. You have a good heart and your words will be in print for all the right reasons."

In one sentence she had summed up his dearest wish, to write for the right reasons, to be published for good writing, not this, not the rubbishy articles he was writing for an incredulous audience. He wanted to write with feeling, for the beauty of the language, to communicate with style and worth. This, he now realised, was the core of his unhappiness, that the talent he had once felt he had was being cheapened, and that his mind was becoming closed when it had once been so open and receptive.

Gradually, softly, she spread a blanket of knowledge at his feet as she spun and wove the basic tenets of life, as she knew it. And as he listened, hypnotised by the sense of power and deep truth in her words, he knew that *he* would never see life again in the same way. He had too easily become disillusioned with his young life and given up on his dreams, to become like those around him who had lost their imagination, spirit, or the meaning of the intensity of life that she now imparted.

They sat and talked as the afternoon shadows lengthened. As she talked, he began to understand how life was really a three dimensional experience. It could be viewed and lived in so many different ways. Whilst his own view had no understanding or experience of the Mysteries that were to her, an integral part, he did feel a pull of fascination and a sense of homecoming as she questioned him.

"Why was William Rufus killed in the New Forest? Some believe he was sacrificed like the Barley King in the thirteen year of his reign, or that the church had him killed because he was a well-known pagan, a witch. Ever thought to yourself why Edward IV married obscure Elizabeth Woodville under an oak tree, in secret? Why his Order of the Garter numbered thirteen. The size of a coven. Why the garter? The witches garter? Everybody used magic. Mary Queen of Scots used one of her noblewomen to craft a spell so that the pain of giving birth to James I was given instead to one of her enemies. Good ol' Queen Bess had Doctor Dee at her side practically the whole of her reign. He's alleged to have organised witch covens the length and breadth of the country to summon up the great winds that smashed the Armada. That was all that saved us. And when the threat came from Hitler's invasion why do you suppose he suddenly changed his mind? The New Forest coven of 1941, that's why. They repelled him with so much energy half of them died within the month. No two people view anything in the same way, Jake. That is what keeps the world turning, the dynamism of life. It was never meant to be flat, straightforward. If it was, we wouldn't have anything to learn. Write from your soul, what you see here," she added, pointing to her stomach. Eyes were not her way, it was her heart, the gut reaction, the way of *feeling* things that mattered.

When the bats began circling like moths around the kitchen window he stood up to leave. He left agreeing to write about what actually happened. He would probably be sacked for stating the obvious, the mundane, but he hardly cared anymore. A great sense of calm had gradually enveloped him throughout the day and everything seemed to be swimming into focus. She had drawn out his unhappiness and he had shed his disillusion.

As if reading his mind again, she led him by the hand into the garden. "Look, *everything* in nature is simple. Believe in yourself and you can't go far wrong. I know it's difficult in the big city to stand still and listen to yourself. But if you try, you'll be all right. Lydia is in the same mess as you, feels she can't escape doing the right thing, a career and all that, and she just isn't happy. And neither are you, are you?"

She had breathed life into his senses, which had up until that point been numb. He briefly thought back to the pressures of my own family. How they were so proud of his job, and his life as they imagined it. He felt hemmed in and under so much pressure to please them by taking the conventional pathway. He gave her the barest reply for fear that his emotions – which had for so long lain dormant – might spill over and embarrass him. Her kindly eyes and her humour, her deep and earthy knowledge had gone some way to re-instate his temporary lapse as a man.

"I have really enjoyed talking to you, thank you for spending so much time with me."

As he was leaving the kitchen that had started exude the security of the womb, he noticed the rows of drying herbs, and shelves of labelled jam jars. Without being asked she said "Oh, yes, I took to healing about ten years ago." And it was nothing she actually said, but a feeling persisted that she had been the mother of Morgan.

He decided to take a look at the farmhouse before driving back to London. The thought of the city suddenly filled him with revulsion. It would have been so good to curl up there in the heart of the courtside and sleep, hidden from all the pressures of the world, but instead he drove on to Home Farm.

The car carefully made its way up a long sweeping driveway lined with mature horse chestnut trees, until the house finally came into view. In its day, it had obviously been an impressive building, originally built with the rational clean lines and symmetry of the 18th century. Now, the sloping roofs and added wings gave it a lopsided charm. The charred east wing completed the disorder. The sky was almost blood red, providing a dramatic backdrop to the blackened charred timbers jutting out against the sun, falling like a ball of fire crashing into the meadow to the west.

Suddenly, men's voices intruded on the stillness of the cattle munching solemnly in the meadow. "That bloody dog's gone again. I told you not to let him off his chain."

A rusty old chain, connected to a raised shelf inside a garage lay discarded. The red-faced owner was striding towards the house, and Jake made his tactful exit, not a little pleased at the dog's bid for freedom. The prospect of interviewing the aggressive owner, was less appealing, more now from a sense of the ridiculous, rather than his obvious bad temper. With a reckless whoop, he turned the car around at the end of the dusty farm track and sped back towards London, mentally discarding the trivial story-line along with his slavery to the job he hated.

CHAPTER THREE

The artificial lights of London did nothing to dispel Jake's brief, but heady taste of intellectual freedom. Armies of strangers swirled around on the periphery of his vision, swarming like ants through the traffic. Soon he would have to participate in the tinkling small talk and get back in the 'real' world but his mind was still pre-occupied with the fire and its weird aftermath. It had all seemed so strange, but after his meeting with Nel, the evening promised to be almost mundane by comparison. He wondered what Lydia would be like. It was funny to think she was here somewhere, but the chances of meeting in the vast expanse of the metropolis, with its thousands of inhabitants, was unlikely.

It was already past ten o'clock and all he wanted to do was sleep, but he had to change for the partying he had promised Clarrie. He knew that she would have given up waiting for him at the flat, having prowled backwards and forwards, waiting for him angrily as she clock watched. Yet he did feel guilty about the way he had been that morning. As he put his key in the shabby looking front door, he half wanted to turn and run away. He was in no mood to answer trivialities like, "Why are you so late?" and "Where have you been?" Questions that demanded untruthful answers, responses of an 'auto- man'.

Not after today.

The house was silent. The rooms were stale and smelt of cigarettes. Wine bottles from the night before still littered the living room. Walking into the bedroom, he saw Clarrie had scrawled a message on the mirror in red lipstick. His good intentions vanished as a wave of annoyance arose. He hated it when she did things like that. It read *"Meet me at the party darling, couldn't wait any longer. C xx"* It seemed all so affected and with a further sinking in his stomach, he privately acknowledged that even a night with Josh and Imogen was preferable to being on their own together. His early morning's thoughts about Clarrie had returned, and if anything, instead if blowing away any doubts, a day in the country had intensified them.

If he had been stronger, he would have stayed at home and faced the loneliness, but even though he dreaded the party, he needed to lose himself in a throng of people and trite small-talk. The taxi passed rows of identical mansion blocks, identifiable only by the incongruous names of Buttercup House, Hawthorn Mansions, and he speculated on how many hundreds of people they housed. All with the same bedrooms, bathrooms, kitchens, the same lives, sharing the same perspectives on their limited safe views of normality.

The bell on the shiny blue door to the flat gave a shrill alarm. An upstairs window was ajar and voices floated out into the humid summer night. The buzzer sounded and released the door - and Jake was inside. This was the worst kind of party: an engagement party. Why did people have them? Just to gloat? They would soon be sending out photographs of themselves on Christmas cards!

The huge reception room was perfect for Josh and Imogen and their kind of party. Polite conversation, glasses stiffly held. Nothing too outrageous, no dancing. Lit by Rococo wall sconces, which threw a golden glow, the room had a soft, romantic air. Flickering candles shimmered along whole walls of gilt-mirrored glass, creating the illusion of 18th century Paris or Vienna, and transforming even the dullest guests into glamorous creatures of the night. He scanned the room for Clarrie but the first person he recognised was Rupert de Villier. They had known each other since Cambridge, where they both read history and sat out the final years of the war.

Rupert's success with the ladies was legendary. A rugged blond with film-star looks and oodles of confidence, he was now leading an archaeological dig in Africa. "Jake, good to see you. I only flew yesterday. I've had a touch of malaria, but the project's going well."

Jake knew that this was his invitation to ask dutiful questions about a remote excavation in which he had no particular interest. As he painfully remembered, Rupert loved the sound of his own voice and was probably the most insensitive person he had ever met, which meant that once his stories started it was hard to escape, or else one had to sit there until they finished. Tonight he wasn't in the mood for Rupert's megalomania, but his friend carried on regardless.

"See that blonde over there, Jacinta, she's not wearing any knickers. She's such an old tart, she's married to Justin, my best mucker from school. We had a blistering affair a while back, poor thing was totally besotted in the end, so I had to break it off."

The woman looked over at that moment and saw him laughing, raising a glass to her. The poor girl was obviously *still* besotted by him from the way she kept flicking her hair and blushing whenever she looked across at him. Instead of walking away, Jake stayed because it was easier than striking up a conversation with someone new. The room was filled with clones who all lived in flats like these, with the same taste in furnishings and social standards. Their sentences would be limited to careers, and who knew who, or where they had been holidaying. Jake began to wish he had stayed in Norfolk with the old woman. At least Nel had offered intelligent, meaningful conversation. Her personality would have danced around the room, shocking them all with her primitive home-spun philosophies.

"Rupert, Jake, what can I get you to drink?"

Rupert eyed up the drinks cabinet and said, "Dubonnet and soda."

Josh squirmed behind his thick-framed glasses. "Sorry chaps, don't have any."

"What about a large scotch then?"

"Oh, God, Rupert, so sorry. All we have is vodka, wine and champagne."

"Oh. Vodka on the rocks will have to do." Josh scampered away to the kitchen like a slave. Rupert chuckled. "The secret is to eye up the drinks on offer first and ask for something you know they don't have. They always squirm. He needs to be shaken up a bit, he's as wet as tripe."

43

At that minute Imogen came mincing over and Jake winced at her sickly greeting. With her high-pitched, mouse-like voice, she was never still, always squeaking and squealing with enthusiasm over something, running here and there, never still. "Who's a naughty boy then, Jakey? Poor Clarrie was beside herself when you didn't turn up. She waited for you at the flat for *aaages*." She was enjoying this, belting out the fact like a steam train, that he had let Clarrie down. A few faces turned to stare.

"As a matter of fact I was just about to ask if you'd seen her. I've just driven back from Norfolk. Is she still here?"

Imogen started giggling and turned around to stare pointedly in the direction of the sofa by the wall, where Jake could just about make out a couple kissing passionately. It seemed shocking at a party like this. "Oh yes, Jake, *Vewwy* much so"

"What exactly do you mean?" Her lisp was annoying him.

"Let's just say that Edward is giving her a birthday to remember!" she shouted this out, almost as a dare to herself, to let it be heard by all the guests.

Rupert compounded the scene by booming: "Let's go and teach this Edward guy a lesson, Jake. Let's get him out."

He had visions of blood being splashed over Imogen's pristine white walls. And again he realised how awful his life really was, when the reaction that was expected of him (and *by* himself included), failed to materialise. At first he presumed it had been the surprise of seeing Clarrie entangled in a passionate embrace with another man, and then a great relief came over him. *It was finished.*

Thank God, for an excuse that offered him the perfect way out. In one day he had been liberated of the slavery that had tied him to his job, and to the sham that was his relationship with Clarrie. He caught his own reflection in the mirror and was surprised to see that his mouth was twisted by a diabolical smile. At the same moment Clarrie saw it too. *There was no going back.* He expected the inevitable outburst, but instead Clarrie got up and haughtily led Edward out of the room. After all, Edward had a flat in Kensington and was training to be a doctor so she, for her part, had traded up and was obviously quite pleased with herself.

44

Imogen was transparently dying to catch up with her and explain why her tactic to make Jake jealous had gone so badly wrong but when Jake and Rupert resumed their conversation, she lost patience. Jake wasn't going to react, so why waste time. Instead, she couldn't resist waving her hand back and forth across her face to prompt them into commenting on her ring. "Do you like it? Josh said it's too big, but I think they can *never* be too big. Anyway, it was Josh's grandmother's." They looked at the formulaic diamonds dutifully. "I really couldn't recommend being engaged highly enough," she lisped smugly as she simpered away.

Rupert lit a cigarette and rolled his eyes. The party was turning out to be better than expected. "Well, that puts you back in the running. See any foxy girls you fancy?"

"No chance. I think I'm going to need a long recovery period away from women. What about you? It's not like you to be on your own for five seconds, you usually have girls all over you."

"Funny you should say that but all I could do when I was in Africa was think of a girl I met at Luke's wedding, remember? We saw quite a bit of each other about a year ago, lasted quite a long time by my standards. I might even ask her to marry me." He added as an afterthought, just as you might say you were going to buy a pint of milk, or something as equally trivial.

Jake vaguely remembered hearing about a brief affair, mostly conducted in secrecy, or perhaps in Rupert's bedroom. "That's great news, but I can't remember which one she is."

"She comes from Norfolk, bandit country. Lives in town now. I thought you might know her, Lydia Chatteris."

The name hit Jake like a speeding train. It *had* to be more than a coincidence. As casually as possible he asked if she were there. A few moments later Rupert stood staring towards the door as some late arrivals filtered off into the party, leaving one curiously dressed girl standing out from the crowd, like a glorious tropic island. Swathed in a large coat and an exotic shawl, she remained transfixed, as though she was experiencing some private rapture that couldn't be hurried. It was curious how many layers she wore for a summer's evening. Later it became apparent that this was her way of erecting a barrier between herself and the world. As if in slow motion he watched Rupert walk towards her. She looked up at him and gently he removed first the shawl and then the grey velvet coat. He still couldn't see her face from that angle as it was masked behind long straw-gold ringlets. As she turned, he was struck at first by the medieval look about her, caused by the grey gossamer dress. She just didn't fit in this room.

Rupert was now towering above her, and picking her up in a giant bear hug, lifting her feet off the ground. From there he carried her towards Jake like a trophy, setting her down on the ground like a prize he had just found in the jungle. Her descent nearly knocked the drink out of Jake's hand.

"I'm so sorry. Rupert, who's your friend we nearly pushed out of the way?"

"This is Jake Hammond, you'll like him, he's a writer."

"Oh, and what do you write?"

Time had suspended itself on a silver thin wire, vibrating with tension, the atmosphere was electrified with pulsating energy. Her eyes were huge, almost black, almond shaped and over powering. Jake felt as if they were boring down into his soul, producing the same sensation that he had felt with Nel earlier that day. He wanted to speak but the words would not follow his thoughts. It was as if he couldn't get the words out, or that she was searching out the answers for herself. Her eyes overpowered everything.

"Anything really." He said like an idiot. She smiled encouragingly. It had to come out. "Actually, I've just spent the day with a lady in Norfolk, I think you may know her."

"Oh, and who would that be?"

"Mrs Nelson, from Eadonhoe"

"Ah, it *was* you then. There's a word for people like you, you know." She was straight to the point and razor sharp. He had blown it. His stomach lurched and before he could think of a reply she burst into giggles. "I've heard you are some kind of pyromaniac, fascinated by fire. Isn't that fair?" She raised her eyebrows innocently and took his breath away.

"How did you know it was me?"

"I spoke to Nel today, and she told me all about you. She liked you very much. When she told me about your day I felt so homesick, I love it there. It's home. I actually wondered if we would meet. I wanted to find out what you thought of it all, of her, I mean." She was becoming more and more animated.

Rupert was getting impatient. "If you'll excuse us Jake, there's someone I want Lydia to meet."

This abrupt departure, annoyed Jake as he reeled from the blow the amazing hand of Fate had dealt him; that they had met like this when the probabilities were so remote. If somebody had asked him yesterday what he thought about Fate he would have laughed at them. But now, although he didn't like to admit it, there *had* to be a larger force at work, because the odds against them meeting, coupled with the events of the day were too huge to ignore. He was even enjoying the sense of anticipation at what hand would to be dealt him next. For a while he no longer minded being swept up in trifling conversations because his mind was still marvelling in the certainty that *something* was about to be unravelled, and he was to have a part in it after all. Some journey to begin, a road less travelled.

He tried to find her in the crowd but it seemed as if Rupert and Lydia had vanished. A group was forming around a well-known artist. He was like a toad, and the ugliest man Jake had ever seen but he had a gaggle of girls around him, one cavorting on his knee. An art dealer was discussing the merits of using more colour when the huge, rotund artist rose up and attacked him. His verbal onslaught was brilliant and a group formed around them.

"You are nothing but a vulture. You are like all of your caste, you feed off the creativity, the life spark of others. It wouldn't interest *you* if we used dog turds to paint with as long as *you* could make money out of it and exploit us. You know nothing of colour, of art. You are vermin ..." The attack went on and at least the artist was eloquently creating a sideshow.

Then he noticed Lydia and Rupert standing to the rear of the group. Rupert had turned his attention to some woman claiming to be a Russian aristocrat who had escaped to become a trapeze artist in the circus. She now boasted that she *only* ate caviar, and was widely known to sleep any rich men (generally over the age of seventy) to pay for her Belgravia flat. Flirting outrageously with Rupert, she had deliberately used her broad back to sideline Lydia. A man in spectacles was dribbling smoked salmon down his jacket as he listened to the circus woman dumb-struck and incredulous, his open mouth threatening to loose its contents all over the floor at Jake's feet.

As if reading his thoughts, Lydia freed herself from the mêlée. Tucking a bottle of wine under her stole, she came to find him as he knew she would. She whispered conspiratorially in his ear.

"I'm not enjoying this, do you want to go for a walk?"

There was no other option. "I'd love to."

Opposite the flat, the Park was shrouded in darkness and silence. Jake and Lydia picked their way through the shadows to the Chinese temple on the far side by the river, where the boats could be heard swaying softly in the current. Like children enthralled with a nocturnal adventure, they climbed the steps and sat overlooking the inky blackness of the river, and the illuminated bridges in the distance.

There were no words until now. She broke the silence.

"So you've been sniffing around looking for our coven then?"

The word 'our' reverberated around his head as he took on board the meaning. So she *was* part of it. This 'thing' he had tried to understand in the graveyard with Nel. She had read his mind once again.

"Don't worry, I know you won't understand and *I* wouldn't tell you about it even if you could. That is *my* secret. But perhaps you are ... sensitive ... Nel liked you, and she's usually right. She told me about it today. The wryd sisters are very mischievous, they have a habit of throwing people together in situations like this." She hesitated for a moment and then carried on, the words tumbling over themselves in her anxiety to make herself understood.

"I hope you don't think I'm mad dragging you out here, only do you ever feel that you're about to burst? Scream with frustration? So much falsehood, everything so expected? Charlatans nobody can see through, like that woman in there. Everything is *so* predictable, everyone's a passive spectator. Nothing is done on the spur of the moment. It's all running commentaries on nothing at all."

He guessed she might have meant being with Rupert. As his girlfriend it would be like being confined in an underwater tank, trying to scream with no sound coming out. "I do know what you mean, working and spending ninety per cent of your time with people with whom you have little in common."

She carried on as though he hadn't spoken. "Have you ever thought you would fade away to nothing, be broken by complete and utter inertia? When I first met him, I thought he would marry me, but like most other superficial men he couldn't commit. Always on the move."

Was she was talking about Rupert? He had no way of knowing how much of this was prompted by her earlier conversation with Nel and how much was spontaneous. Then she was rushing on again.

"He'll probably find some nineteen-year-old, settle down and produce his children when he's seventy. I love him now as a friend and yet sometimes I think of what I would have done for him. Instead we coast from party to party, painstakingly avoiding anything that's important. It's not done to talk about things. Not even the war. But if I'd been sent away to school at six, I'd probably be numb. How can you have feelings after that, let alone express them?"

Jake wondered why she was telling him all of this. Perhaps she thought he and Rupert were closer friends than they really were. Nevertheless, he admired her way of being so open. It seemed almost childlike. A mixture of vulnerability and a measure of hardness like pumice underneath. In the darkness, he thought he saw the glimmer of tears on her cheek, but if she was crying over her lament of love she didn't let him see. She turned her face instead to the bobbing boats on the Thames. They were just discernable in the darkness by the sound of the rigging echoing like a bell across the water.

"One day, in a room full of people he suddenly announced how great it was that he had this dig in Africa. I had no idea he would go back there. It felt as if I had been stabbed. He was running away again. Imagine the shame. I had to smile and congratulate him along with everyone else. Of course, it wasn't 'done' for me to have had a scene, being a girl I had to be passive and smile. I find it quite funny now, unbelievable.

"What you have to do with men is catch them unawares, sort of stalk them as you would an animal and without them knowing, so you don't put the wind up them. You are *meant* to pretend that you don't want them to want you, that you don't care about being loved and hopefully, fingers crossed, they *might* decide to give of themselves before the moment passes. Of course, the moment *has* passed with Rupert and I have gone passed hoping and waiting for him to say he wants to marry me, and I can't play the game anymore. Play acting has never been my forte."

Jake marvelled at how anyone could have let her down, she had such an *inner* beauty. Lydia was looking far into the distance, her hair blowing gently about her face. They were only a foot apart and he could have easily brushed her face with his hand and tenderly hold her. The whole thing was unreal. She was at her most captivating then, the depth of loveliness within shining out so that only kindness permeated everything. This was perfection, and in one preternatural second he began kissing her softly, holding her thick hair entwined in his hands as if to keep her there ... protective ... protected.

She moaned and pulled away, then as if nothing had happened between them, she continued with her obsession on the theme of loneliness. "And what about you? Have you been a bastard too?" At least she was laughing but her eyes were childlike, her breath held in as if she expected the blow.

"No, I don't *think* so." What a liar he felt, thinking of Clarrie.

"But do you believe in love? The *true* meeting of souls?" It was like an angry demand. Before he could answer she spoke again. "Close your eyes and listen?"

"To what?"

"Shhhh."

It seemed like an eternity. He just watched her, eyes closed like a child as if she were again in a secret rapture, sniffing some secret vibration on the wind, like an animal. He later remembered the image of her like this — for always. Time was standing still, the evening had no set course, yet all around the air was filled with the vibrancy of life, surging and charging throughout the dark earth until it seemed to pulsate through his veins. The trees became watchful, the inky surface of the river murmured. The lilting wind animated her hair. Clouds quivered across the sky flitting around a pink moon. They could have been in Italy watching a sunset die behind a lunar landscape. It could not have been more beautiful than this moment. They swam through ideas as thick and loaded as the murky river, and he was lost in the intensity of her thoughts, dancing from this to that in fearsome leaps of imagination.

"I didn't think London could be so beautiful."

"No, it often isn't. What did you think to my world?"

"You mean Norfolk?" *Or the one he'd just glimpsed?*

"It's like a lost world. I didn't want to leave."

"You must miss it."

The journey had begun. She started to weave her web.

"Have you ever sat in the middle of a wood at night? There is a place, not far from home where Ann Boleyn was born. I used to fancy I heard magnificent hunts tearing through the forest. In the centre you can sometimes find a grey mausoleum, built like a great pyramid to the stars. Great yew bushes line the avenue enclosing and echoing death. I tore through the branches with them, with the great torches of fire chasing death, the ghosts, the essence of that place and the grandeur that could be life. I was obsessed by the spirit of Anne Boleyn and that place as a child, because love was the highest ideal there.

"I would try and reconcile the loss of a man's love – if it was true - in her case. I would reason that she was done to death by treachery, not by the loss of all that I stood for, the everlasting nature of *real* love. All my childhood I sought it, climbing forbidden terraces under the light of the stars to seek it out ... and it was there for the taking, the ghosts of young lovers, of old souls singing in youth. Old, because they had loved. Wise, because love is the highest essence of life, the highest state of man. That is what shines out from the soul to the gods and that is the only thing I feel that can link us to heaven, to the great plan of the universe.

"Often the moon would be like this, very still, hypnotically beautiful ... There's a place not far from the yew grove, where a lonely tower stands, the sole testament to a lost world: a village burnt during the plague. I would climb under the broken flint battlements at night, creeping along the mossy aisle until I would lie under the bell tower, or climb up its broken steps to the moon. It was there that the ghosts came to me most strongly. The shadows of centuries, burials, births, deaths and most terrible of all - because the power of it still abounded - weddings, of fantastic loves lost by now ... but still echoing among those broken walls. The energy remains, the great circle of life still unbroken so powerful and terrible in its dimensions. That level of life always remains lost to most of us who cannot believe or feel that kind of intensity.

"I was a voyeur on the sadness and ecstasy that was their life. And every now and then the same pair of lovers would show themselves to me. Real love can never be lost. I have seen too much. The earthy smells of the rhododendron bushes, the hoot of the owls just as now, only more charged with emotion. I long to be back in that world, as far from all this drabness, this great world of change we live in now. I feel so often as if I don't belong in the here and now, as if I'm no more than a gossamer shade ... as they were to me. I was determined to keep going back there, hungry for more proof it all existed, perhaps to offset the bitter soullessness I discovered with time.

"Do *you* believe we have lived before? I know I have. I lived in the countryside with ... Oh, such great passions, such grandeur of emotion and purpose you wouldn't comprehend. Perhaps I'll never find what I am searching for, to replace that which I know I *have* had before. So I just exist, sit and wait really, for someone to really set my soul aflame."

She turned to Jake after her soliloquy and laughed, but her eyes were focused on the dark shadows beyond and he could sense a tragic longing in her. It wouldn't have mattered to her if there was someone there or not, she was not talking *to* him as much as affirming something to herself. And at the time, although her essence of her words had etched themselves into his brain, he could only perceive the true meaning and force in a fraction of them. He marvelled more at the eloquence of her words, rather than understanding the old wisdom of their content.

Was she mad?

Touched by madness perhaps, but with such resolute bravery, such openness. It was madness of a kind but with so much sense and genius that she really did belong in another time and place. Yet, he was amazed that as she talked, the persistent hum of the night traffic had been completely silenced. Even the stirrings of his own logical mind had been stilled for that long moment, when she spoke and guided him through her reality. He felt afraid for her, fearing that this wonderful, beauteous world she belonged to and sought out, didn't really exist. With a man's objective conviction, he pitied her. It was as is if she had condemned herself to a life that would be always unfulfilled for her emotionally. She was already an island. Who would take on, or understand, this high frequency of feeling and nurture her? It seemed as if she had decided that the modern urban world had no romance, beauty or poetry, no place for her.

He sat beside her, saying nothing and, regarding that sad face silhouetted against the moon, he let her envelop him by the sheer life force she exuded, flickering and dancing over the length of his veins, bristling the hairs on his neck with electric shivers. If she wanted to go on and shout at the defilers of beauty, he would listen. *He wanted to believe in her.*

He stroked her face gently with his finger, willing her to turn to him again. A breeze suddenly floated off the river and she shivered, turning at last with an expression verging on panic. As if she had recalled something that was distasteful to her. Almost audibly he saw her body snap forth from its dream state. The moon had vanished behind a cloud. All that illuminated them now were the lights of the bridge. Suddenly she rose, shaking the leaves or imaginary creases from her grey dress.

"Surroundings fool people so much of the time, they can charm you into deception, don't you think?"

Smiling and without warning, she turned and started down the path towards the road and the world outside, slamming the door shut on what she had revealed so unexpectedly. He wanted to run after her but sensed she didn't want him to. Why thrust him back into that miserly cold evening where the twinkle of pub lights obliterated the stars and pervaded their island solace in the park? He was an intrepid rider into her world. Why tempt him into it , only to leave so abruptly?

As if his thoughts had sailed into the back of her head, she spun round on her heel and called out. "It was nice to have met you." Slamming the barricades even more firmly shut, as if to settle any doubt with the finality of her tone.

Angrily he threw the empty wine bottle into the river. Perhaps she had been drunk. *Perhaps he was drunk.* Was her hasty departure due to him, he wasn't even sure. What right had he to expect anything after just one conversation? But then it wasn't an ordinary conversation between two strangers. And still he watched her gliding back towards the road, trailing the wet grass with her dress.

"Can I see you again?"

His pathetic plea fell on deaf ears, or perhaps she was in that other world again. Years later he understood that no one really came close to entering it. Mystified, he watched her go back to the people, where she had been so out of place, even more than himself, but at least he made a pretence at the charade. Perhaps she had nowhere else to go. He tried to identify her among the bird-like silhouettes behind the windows, until the chill wind rose over the water and drove him from the Park.

CHAPTER FOUR

Clarrie had already cleared her things out of the flat by the time Jake returned. She had arrived with a bag one night seven months before, and had ended up staying. He felt a great sense of calm in the flat, and relief at her absence, but the smell of her musky perfume lingered in the airless bedroom, and on the sheets, which were still stained with her make up.

Through the long hours, he retraced the conversation with Lydia. He tried to remember her face, but it was so ethereal and changeable, he couldn't summon her features in his mind's eye and she appeared like a shadow in his waking dreams. Every time he tried to sleep, her disjointed, madly intense words came to haunt him with their strange power. He tried to imagine her in the daylight, but kept returning to the image of her laughing at him by the light of the moon, as if she had some secret knowledge of his life. In dreams, he felt the panic grow as her great power drifted into his mind and left him nauseous.

Sunday mornings were the only time of the week that there was a lull in the ceaseless drone of traffic beneath the window. He placed his face to the cool pane and observed the quiet, empty streets. Even the cafés were still closed, and it was one of his favourite times to reflect. Taking a plate of eggs and toast to the balcony helped to ground his thoughts until he could reflect upon his meeting with Lydia a little more objectively. He tried to imagine her as a day-to-day person: what she ate for breakfast, how she dressed, her job. She must have a more normal persona at work he mused. Perhaps last night he had been too romantic and more to the point, drunk, and much of it could have been imagined. In the cold light of day he relived the events of yesterday and was less confident about giving up his job, for all his strong intentions. Change unsettled him, and with Clarrie gone, he decided that he would take things a little more slowly. His head was beginning to hurt, and ruefully he reflected that this followed a rigid pattern of predictability which had come to rule his life. Drinking too much was almost a daily ritual, and the box that he called home still seemed claustrophobic and soul-less for his writer's creativity.

How *could* he write properly if he had no stimulation, if the excitement with life was gone at twenty-seven? Life should be about shaving the edge, pushing limits, exhilaration for the soul. He determined that he *would* find Lydia. He would call Rupert before lunch and make up some pretext to see her.

Only after reading the entire batch of Sunday papers did his resolve begin to ebb. The sun was almost overhead, and the little cafés below were starting to fill with couples out for brunch and coffees. They made him feel isolated, and ridiculous for thinking he could just telephone the boyfriend of a girl he had suddenly developed an infatuation for and ask for her number, even if they were old friends. She probably wouldn't even remember him, let alone welcome the call. He decided, out of curiosity to look up the old family seat of the Boleyn's in Norfolk. That way he could determine whether Lydia had been talking sense, or whether he had been drunk and imagined everything.

Taking down a local 18th-century account of Norfolk life he'd bought from a second hand book dealer when doing research on the Duke of Norfolk for his degree, he slowly read with excitement about the Boleyn family home, Anne *had* indeed visited. Lydia was right, and it would have only been a few miles away from Eadenhoe. Furthermore, he read of two witch trials at the village of Pemberton during the visit of Mathew Hopkins the witch-finder. The hairs on the back of his neck were starting to stand on end again. He went on reading and almost missed the crucial entry: under the section entitled 'Eddleton Hall', he learned that the magnificent house was built on the site of a village that had been burnt down. Everything was cleared for the newly rich baron and his desire to create a parkland to surpass all others in the region.

What he found curious was that he even took down the church adjoining the village of Pemberton, the village of the fire. To tear down a church in the 17th-century seemed not only curious, but extremely odd. Why had it been allowed? He read on to find out that the village had been struck by the Black Death, which killed most of the inhabitants. A fire had been lit to cleanse the disease-ridden village and consumed a young couple with their baby who were locked in the church. It was said that they haunted the tower that was left standing, and that the site was feared by the locals, as a local coven was reputed to gather around its base to call the spirits of the dead who appeared at times of great tragedy.

He closed the book, hands shaking in disbelief, for events were out-pacing him. More importantly, they proved that there was a precedent for some kind of magic, for good or bad in the area, which disturbed him even more. Still his rational mind had trouble accepting it, for all Nel had explained to him.

Deep in thought, he nearly missed the ringing telephone. Almost at the same moment, he was distracted by a strange black bird swooping over the balcony against the brightness of the sun. Jumping up in alarm, he knocked over the coffee cup, so that the dregs threatened to stain the book. Swearing, he swiped at the bird with the paper but it had gone. Breathless, he belted to the sitting room and picked up the receiver in the nick of time.

"Jake, sorry to bother you so early."

Her voice stunned him into silence and his heart lurched. Grabbing a cigarette, he squatted on his haunches next to the telephone table with the broadest of smiles, to let her voice wash over him. The drabness of the flat seemed to melt away in seconds.

"I'm sorry, I've probably dragged you out of bed. I got your number from Rupert. I told him I'd been awfully rude to you, and then I thought about what I'd told you and I was mortified. You must think I'm mad. Sorry for bombarding you with my intense dissatisfaction of life. I think London is getting to me and I was in a fey mood, I suppose. I *did* enjoy talking to you. Thank you for just listening. You must have thought I was drunk, or boring you to death, going on like that. You just listened, and I dragged you away from that party. I wanted to thank you for not even mentioning the fire, for not writing it up as you were going to. It was brave of you. Anyway ..."

"Stop saying 'sorry'. I loved listening to you. It was amazing ... really. You absorbed me totally. And you saved me from that party. I have to thank you for that. I just didn't understand why you left so suddenly. Did I do something to offend you?"

There was a echoing silence. *What was on earth was he doing?* He had no claim on her, they had only just met and he thought how pathetic it was to have felt so lost when she walked back into the party. Then the voice came back.

"Would you like to meet up? We could go for a coffee."

They met two days later. The rendezvous was a run-down Italian café, near the British Museum, following Lydia's meeting with friends in Museum Street who dealt in rare occult books. She had been reading hungrily all morning and now with her head swimming with the information she had sought, she looked drawn and tired. The little café warmed her, with its steamy windows and the chorus of coffee machines spraying jets of steam like geysers. Rupert had left for Africa in a flurry of chaos the day before. His mania always left her depleted, and although the first few days together was always filled with excitement, by the end of the week the strain began to take its toll.

Edgily she looked about for Jake, peering across the huddled groups for sight of him. He was seated in the corner reading. And there was a glow of warmth when she saw him again; he was even better looking than she remembered. His face had a look of serious concentration as his blond hair fell over one eye as he read. Although he was strongly built, and tall, he was not colossal like Rupert, who seemed always to take up too much space wherever he was. Jake gave the impression of being more sensitive, with real depth to him - which she found attractive.

When she arrived at the table, he was so deep in thought she had to speak to arouse his attention. "Jake ... it's me ... Lydia. I'm early."

He looked up startled: grey-blue eyes she noticed, now she could see him in daylight. She had expected him to have worn a suit, it being a weekday but instead he looked incredibly free somehow, in a white shirt which showed off his tan. "Have you got the day off then?"

"No, I decided yesterday to tell them I wouldn't be going back. I need to get my life back on course again. I'd lost sight of my ambitions, and in a funny way the trip to Norfolk made me see that."

"What will you do?"

"I'm going to rent out a room in my flat, which should keep me going for a while, and then try and get my poetry published, followed by some research into 'The Stuart Kings', and I will then embark on my life's work, a book on James I." He said with mock seriousness, but the overall plan had a ring of truth in it. There was a new lightness, a humour and happiness about him that she hadn't seen at the party.

With the camel coloured wool skirt and shirt, and sitting with hands folded demurely in her lap, Lydia appeared so very young and unworldly. So unlike the *femme fatale* he'd met at the party. She sipped her hot chocolate, leaving a brown streak on her upper lip, which again made him feel protective towards her as if she were a child. As he handed her a paper napkin, they both caught sight of her reflection in the stainless steel of the coffee machine and giggled until they had tears running down their faces.

"Do you know what I tried to do for a job here?"

"No, but it can't be worse than being a reporter for the *Standard* can it?"

"*Yes.* I was employed for a while as a publisher's assistant. He had the worst temper, and I only lasted a few weeks. My parents still think I am working there, and I don't have the heart to tell them what I really do."

"What do you do?"

"I make a good living as it happens, from the cards. I get by, I mean, it pays the rent. I only charge a nominal amount to cover my time for those that can afford it, but some days I'm so busy I don't know where to turn. I think it's been word of mouth and I really enjoy doing it."

"You mean the *tarot*?"

"Yes, and I call the spirits, too." She said in a matter of fact way, as if she were saying something ordinary. He didn't know what to reply. "You probably think how lucky I am, how free it makes me seem. But I am so restless, I feel so caged up here in the city. I want to go back to the country but I can't go back to living with my parents and I have no money to speak of, so I'm afraid I'm trapped here for now, unless I meet a rich husband of course, who could whisk me away. I keep dreaming of it."

"You must miss Nel a lot. The country. Why don't you live with her? If that is where your heart is."

Suddenly tears of sadness now started to fall, spilling into the dregs of her mug. "Because I'm supposed to wait here and work until I find a man and marry, that is what's expected of me. They would disown me if I went back now, without a husband. What would I do there? It is so much easier for men. But for a woman to do what she wants, it's so hard unless you have the money to be independent. And who am I going to meet around Eadenhoe? There are so few men left."

He reached for her hand across the table. It was true, if a woman carved her own way in life, some pockets of society still thought it strange. Then as he looked at her, her eyes glazed over and it seemed as if she were fading from him, that her mind was drifting somewhere else. She suddenly seemed so deeply unhappy. How could such a young girl feel such sadness? Absent-mindedly she fingered the cigarette packet on the table, and started to tell him again how isolated she was; that she belonged nowhere except in her great imaginings and with the few who could understand her.

"I feel so lost Jake. People are so shallow; they have no depth, no soul. I am not interested in this world, in money, in their stupid parties. I want to hear their innermost thoughts, their dreams; their secret wishes. If I could find a man with imagination, who still had the strength to dream, then I *could* love him. I know you probably don't understand but if you can tune in to what people are thinking and to the spirits, who are everywhere, then your nerves can get pretty jangled. I can't talk to anyone about it here, and sometimes I need to. I miss Nel so much, she understands. And because I am sensitive in that way, I seem to feel everything so much more intensely than everyone else. I just wish I could find a man who felt the same way; who could really love me, not just pay lip service to the word."

"I imagined that mediums were old, rotund ladies, not petite and pretty like you. I don't doubt you have a gift if you say you have, but I can't understand it, and I *am* a little sceptical, if I am being honest."

"That's all right, I can cope with scepticism, it's ridicule I can't take. I just knew I could talk to you without being judged, but I have to hide all this with Rupert and his friends, or they'd think I was nuts."

"And in Norfolk your friends are more accepting, or gifted in the same way as yourself?" He thought of the sense he'd had of Nel peering into his soul.

"Yes, in a way. There is no doubt I have to go back – if I stay here I will certainly go mad – it's just a question of how, and when. The going back, I mean, not the madness."

It slowly dawned on him that ironically, there was one thing that was drawing them together, the sensation of isolation they both felt although for different reasons. He wondered how, at the same time, that one couldn't be isolated growing up in the isolated wilds of the Norfolk countryside.

"What was it like, at Home Farm? You couldn't have had many friends there as you were growing up?"

Lydia knew it would be stupid to tell him that for her, the trees and the streams were alive with spirits, but told him instead of those first days there in the wild. Fifteen years earlier, and she could still summon the smells of the musty kitchen, overlooking the meadowland shimmering in the July heat. She remembered how the power of it bought out her own perceptions and magical ability.

It was the day she had cycled from Home Farm with Lily's son, Dan, to the village of Catley. They had known each other from when Lydia's family had first rented the gate house at Eddleton, and eased back into their brother-sister banter effortlessly. Catley was five miles from Home Farm, in the direction of the sea, and it had taken them most of the morning to cycle there. Apart from a few cottages, she remembered the austere grey church set on the edge of a steep bank, with lichen-strewn tombstones tilting away from the church. The graveyard was knee-high with meadow grasses and wild flowers, and that's where they flung their bicycles to eat their picnic lunch. Her mother had told her that this had been the birthplace of the famous knight; his great manor replaced by wild meadows and the village gone. It was sad to think that even his tomb wasn't to be found, but the huge imposing church was still an echo of Catley's greatness and rise to fame.

When they had eaten their sandwiches, Dan went off to look for adders, and the morning had grown so hazy that Lydia leant against one of the old broken tombstones in the bright sunshine. Poor Sir Thomas. Had he been killed in battle, and would he think back fondly from all those miles away and think back to the church he had endowed? Now its only visitors were adders and the odd child. Suddenly she felt the urge to walk over and try the rusty handle of the great door.

As the latch turned, it created an echo throughout the vast empty space inside. The building had been stripped of its altar and pews, leaving nothing but the dry font and a few dead pigeons that had become trapped inside. The once fragile windows that had illuminated the proud columns had been replaced with stiff sheets of grey corrugated iron. Yet, without remembering how or exactly when the desecration happened, she suddenly became aware of music and the flooding of colour into the aisle, as if she was stepping into another world. It was the first experience she'd had of the overlapping of time, and the thrill of stepping into another dimension. As the outside world seemed to fade into the distance, she was drawn into the vacuous cavern, which seemed to be alight from within, complemented by the music of psalms, pilgrim's prayers and the sultry smell of incense.

Although she was aware of her physical surroundings, the whir of the coffee machines and the dreary murmur of the people on the next table, of Jake's intense concentration on what she was saying, she was running with the rain and summer winds of her youth. More than just memories, she could see the dappled water in the sunshine, hear the noise of the mill race on the edge of Catley. She could even see how the winds had torn off part of the church roof, as she hovered above the children who now played on the old rickety bridge above the reed beds. She was used to being in two dimensions at once, but it still drained her and sometimes she moved from one to another, without knowing or realising where, or when, she was.

It was also that summer Dan had introduced her to the ruined tower at Eddleton — a solitary mass of ancient stones reaching up into the azure blue sky. It stood as a lonely witness to the lost village and the rich baron who had laid waste to all around it.

"How many do you think were killed?" she asked Dan

"Thousands, probably millions, all meeting a grisly death," he answered with a child's grisly relish.

They crept among the flints that once called the workers from the fields with harsh regularity. They shared the shelter with the straggling sheep, and it was here they camped out under the stars, and she heard the stories of the people who had lived, worshipped and loved there. Scores of them had only paid lip-service to the Christian ethos and had entered the church – as it then stood – through the north door. They told of how they followed their own religion under the stars, in the coverts of the wood and by the sea. And through them she reconnected with the ways of her own ancestors and the Old Religion.

Whilst she spoke, Jake marvelled at the same ethereal beauty and vibrancy in her features that he'd seen in the Park in the moonlight, as she told him of her childhood a decade ago. Her face flushed and her eyes shining with excitement, he realised that somehow she was really re-living those moments. When she had finished, it took a moment or two for her to look into his eyes. Until then, her gaze had been up and over him, somewhere else. To tell him all this and to drag herself back to the drab world of here and now and bereft of her mind's magic, seemed to have drained her energy. He could not know that for her part, she had gone in spirit to oversee the desolate graveyard and the minute movements of the animals in the grass, from a birdlike vantage point.

"And what of Dan, do you still see him," he asked.

"No, everything was ruined. We grew up of course, and he ceased to see the things I continue to see, and he thinks it's all far too stupid now. It's difficult for him to speak of it."

"God, it was as if *I* were twelve years old as you were telling me about it. I could have almost been there myself."

She laughed, but her eyes were serious as she sipped her fresh chocolate. "But that's as it should be, isn't it? To immerse yourself completely so you loose sight of being sceptical, or whatever."

"If you say so," he teased, eager to change the subject.

"I am so sorry, you should have told me to shut up, but being as you had been to see Nel, I thought you would be interested."

"I'm very ... honoured that you've shared it with me."

"Especially since you originally came to quiz me about the fire. I think I've done a pretty good job of side-tracking you," she said mischievously, but even though interest in the job and the story were finished, he realised that if he was no closer to the source of the fire, he was closer to Lydia by what she had told him. There was energy about her now, a spark that made her eyes so remarkable. She was blooming with youth and happiness again.

She looked at her watch. The time had flown. "Look, I'd better get back, I've got somebody coming over later. They'll be wondering where I am. I'm sure I'll see you soon."

He watched her cross the room, half-obliterated by the steam from the coffee machines and the throng of customers, stunned again by the abruptness of her departure. She strode away, just like before and all he had planned to say was lost. He felt that she had two personalities, one for this mundane world, and another for a more distant realm.

He followed her out of the café to wave goodbye, as he couldn't eject the images she had rained down upon him; her loss of innocence under the stars, by the tower, the power of the surroundings, the freedom of youth. She had brought it all to life in that wonderfully fierce way she had, whenever something had struck her soul. What experience had he to offer her on those terms? He watched as she walked out into the traffic, to what should have been a space between a hill and the setting sun. And then, whilst counting the mini-seconds after she had left, as if by magic (for he was willing for something to bring her back), she turned and ran back to him.

"I was planning on going to Norfolk for a few days. I was too embarrassed to ask, but I know you found it beautiful," she stammered breathlessly. "Would you like to come with me?"

"I would love to, thank you."

There was a long silence. "I think I can trust you not to write anything for that bloody article. If you do, I'll never talk to you again."

She was serious. But it had never crossed his mind since he had handed in his notice at the *Standard*.

She lived by the river in Battersea. Her flat was small and dark, like Nel's cottage, not like a London flat at all. It was on the ground floor and the door opened onto a large room draped with coarse, red silk curtains. A painted wooden bishop stood at one end and primitive gargoyles were perched on every corner. A mirror reflected a huge painting of a green man, leaves spilling out of his mouth. These were, she said, her 'truths'. There was a small garden and a huge rowan hung with pieces of coloured ribbon and flints. Primitive sculptures hovered in the flower borders, partially visible and therefore menacing to him. They loaded the last of her luggage into her battered green car.

"How long did you say you are going for? What do you need a vanity case for in Norfolk?"

She grinned shyly. "You never know who you're going to meet, do you? You'll have to have Mabel on your lap I'm afraid. I never go anywhere without her." He was imagining a large buxom best friend with glasses, who wouldn't stop talking.

"Who is Mabel?"

Struggling to contain her hair in a long black scarf, she whistled, and Mabel came hurtling around the corner headlong into his leg. Mabel was a black and white Jack Russell terrier, with a saucy patch of black over one eye. Resentfully she sat Jake's lap, growling at him in intervals to remind him that he was a usurper, who had taken her place, as they weaved through the grimy streets to freedom.

As they neared Thetford Chase, Lydia seemed to glow with excitement. It was like watching a changeling blossom from cool intense concentration to a young child, brimming over with happiness and emotion without a care in the world.

"I know it feels like an age away, but we'll be there soon." The wind had buffeted her mascara, producing ink-like smudges below the eye.

"Are we going to your parent's?"

"For a bit, if that's okay, and then we'll go and stay with Nel."

"She scared me almost as much as you do, you both have eyes that pierce through you! Is her surname name really Nelson?"

"Yes, Nelson was a distant ancestor on her father's side or something like that. He came from these parts. The funny thing was, on her mother's side she is also descended from Napoleon. One of her female forbears took a ship to the continent to become a nanny for a rich family in France and got 'caught' by Napoleon who was on board. Funny to think of the irony of the two men entwined by destiny in the end, and by such a small coincidence."

The irony, he reflected to himself, was that Nel couldn't have been further from either in character. The sun was shining and he too felt carefree, exhilarated by the wide open spaces and sense of escape. Suddenly, a car veered out of nowhere around the small sharp bend narrowly missing them. He grabbed the steering wheel and pulled them to safety.

"I was fine, I saw it," she said, laughing. But he noticed as she accelerated out of the skid, how afraid she had been: her complexion had turned grey and her lips had lost all of their colour.

"A long time ago, Nel had a daughter, Morgan. She was killed in a car accident. A tractor ploughed into them on a bend. It was harvest time, they didn't stand a chance. Nel was driving." He shivered. His instincts had been right, after all. She went on, oblivious. "They carried the tiny orange box up the hill to the church and buried her themselves. She was only two. It was a pagan ceremony. They accused Nel of devil worship because she didn't want a Christian burial for her little girl. And so the so-called Christians made her bury Morgan outside the boundaries of the graveyard, on the edge of the field. They still don't understand. Nel was nearly paralysed and when she could walk again, her heart was broken. Nel said that it was such a horrific crash, the powers that be said let's not bother giving her another life. Let her complete it all this time around. Dying in bed," she said, "must be such a relief. If only I could be sure death were like that. If the divine power had given us all the gift of a peaceful death, then life would be worth living."

"Was she married?"

"No, she started off as an opera singer. She gave it up because it got in the way of her lover's own ego. He couldn't compete, you see. She got rid of him after the crash."

Jake must have looked horrified. "No silly, witches don't go around killing people. She gave him the elbow; he's not under the vegetable patch."

"Her life sounds like an opera."

"It's not been all tragedy. Nel has told me that her real blossoming has been over the last 20 years; after all of this happened. Well, that's what she says. She came into her own as a healer. She's quite famous around here. People come from as far as London to see her sometimes. Of course, you must have known all that. Her beauty shines with age, with every passing year I've known her. By all accounts she was a stunner when she was on the stage."

And here he was with the most beautiful person he had ever seen, totally unaware of the effect of her own presence on him, laying her world open like a book at his feet.

CHAPTER FIVE

They eventually arrived at the Home Farm. The young horse chestnut trees Lydia remembered lining the drive when she had first seen the house were now sturdy enough to almost canopy the driveway. She felt a sudden longing to be alone, safe and happy with her mother, as they had been for so long before Isobel had re-married. As the house came in to view, it never surprised her how just how daunting it looked. How it recalled the countless wakeful nights because of the nightmares she had experienced in that cold room overlooking the meadow. That first dream of the fire had re-occurred over the years, but since it had actually happened, the dreams had ceased. Nevertheless, the sight of the charred timbers caused a chill, making her wonder whether somehow *she* had actually caused it to happen ... whatever had happened between her step-father and the locals.

From Jake's point of view, the daylight had transformed his brief recollection of the farm as he had sped away it at dusk just over a week ago. He remembered what Lydia had said about the driveway, but found it hard to imagine the demons that haunted her, while the sun shone down over the blackened beams. He did not notice how the trees swayed and bristled despite the stillness, and he was oblivious to the ominous flight of the large black birds following their progress in the car. The fire had only ravaged one end of the house, and so the overall appearance of the farmhouse was still impressive.

"What did you say the fight was about?"

"My stepfather wanted to buy the meadow over by the Forge to graze a few horses. Well, he *did* buy it from the church for a pittance, by all accounts. The villagers said it was common land, and that it would be sacrilege to allow it to be churned up because it was an ancient site full of rare meadow flowers. When the records were checked, it turned out that they were right, the land never belonged to the church; it had escaped enclosure and so it seemed that the church had wrongfully taken the money for it. When they were publicly denounced in the local paper, the church tried to escape implication or blame, and shifted it on to my poor unlucky stepfather.

"The vicar let 'slip' to the villagers that Michael had tried to deceive them all, the church included, and that no money had passed hands, which of course was a lie. They came by night, a whole band of them with flaming torches demanding he admit what he had tried to do. What made matters worse, of course, was that not only had he had dared cheat them of the land they had held for centuries and now still refused to admit it, but that he was an outsider. Someone smashed a window and lobbed a torch in. I think it terrified them all how quickly the fire took hold and most of them left before they could be accused of arson or murder. The braver ones stayed to help curb the fire, after all the house is still part of the estate and they wouldn't have dared destroy it."

"It must have been horrifying for you, were you hurt?"

"No, I was away in London."

"But didn't you feel sad with what happened to the house?"

"No, not really. It was a refuge at first, but I never felt part of the house and I never managed to conquer its omens and cold spots. I never really belonged here, I suppose. Even now I feel strange coming back. I love the meadows, the woods, and the streams, but the house is ...well I can't explain it, but so much has gone on here over the years, I feel it has a cloud over it.

"Still, I reckon you were upset when you found out about the real cause of the fire. It's hardly the story of the century, is it? They must have been a bit desperate for news, dragging you out here for this! But then you could mix the occult with anything and it would have front-page news after the recent furore with Gerald Gardner. That was what was important for you, Jake, wasn't it?"

There was an underlying anger in this last sentence, an accusation almost. "Lydia, I'm not writing it."

"Well, someone else is simply going to be sent here, and it's going to start all over again, isn't it?"

"Look, I've given up my job. Does that please you? And before I left I told them it was nothing, just a hoax. Don't expect me to have converted them and half the world to whatever you believe when I don't understand it myself."

He shouted this at her and registered her shock by the way she looked. He was becoming increasingly irritated by the insinuations that he was unseeing, unfeeling, and callous. Maybe he had been in the beginning, but that had changed and he felt guilty for shouting at her. His reaction had also taken him by surprise, since he hardly knew her. Why did his emotions feel so taut?

As the car slowly drew in the yard at the back of the house, a woman walked out to greet them. Although it had to be Lydia's mother, Isobel, he thought how so very small she seemed even compared to Lydia, who was herself petite. Instead of the golden curls he had expected, she had short dark hair and dramatic red lips.

"Lydia darling, come in. Don't lurk by the stables with your poor friend."

There was a moment of awkwardness, as it became clear that Lydia hadn't thought how to introduce him to her mother. He wasn't even a friend, they had just met. "This is Jake, Ma, the friend I told you about who was going to do the write up about the fire."

"You mean my husband's idiotic and greedy little scheme that nearly lost us everything? God, that man is such an embarrassment. Come, you had better meet him. So ironic to think that we survived the war, not a single bomb landed anywhere near us, and now this had to happen." She said with a wry smile. Obviously there was no love lost between them.

It was surreal to be ushered passed the blackened oak timbers, treading in the piles of ash and debris that were still left. Jake smelt the burnt wood and suddenly felt sorry for Isobel inhabiting half of what had been her home. The kitchen door had now become the means of entry now that the scullery and outhouses were gone.

"The estate says it will be mended, but of course there are few men working now, and I doubt they will repair it for years to come."

The kitchen itself was huge. It was decorated with a crude cream limewash and there were few items on the bare walls, but glowing range made it feel cosy and warm. Bent over the crooked kitchen table topping up a wine glass, was a refined looking man, but whose gruff voiced betrayed him to be the same person Jake had heard shouting after the dog on the day he had sped away.

"About time Lydia, you're late as usual. We were expecting you for lunch."

Ignoring her husband's rudeness, Isobel introduced them. "Michael, this is Jake, a friend of Lydia's from London. Lunch doesn't matter it's just so nice to see you, I have missed having you about the place, I am so lonely without you here, darling."

It was not surprising given the rough manners of Michael, whose courtesy hid a constant annoyance and impatience. A 'velvet fist in an iron glove' Lydia called her stepfather, whom she detested. Isobel had even finer features than her daughter; she was smaller boned and had a gentler manner. Lydia's manner was forthright when she wasn't dreaming. It was her inner beauty that was soft and rounded.

"Are you both staying for dinner? I have to warn you, although Lydia's probably said, I'm a dismal cook so you'll be taking your life in your hands. Actually Lydia's no better. Did she tell you she nearly killed eight people with uncooked kidney beans at a dinner party last month? I made you study Latin instead of domestic science at school, didn't I, darling? Poor girl was the only one, but I think it was more useful."

"But Mother, you never even showed me how to cook bacon. I *still* don't know how to make an omelette. I'll never catch a man like that!"

"Oh, tosh Lydia, they'll just have to take you out to eat. I know which I would rather do."

After the early start, Jake was secretly dying for someone to ask him whether he wanted a piece of the game pie he had eyed on the range, but with the array of wine bottles on the table, he guessed it would be a long time in coming, if at all.

"Can you stay for dinner?"

"Actually, I hope you don't mind, but I'm taking Jake over to see Nel. He's writing a story on her."

Michael muttered something about it being a waste of time writing a story on the local imbeciles, and walked out of the kitchen in disgust. Both women ignored him, as if he didn't exist.

"Oh! How interesting, and on what exactly?" Isobel rounded on Jake, and fixing him with her commanding eyes, he couldn't think of what to say. How much did Isobel know?

Lydia piped up. "Opera."

It didn't deter Isobel who darted straight to the heart of the matter instantly. "Oh you'll love it. You are very honoured because no one gets an invite to Nel's coven, Lydia says. Well, there's no law against it, not anymore, is there? There's probably loads of cunning folk who will now start to emerge. I find it exciting, not that I know much about it. It's all kept so hidden still, but I shouldn't wonder at some of the things they get up to in the villages around here. There is a sense of the old power everywhere in these quiet places. Do take care though. I'm all for enlightenment, but there is shadow and a great deal more 'truths' that most of us will ever understand. And there's no going back." She said all this with a sad smile, perhaps remembering her own mother.

Jake was having trouble digesting the fact that Isobel was - in a very subtle way - acknowledging that her daughter was a witch. His stomach fluttered with anticipation now that he sensed he was getting closer to those hidden things that Lydia had hinted at, of the unspoken of mysteries.

As if reading his mind, Isobel added: "She always was a strange child. We gave up in the end. Have you not heard of this area, its strange power that pulls you here again and again? It makes you never want to leave."

At that moment, Michael walked back into the kitchen. "For Christ's sake, not AGAIN! Every time you two are together, all you talk about is this ridiculous gobbledy gook and devils in the night. You should be locked up with the rest of the village mad hatters. I do think that you should accept that we are not in the Dark Ages, *this is the twentieth century, woman!*" He raised his eyebrows dramatically and roared with forced laughter, looking at Jake for support.

"Come, I'll show you Lydia's garden," said Isobel leading them out of the kitchen.

No wonder Lydia doesn't like it here, Jake thought, following Isobel through a red brick stone archway surmounted by a carved stone image of the Green Man. There was a green gate, painted with another green man. They walked along a dark narrow passage that was walled either side and roofed by an arbour of roses and wisteria. It seemed unbearably long and claustrophobic to him and he was glad when they emerged inside a sunken circle, enclosed by grassy mounds carpeted with daisies and feverfew. A wizened blackthorn bush held pride of place, and from one of the branches, a blackbird sang above them.

"She built this garden herself," Isobel stated proudly, "when she was sixteen." It was clear Lydia was more relaxed here than inside the house, more confident, perhaps but a heavy look passed between mother and daughter, signalling that Lydia desired to end Isobel's flow of talk. Jake guessed that they had trespassed too far into her sacred space, her magical garden.

"We really have to go. Sorry. I'll call you tomorrow. Can I leave Mabel with you?"

"Of course, put her in the stable with the others."

They journeyed the few miles further, to Nel's house, which seemed much more romantic and remote to him, viewing it for the second time. The overgrown path seemed wilder still, reaching out as if to capture straying visitors by the ankles. A casement window stood ajar, wafting merry peals of laughter across the balmy afternoon, and also an ethereal chorus of music that seemed otherworldly, yet had a familiar tune as if it had came long ago in a different era.

It was strange to see another piece of the jigsaw slot into place as Jake wryly observed Nel and Lydia hugging each other with laughter and affection. Nel brushed the loose curls from Lydia's hair like a mother would have done, as she listened intently to Lydia's animated talk.

She was so excited to be with Nel that her whispers in Nel's ear were quite audible to Jake. "Did you send him to find me? How strange for us to meet like that, the *same* evening. I think we've convinced him to ditch the story but I wanted bring him tonight to experience something of what we've told him. I had no time to ask you, I just thought it would be all right. You can tell him to go if it's not."

He saw a mixture of tenderness and quick anger cross Nel's eyes, but she for once was too polite to say anything further, having grasped that he had heard them. "Welcome back Jake. I am glad you found each other. Come, meet the others."

Glass lanterns were strung up from the rafters of the kitchen and in a continuous line out to the apple trees, as if in readiness for a party, or what looked to be a party of people engulfing the small cottage by their numbers. For a moment, he couldn't quite place what it was about them, but it didn't seem like a normal social gathering. And then, it was obvious. He had never seen such an odd grouping of people thrown together at such close quarters. Some were laughing loudly, others talked quietly in dark corners, and it was marvellous to him, after the boredom he now felt for his London life, to see a lady in her seventy's talking to a young man in his early twenties, or the aristocratic man in his tweeds laughing with the labourers. As Nel drew him further into the sitting room, the group stopped talking. Dozens of eyes bored into him, through him, and he looked for Lydia to dispel the silence. Suddenly, she was by his side but was conscious of the hesitation and the fear that was now almost tangible.

Finally, one of the stout labourers broke the deadlock. "What is this? Why have you bought him, a stranger to us? How can we trust him? Last week he comes here as a reporter and now all of that is forgotten? You must be crazy Lydia, and I for one won't stand by and let you destroy everything. Are you lovers already? Is that what has made you forsake your sacred oath? Is your conviction so weak that it blows in the wind, or have you lost your mind with lust?"

Lydia had slumped against the doorframe, ashen with the shock of this unexpected assault. Before there was time for anyone else to respond, Jake had crossed the room and, grabbing the man by the throat, threw him against one of the gnarled oak pillars.

"Never insult her in my presence. That goes for anyone here who dares insinuate that Lydia is fickle or loose. I assure you she works from pure intentions, and as I have bought her nothing but trouble I will leave, but not before you give her an apology."

At this he slammed the man's head back against the beam with a thud, jerking his face toward Lydia by seizing a fistful of dark curls. There was a shout of pain, and the muttering of something unintelligible. Jake tightened his grip. "Say it damn you!"

There was a manic look in his eyes, and it was obvious that he would soon be pushed to the edge of all reason. Both men towered over everybody else in the room, and were evenly matched for a physical fight, but Jake's fury made him deadly. Nel's voice broke up the stalemate. It was deeply resonant and seemed to echo about the room with power.

"Will, apologise to Lydia, and Jake, let him go. There shall be no more talk of this. I understand your concerns Will, but you have shamed me. You stupidly attacked them without waiting to hear what the position was. Do you think I would let any harm come to any one of us? Where is *your* trust and loyalty, Will?"

Jake let go of the dark fistful of curls and stood to one side.

Will, red faced but shamed, walked slowly forward to where Lydia stood. "I am sorry for my hasty words."

She reached and rested her fingers lightly on his arm. "Will, I would *never* break an oath. You should know me by now. Do I not come from a long and ancient line of those who have trodden the way of wise against all perils and dangers? I bring Jake as a friend, because he seeks to understand and he *is* making an effort to do so. You can't return to the shadows, Will, there is no point. People are beginning to know about us, and it is best they understand rather than spread lies. It *is* the best way. I vow he will not betray us. I also know Jake has a need for someone to show him the shadows, but let him see first."

"She is right, there is something special about him," added Nel. "I don't like being surprised either, but Lydia has shown courage and foresight. What is more, Jake has given up his job, there is no story to write anymore, he comes here for himself. Now let us get on with what we are here for and forget it."

A young girl stood up. She was plain and looked unexpected worn for her age. She had a long running scar running from her cheek to her ear which was partially hidden behind a curtain of long dark hair. "There will be those who remember this beyond your lifetime, Lydia. I just hope you know what you are doing, because I feel that both of you will bring each other nothing but heartache, and to us you bring nothing but trouble and unease."

"Megan, keep quiet or get out. I have said my piece, and that applies to anyone else who chooses to ignore my warning," snapped Nel.

The girl walked sullenly out of the cottage on her own, looking back to cast Lydia a sly and resentful stare.

Nel added "That girl has no witch-blood in her and not a great deal of power, but she is motherless, and I promised her mother that I would guard her in the Old Ways. Not all families pass on the blessings the way that yours have, Lydia, so don't feel angry with her, feel sorry. Now come, drink to the long night, and to friends."

A horn of red wine was passed to Will who tilted his head to drink and then offered it to Jake with a smile. "Apologies to you both. Drink and be merry, please. And welcome."

As Jake took his share, the rest of the crowd echoed the sentiment in a subdued but meaningful chorus. The tweed-clad aristocrat came forward to Jake with a grin. "Welcome then. You know we go skyclad don't you?"

"Sorry but I don't know what you mean."

Lydia whispered in his ear.

"Naked!"

He looked around the room for affirmation, aghast, until the room again burst into laughter. To his relief he discovered it had been a joke.

Nel added fuel to the banter. "Jake do you honestly think that old Martyn here would risk catching his you-know-whats on a blackthorn tree in the middle of the night, or would really expose himself in the cold of a February moon? He'd probably drop down dead with the cold, and we would probably drop down from laughing. You have to use your common sense and not believe everything you hear. Not when we live at the mercy of the Siberian winds here in north Norfolk! Try to keep an open mind. We are going to celebrate Midsummer, that is all."

By the time they filed out of the cottage, darkness had fallen and the lanterns glowed, throwing shadows across the lawn. They silently passed the last house in the village, along dark narrow lanes and hedgerows, no one uttering a sound. For Jake, it intensified the noises of nature: the hooting of the owls and the scurrying in the undergrowth taking on a new resonance. They tramped through the ripening corn toward the shadows of the great wildwood standing on the brow of a hill.

At the head of a deep gully, Will stopped and delved into his rucksack, taking out a coil of thick rope, which he secured to a large tree. A very large witch was solemnly handed the rope. She tied it round her ample girth and beneath the shadows of the trees all they heard was her grunts and wheezes as she made her descent. A few of the younger men started to snigger, until Nel chastised them under her breath.

"It's fortunate for all we're not in the burning times now. What happened to silence and secrecy?" A crashing in the shrubbery below signalled the descent had been safely accomplished. Nel again quashed any mirth. "I'd like to ask all of you to be silent and pray that the spirits accept us, for we mean them no harm. We are now entering their sacred place, in their time of night."

There was now a reverent hush and the rest of the party made the descent in silence. The close proximity of the spirit of the old trees was now unmistakable, even to Jake, as they wove their way through to the sacred grove. From the sidelines, Jake observed as the circle formed with each shedding day-to-day personalities like skin, in order to revere the Old Ones. By now they had all donned black robes. Flaming torches marked the quarters, with Nel presiding at the north with the aristocratic man serving as her 'priest'.

Two hours flew by for Jake in a heartbeat. He watched, entranced by the beautiful simplicity of the ceremony, the great happiness and rejoicing, the lyrical movement and energy of the circle, the fusion with the earth and sky and that great moon shining down through the trees. Reality had been shifted. Lydia came to the centre, surrounded by rhythmic chanting, and bringing waves of tangible power to the edge of the circle, until he was sure he could see currents of azure blue pulsating all around them, yet it seemed to flow from one to another. With fierce concentration they were willing it upwards and outwards, until it was released with whatever intentions were sung in their thick guttural callings. The release of tension in the air was like a crack of lightening, it happened suddenly, and there was a new lightness.

    He followed their gaze upward through the trees, and heard himself sigh at the splendour of the full moon. He had never noticed how strong its pull had been before, and how awed and reverent he felt towards it all. Lydia was waving her arms like the waves of the sea, gently, coaxing. Her words suffused with power and their meaning, although not clear to him, were part of a beautiful call which he felt spoke to a part of his soul that had lain dormant for most of his life.

    He sensed unnamed, faceless beings being drawn closer to the circle from the surrounding shadows. And with a shiver he realised that the light of the moon was being coaxed down so that Lydia herself began to glow with its beauty and power. Her words slowed. They became deeper, more urgent and it seemed that her voice had changed until he no longer recognised the words as coming from a human, but from the moon itself, resonating with universal truth. He saw how Lydia's face took on many aspects, from young girl, to mother, and finally, he saw her as she would be at the end of her life, in old age. Yet her power and beauty increased, until even the blade of the dagger held at her heart had become imbued with moonlight. Only afterwards, on reflection, was he sure that he had seen the outline of a stag's antlers to the edge of the clearing where they worked.

    Shivering with cold and hunger, the party tramped back through the wood, ascended the hill and over the hard fields baked by the summer sun, to the cosy cottage. "Let's have a bloody drink then," Nel ordered.

    Lydia handed Jake a mug of cider. "I'm sorry if it went on a bit. I just wanted you to try and experience what it all means to us. We don't worship the devil, you see!"

    They were all laughing at him and he suddenly felt like an ignorant schoolboy, patronised and stupid. He spun round on her angrily.

"I'm glad I provided you with entertainment, I've had enough at your expense. I'm going." He glared at them, daring them to speak to him. Instead, he was met by murmurs of innocent concern. Immediately he could see that he had once again been too rash. They meant no harm. "Jake, don't go, please. You should be flattered that we wanted you to see, that you were invited in. We thought it would help you to understand."

The whole company held up their glasses, proffering a peace offering and he couldn't but help be placated by circle of smiles. Relaxing in their cups, the rest of the night soared, danced and crashed as if Dionysus himself had descended into the spirit of the group. They drank, talked and sang until dawn; until the small cottage windows were steaming with condensation, and the dew was glittering brightly on the grass outside. As Jake opened the door and inhaled the sharp cold morning air, he saw that the sun was rising whilst candles still flickered in the coloured glass lanterns hanging from the trees. Behind him, voices continued a half-hearted, drunken debate on the pros and cons of sleeping in the barn versus the house, and he wished only for sleep, exhausted by all he had been privy to during the long night.

Lydia followed him into the chill of the garden; one of Nel's grey cats eyeing them suspiciously as they crept away from the cottage. Grabbing blankets from the car, they walked to the copse of ancient oaks at the bottom of the garden, by the water meadow. The stream was burbling soothingly and the birds were beginning their morning song. Laying the blankets on the damp ground, they were too numbed by wine to feel much of the seeping cold. She nestled in the crook of his arm, and his heart boomed with joy and excitement, spurred on by the still visible moon showing through the leafy canopy above them.

Jake was on edge, taut with desire. He had watched her loveliness unfold all night and was sure that it was she who could take him to his life's purpose — sure that they had to be together. He had never been so enchanted, but now there was beauty in everything, even the toads he saw crawling by the brook.

She turned her head to him as she lay and whispered into his chest. "I wish time could stand still, where you want it to. Today has been so perfect. I feel so close to you now that you understand a little more about me. Most of my friends have no idea but with you, it's as if I've known you all my life. Thank you for not judging. It means so much to me."

Everything *was* perfect and the moment went on and on like the sinuous thread of a spider's web. In the year's to come, he would try to re-live bits of this time with her, again and again, throughout his life and long after it had all turned to dust. He pulled her closer to him, kissing her with all the tenderness and love he felt was her due. She began to kiss him back, grabbing his hair but then stiffened and stopped, turning the other way. All of a sudden, she seemed sad and the moment was gone.

"Jake, have you ever been in love? So much in love with someone that you felt you could die for them?"

Frustration and tiredness, coupled with drink, replaced desire with irritation at her sudden shift of mood. "No, I'm afraid not. Maybe I'm just one of your regular bastards, or maybe you just like to dramatise everything."

"Jake, don't talk like that." The wounding had been intentional, because yet again she had wrong-footed him. "But do you think you could love someone totally and utterly, be capable of the purest love, to put that person before all else?" she asked in a small child-like voice.

"Let's just go to sleep" he replied wearily, pretending to sleep for what seemed like hours accepting that he was falling in love with her; that he felt a physical pain every time she walked away, or retreated into her own world.

Through half-closed eyes, he watched her move off across the lawn, turning at the last minute at the corner of the barn and smiling, as if she were party to some knowledge he could never share in. Again her inner light hit him sharply like a dagger, twisting all reason, and giving rise to the fear that he could never have her. He wanted to make her realise that *he* was the one to love her in the way she was searching for but there was something in the way she had walked away from him, which had made him shiver with foreboding. *This wasn't the time: something else had to take place — they had to wait.* Perhaps this was his cowardly way of saving himself from further rejection, but it was strange how strong this impression had come upon him.

After a time, he followed her into the barn and found her asleep on one of the mattresses, huddled under the dusty blankets like a child. He wanted to hold her protectively as she slept, but his dark thoughts twisted around and around in his head so malevolently, that he gave in to the heaviness of his body and allowed sleep to take him, giving him some respite.

There was another who had seen them by the brook. And now she smiled triumphantly having settled her score so swiftly with Lydia. She had seen that Lydia had finally found her soul-mate in this attractive young man, that her quest was all but over. She had felt the heat between them but old jealousies linger and she had worked her limited but focused intent against their union. She had watched the old rituals carefully, time and time again, and now she mimicked the movements and gestures, made them her own to soothe her hatred. Let their love consume them; let them be like islands to each other, unrequited, their passions burning whilst they could never be as one. She crooned her dark spells softly in the air, the moon throwing back her scarred reflection in the mirror she held above each of them, as she performed the final rite. Megan then quietly crept away to watch and wait in the still cottage.

Jake still remembered the call of the thrush that first broke his sleep. The sun crept its way across the stained floorboards of the barn floor to where he lay cocooned in the grey scratchy blankets. A pair of white doves watched, all knowing. The smell of frying bacon dispelled his solemn notions and despite the rough blankets, he had had one of the deepest sleeps he remembered. Where was she? He recalled her so clearly sweeping off into the dawn mist only hours before. He got up and searched out a cup of tea. The door to the kitchen was open and the grey cat, who had looked so menacing the night before now grinned serenely in the sun. Nel was frying up a colossal breakfast on the stove humming to herself.

The few who were up were silently nursing heavy heads. Obviously, no one was permitted to mention the night before. That was the rule, even though a window in the kitchen had been broken during the night's high spirits. He had not seen Lydia at first. She was leaning against the door frame, staring out across the meadow, where a strange kind of sea fret had come to sit in the hollow, obscuring the trees beyond. She was wearing a linen dress and her unbrushed hair had fallen into ringlets. He willed her to meet his eyes, but she seemed lost in the strange fog that had come from nowhere. Lydia was watching a white horse that was only just visible through the veil of mist. Finally the animal dissolved into the blanket of white, and Lydia felt a sad longing for it to reappear, for she was sure it was the same one that often came to her in dreams.

"Did you sleep well with the pigs and chickens then, my man?" Nel asked, shaking him out of himself. "What are you both doing today? You're welcome to stay."

Jake looked at Lydia, praying she wouldn't subject them to another night with all these people. He needed some time with her alone. "Jake, I had my fun yesterday, what's it to be? Please don't say a family lunch. I can't make decent conversation."

He suddenly had an idea that would take them away from the cottage, without appearing rude. "How far is Thetford from here?"

"About an hour away, why?"

"This friend of mine is a captain in the Life Guards, they're on summer camp and he's invited me to an open day. Jousting, horses, that kind of thing."

He could see the response was not good, as the whole room seemed to roll their eyes in unison. "Since when has watching a load of cavalry officers showing off in tight trousers, been fun?" one lad asked. Sam was about Jake and Lydia's age and had been apprenticed to a farrier since he was thirteen. With a fount of knowledge about his craft, Jake envied him for his focus and love of what he did. His humour was down to earth and Jake secretly admitted that had it not been for this weird occasion, they would probably have never spoken under normal circumstances.

"Oh, I don't know, Lydia might quite like it!" Nel said bawdily.

"Nel! I'm not *that* desperate, besides I've had my fill of army men, they only talk about themselves. Every regiment, it's all the same, mess dinners, pompous majors and manly wives. And the lifeguards are the worst!"

"Oh, come on Lydia, you like horses don't you?"

"Yes, the animals, not the girlfriends and wives. Well all right, as long as we can just look at the horses. And don't expect me to dress up. I refuse. I've come to relax this weekend."

"There'll be free champagne and a free lunch."

"There'll be some price to pay, I suppose. Oh, all right then."

Twenty minutes later, they were on the road to Thetford. Jake still couldn't shake off a sense of foreboding and although it would have been easy for him to have changed direction – after all, she had no desire to go there – he was powerless to stop and so he kept on course for where the camp was stationed. The gates of the military camp were festooned with brightly coloured flags. A soldier stopped the car.

"We're here to see Captain Seligman."

"*Captain* Seligman," Lydia drawled, mimicking him. "Is he a chinless wonder then? Or a pigmy in big boots?"

"Neither, you'll probably find him charming."

"Oh I get it. Nice chap and all that, but nothing up top. Don't tell me his father was in the Life Guards, and all his family before that, and he doesn't have a clue what to do now, let alone a brain cell to work it out with."

"No, he's not like that. You might even be pleasantly surprised."

"Can we go if I don't like it?"

"Of course. Come on, it'll be fun."

His words were lost over the din of the crowds who had come to see the summer horse displays. It was now hot, and the rows of spectators shimmered in the hazy swell of the heat. They headed for one of the younger looking soldiers. "Excuse me, Captain Seligman please?"

"Certainly. Sir, Madam, please follow me." They picked their way through the field to the officer's tent. "This is Captain Ellews, he'll look after you until Captain Seligman is dismounted. I think he's riding in the rugby round." A team of black horses beyond were pulled into a huddle on the field, their riders trying to wrestle each other from the saddle.

Captain Ellews, a large sandy-haired officer beamed at them, his hair flopping rakishly over one eye. "Lydia? Had a groom called Lydia once, damn pretty filly ,too." He winked at Jake for approval, conspicuously eyeing the outline of her figure through the thin printed cotton dress. Luckily she was too distracted by the horses in the field to have noticed, and wandered away from them.

As the conversation wound down, an even taller officer, sauntered over, hot and sweaty from the match. "Just been bloody knocked off. I say, who that is over there talking to Paddy, haven't seen her before."

All eyes followed his to where a group of officers were swarming around a pivotal spot by the open entrance. As the crowd briefly parted, Jake now saw Lydia happily ensconced with a glass of champagne, laughing in the midst of all that male adoration. Mollified by this sudden attention, she tipped him a wink.

The voice on the tannoy announced the end of the round of rugby on horseback. The corporals, not surprisingly, had beaten the officers 2-1.

"And next ladies and gentlemen we have tent pegging. To start the round we have Captain Seligman on Fleetwood."

CHAPTER SIX

1999

Scattering crumbs across the lawn for the birds, Megan reflected on how swiftly the years had passed. The dampness of the early morning made her bones ache and she knew that she was beginning to stoop with the pain of her arthritis. The damp fenlands were possibly the worst of places for her, but she would never leave Martha's Cottage, nor Jake. She had never married. Sometimes she thought back ruefully, at how good-looking Jake had been that day he had strode into Nel's cottage with Lydia. She had never met a man who had attracted her the way he had, and although she had made many things happen in her life, she knew she could never have him. He wouldn't have wanted a plain girl like her and besides, she thought with a grimace, nobody's flame could burn brighter than Lydia's did for him.

She was no longer painfully self-conscious of the scar on her cheek, having long accepted her age and plainness. It was enough to see him, to be with him in whichever way it had to be, every day.

It had been Nel who had thought of the arrangement, and it had worked well, just as she had predicted. Jake had travelled for much of the time that Megan had worked for him; now a highly successful photographer, she liked to think that she had always been a quiet, invisible part of his success. Nel had always looked after her, and saw that Jake would carry on as a protector long after her death. It had been so many years ago, yet a residue of Nel's power still resonated within her. She had inherited some of Nel's most treasured possessions, things of great power, that had come down through long lines of the Craft. Following Nel's death, she had moved away to housekeep for Jake, and somehow never had the heart to find a new coven, or work with others again. The beautifully worked tools bearing their ancient symbols were now safely at the bottom of the lake behind the cottage where Megan knew they would never be found. Sometimes, but very rarely, when the moon was full, she was drawn again to the shadows, to work her old magic, but mostly she had no heart for it. It was enough for her to listen to the animals and the wind; to silently watch and yearn.

They had lived peaceably for all these years, she and Jake. She had seen women come and go. Some had lasted for years, but they all left him empty for what could never be, she reflected with quiet satisfaction. It was she who knew him best, down to every minor detail which she relished, from the washing of his shirts to the making of his bed, menial tasks that kept her close to him. The final bond was Rebecca.

In some way Jake and Megan had come to sharing almost a joint parental responsibility for the girl; Jake valuing her common sense and womanly experience in bringing up his niece. Rebecca had arrived at Martha's Cottage one cold December day at the age of four, and Megan remembered sharply how her maternal instincts had been roused so quickly by the little bundle wrapped in her winter duffel coat.

Rebecca was the daughter of Jake's only sister, and nobody knew who her father was. It had shaken him deeply when Mary had been killed in a car accident, but then there was the little girl who bought so much warmth to the house, so much laughter. In many ways, in Megan's mind, their's had been a 'marriage' cemented by the child's arrival, fostering her own role as mothering by proxy. It meant that he could never get rid of her, for the girl's sake.

The sound of Rebecca's stereo wafting across the garden through the open bedroom window bought her back to earth. Megan craned her neck upwards to see Rebecca laughing at her and waving. She had thick black curls that framed her broad face, tall like her uncle, she didn't have his blond looks or grey-blue eyes. Pretty, but not beautiful, Rebecca's best feature was her energy, Meg thought. There was never a dull moment and perhaps she and Jake had spoilt her, each in their own way. They had given her enough love and affection during her childhood to give her confidence, and now at seventeen, there was nothing in the world they would have denied her.

Rebecca was bored. There were still weeks of the summer holiday to go, but her friends from boarding school were all so far away. Martha's Cottage was her home but now it felt stifling. Built with two curved ends, a vicar had built it in the 18th-century for his daughter, Martha, and the lack of corners was devised to keep the devil out. Martha had died a spinster, no doubt suffocated by all its godliness.

Then there was Megan, who had never even known what love had been, who was always watching her wherever she went. How did she manage to know *everything*, no matter where she went? As a child, she had always loved Megan, but now Rebecca resented her constant protective interference, especially when her uncle was away. She wasn't even a relation, she was just paid help, and still she told her what she could and couldn't do. Recently her resentment of the older woman had spiralled, and Rebecca had begun to notice how odd she was. She fed hares; she talked to birds and walked for miles in the middle of the night. She had accepted these eccentricities as a child, but now they just served to illustrate how different they were and how isolated she had become.

Somewhat sheltered from the world, Rebecca craved romance; an escape from the dreary cottage and her old guardians. Although the cottage was small there were still some areas from which she had been banned. One of these was Uncle Jake's study. It was in the oak folly at the bottom of the garden, filled with dusty old books and a huge oak desk. Its Gothic windows faced all sides of the garden, and so it was hard for intruders to approach when he was at his desk.

Recently these boundaries had become too enticing for Rebecca not to breach. Of course, her uncle had no perception that his beloved niece would have stolen the key. All he saw as he looked on her was the small, fragile little child, with dark ringlets, who had come to him for his protection and love. He did not see the woman she had become. And for Megan she was also an angel, because she mirrored her own circumstances. It was almost as if Megan tried to live again through Rebecca, and this irked the girl even more. And then there was this possessive knowledge Megan purported to have of her Uncle Jake, which she found downright creepy. There was so little to be learnt of her own parents, that she was determined to find out about her past: her uncle's past. Why had he never married? Every time she had tried to broach the subject, she had received a curt answer that showed there was much more to uncover. As she counted the long summer days ahead of her, she determined that this would be her mission. To discover the truth about her uncle. The reason he had Megan, and not a wife.

As she waved cheerily at Megan, she felt a sense of triumph about last night's adventure. It had been so easy to steal the key from the cabinet in the sitting room whilst her uncle was away for the weekend. Later, she had crossed the lawn in the blackness, lest Meg could see her from one of the windows. The grass was wet, and as she ventured out under the sliver of new moon light, a hare darted out in front of her. If she had been of a superstitious nature it might have seemed like an omen. Bold as anything, it sat up on its hindquarters, twitching its nose as if it knew what was contained in her heart. But, being a very practical girl, and one who preferred the sound of her own voice to listening and sensitivity, Rebecca strode purposely across the lawn.

Until that moment, she had felt like a child trapped in the budding body of a growing woman. She had only heard about passion from books and films. Romance seemed a far-off conception, if it existed at all. She doubted it. There had never been anything remotely romantic or passionate up to this point in her life or, it appeared, in anyone else's, to disturb the peace of Martha's Cottage. Even quarrels were sparse and the prospect of Jake or Megan ever having a wild night of passion was almost laughable. The only encounters she had had with boys of her own age were a great disappointment.

Sometimes, when she looked at her reflection in the mirror, she wondered whether her own father had such green eyes. Did her mother have blonde curls, or dark gypsy locks? Were they in love beyond the bounds of human existence? All these things consumed her mind on a daily basis and there was nobody with whom she could share these thoughts.

As she unlocked the door of the folly, she breathed in the smell of rich cigar smoke, and there was a stillness that unnerved her. She shone the torch around the room, until it illuminated a wooden chest carved with a great dragon. She whistled to her self in surprise, she had never seen it before and it was like the carved Italian *cassonne* she had seen on a school trip at the Victoria and Albert Museum. Opening the lid the smell of old wood and earth assailed her nostrils, as the beam from the torch revealed bundles of letters — by the same hand.

The writing was distinctive, with large flourishes ... they had to be from a woman. They were dated from more than half a century ago, yet they had been kept so pristinely, they could have been sent yesterday. There were all different kinds of postmarks. Some from London, some from Norfolk, Glenn Cannick in Scotland. She lit the remains of a candle on the desk and as she began to read, the quest to examine the contents of the folly was forgotten. She was too enthralled to care about Megan, or being seen, and so she stayed there until the sun rose, devouring the letters one by one. Occasionally she could have sworn that she saw shadows move across the lawn but perhaps it was just the reflections of the statues in the candlelight.

When she stepped out into the morning sun, she knew she was changed. It all seemed so different now. She had entered the folly with great intrepid excitement and now trudged back to the house, overburdened with the past. There was a strange sensation that she had aged by years in reading about the tragedy — absorbed in the characters as if she had been part of their lives. The love of two men for one woman, and her heartbreak at the treachery of one, destroying all three in the end. There was so much waste to beauty and love.

It was several days before Rebecca felt herself again; convinced the spirits of the lovers had possessed her. Some girls at school once had experienced awful nightmares after smuggling in a *ouja* board and so she began to stay up as late as possible, rather than enter the dread state of sleep in the darkened bedroom. Even the round 'corners' were party to ghostly shadows that lurked everywhere, watching. On the third day, she could contain it no more and so she confided to Meg what she had done, partly through curiosity, and partly as a way to stop the dreams. Who was this woman? Was she still alive? Megan had only stared at her weirdly, mumbling something about leaving the part alone but from that Rebecca was convinced that she *was* still alive, and resolved to find her. To feed what was now becoming an obsession, and to bring the story to a happy end.

Every night since going to the folly she had dreamt of this shadow-creature with burning eyes and wild locks of hair. Sometimes she would be wailing at her loss, at other times silent in a rapture of love. But always she would ride a beautiful white horse towards the horizon of the seashore, where the sun fell in red fiery pools.

Megan briskly cleared the breakfast table. It was the first time Rebecca had seen her uncle since the previous evening and there was now an awkward silence between them. Eating her toast, head down Rebecca crunched angrily, chewing over her situation. Having read the letters, her resolution to experience 'life' had grown desperate. She had discovered the burden of her uncle's grief, which he had carried around secretly - until yesterday when it had burst its banks. It was too much. In her eyes, he had taken on a new status, becoming a focus of glamour and interest, which also served to make her own dissatisfaction the greater as she was aware that even he had had a great adventure and she had never experience anything close to romance and love.

Her uncle shuffled annoyingly behind *The Times,* at the breakfast table, which epitomised her plight as she saw it. She had to have more, and now she had read about them in their youth, *their* golden time, she would grab it. Her chair scraped on the stone floor as she tried to squeeze out without drawing attention to herself. The paper came down, revealing his face and instead of his usual absent-mindedness, he wore an expression of anger.

"Rebecca, sit down."

She didn't have much choice, and so she obeyed, momentarily shocked out of her self-absorption as his fist crashed down on the table. "Megan has told me that while I was away, you went into my study. You actually stole the key and let yourself in, in the middle of the night. *How dare you?* Nobody goes in there, let alone a silly child like you. You have no right to be there. Did you think I wouldn't find out?"

She was scared, she had never seen him like this before, he was livid with rage, but she would have her say. "Of course you'd find out. I can't even breathe without bloody Meg spying on my every move. I should have known."

"Shut up and listen. Your trouble, young lady, is that I have totally spoilt you. You came here when you were little and turned my life upside down ... and you, you little spoilt girl, dare to invade the *only* place I have as my own. You have no right and no business to look at my personal things and if I find out you have been in there again, you can leave. I mean it. I will take you out of school, and you can make your own way. Have some respect for God's sake."

He spat these words at her, mad with anger and she was scared he was going to upturn the table. His words shamed her, but she felt her own despair and rage boil up too. Why was she always forbidden everything? Her bottom lip protruded petulantly. Pretence was useless, the game was up. Shame made her head and then just as suddenly defiance welled up against this subservience. Why not speak the truth?

"How can you expect to ban me from there and not expect me sooner or later to have a look? I didn't mean to go into the box, I was only going to take a look around the room because I had been curious for so long. I didn't know it contained letters and stuff."

The effect was dramatic. She had indeed opened Pandora's box. Jake's face showed disbelief and shock. She must have unearthed the letters, Lydia's things, all of the ghosts of his past he strove daily to keep at bay.

In trying to offer some kindness, Rebecca dug a deeper hole for herself. "Why don't you find out if she's still alive and go and meet her. I saw her address, it wouldn't take that long. You must have loved Lydia so much."

In the reflection of the mirror Rebecca saw Megan's face crumple into something in between disbelief and anger, showing again she had been listening beyond the open door. In the same instance her uncle spun round to face her, his eyes were fired with disbelief and rage. He formed the words in his mind but nothing issued forth. He was dumb. And then it came, this great shedding of emotion. It stirred up revulsion and terror in her. The words finally came, almost at a whisper.

"Don't you ever mention her name again. *How dare you ... you stupid ignorant little girl.* You know nothing about me, about my past, about her. What have you done with my letters? You disgust me. Get out, before I ..."

She ran from the room, but not before seeing his self-control diminishing as he looked at his huge hands, shaking with anger. At well over six foot, he seemed to tower over her with a strength and emotion that made him formidable, scaring her. After he'd stormed out of the house, she meekly crept back into the dining room and gathered the rest of the breakfast things, taking them into the kitchen. There had to be some way of making it right with him. Perhaps she could get them to make whatever peace they needed and make to make some sense of all those wasted years.

She would find Lydia herself!

By the time she encountered Megan in the kitchen she was almost jubilant with her new scheme. Megan glowered. *Now what?* she thought, trying not to catch her eye whilst loading up the dishwasher. Megan always knew everything that went on but Rebecca had never resented her so much as now. She could sense Megan glowering, her birdlike eyes boring into her back as she bent down with the plates.

"You've done your uncle a right turn, Miss."

Who did she think she was? It was fine to mother her in a nice way, but this was definitely not on. Of course, she felt terrible but there was no need to hammer the point in any further. Anyway it was between her and her uncle ... and Lydia.

"None of this would have happened if you hadn't stuck your nose in and told him!" *There ... that would tell her.*

"You have no idea what those letters meant to him, have you? They were *private,* not meant to be read by a clumsy schoolgirl. There are things in there that should be left well alone."

What did she know? Rebecca glared back at the housekeeper, seething with hatred. Why did she care anyway, she was only a paid help, after all. Even as she thought this, she knew that this was wrong. Megan was like family to them. Even so, she was always set apart by her strange ways; the way she fed the hares, and gazed for hours into a bowl of water. No wonder she had ended up without a family, as a lonely housekeeper. And now they were lumbered with her.

Megan sensed that the girl had turned. Unless she could control the situation, it could end up with catastrophic results: it could even end her life here with Jake. She had no choice but to warn Rebecca and convince her to forget the matter. She had only seen his rage come out once and thought back to the day at Nel's, when he flared up, again over Lydia. *That serpent!* Her old jealousies and insecurities returned as if she were a young girl again.

"I'm warning you, do not ever touch those letters again."

She also remembered Nel's book, which was also in the folly for safe keeping. It should have been buried with her, for it contained such mysteries of which even she had no concept, but although she had not understood its content she could never bear to part with it. It was a link with the old power and the thought that Rebecca could have discovered it, made her feel sick with fear.

"You must never mention that woman's name in this house again, especially in front of your uncle. He goes strange when it is mentioned. I knew her, as a young girl. I know what I am talking about. You must believe me, because if you don't, I swear you will regret it. She is cursed, she brings misery and unhappiness on everyone she meets. She charms them first and then, when it is too late ... well, they just can't see what she's really like."

Rebecca, if she was repulsed by her uncle's reaction, was even more horrified at this display, as Megan shrieked like a banshee, having lost all self-control, she was hysterical.

"She sounded lovely in her letters, I should know, I read them all. I *do* have feelings about people, and I am a good judge of character, you know."

Megan hissed at her like a snake, now beside herself with rage. "That bitch, broke all the sacred oaths of my friends, my family. None of them will ever speak to her again, she took our secrets and knowledge, and we will never forgive her. For myself, I wish she were dead. She has done more damage to your uncle than you'll know, and how *can* he ever forget her with the likes of you stirring up her name again? I have tried for years to get him to see sense, to soothe him, but you have undone a great many years of my care with one foolish sentence, you little fool."

She thought back to how others in the village had felt so wronged and betrayed when Lydia left them. An appointed priestess, she had no right to break the ancient oaths, and she had been sure that Nel had never got over it.

Rebecca viewed her with narrowed eyes. They were both off their heads. It was best she went for a drive. If she gave in to Megan this once, there was no limit to the woman's audacity. How dare she tell her what she could and couldn't do?

"Well, I'm afraid that now I have passed my test, you can't stop me, especially now I know her address. It's called Lemellan, where she lives, but I'm sure you know that, you obsessed old bag! There's nothing *anyone* can do to stop me. You're not my bloody mother and by the time you tell my uncle, I'll have gone, long gone. Uncle Jake needs some company and I think if I can find Lydia it will be wonderful for him. Evidently only I can put an end to this stupid impasse." She went on, confidently. What did that stupid old woman know? She was sick of her possessiveness, over her uncle, and over her.

As she watched the tall teenager stride out of the cottage in defiance, Megan felt sick with dread. She suddenly noticed how loud the clock sounded, as if it were saying the name, it swarmed in and around her thoughts. Her worst fears were coming true. She had to stop this meeting, but knew in her pragmatic way that her way with her Craft was clumsy. She could stop the meeting but it could harm Rebecca, and she didn't know how to ensure the girl remained safe. There was nothing for it but to let her go, for if anything, she loved the girl as if she were her own. But then, there was a noise. She had come back.

"You know what, I think you are jealous. You just want to keep my uncle to yourself, you sad old cow. Because you know if Lydia was back you would have no place in his life. You're sick, that's what I think."

Barely had she finished the words, when a pot was launched across the room and shattered into fragments at Rebecca's feet. Stunned, because she had never seen Megan this way, the girl stooped to pick up the brown earthenware shards. When the shock had subsided a little, she stood up and saw that Megan, too, was shaking. She had cut her hand and now held it over the white enamel bowl, where the sound of the blood could almost be heard in the silence. The beautiful day shone through the window at them, as if to remind them of the unhappy scene that was theirs — trapped inside with each other.

The monologue came, slow and steady, deep and low with meaning. "That woman is the last woman on earth who is wonderful. To raise her up again would be the very worst thing you could do for your uncle. The shock would kill him. It's enough that he's haunted by her every day of his life. It would be like raising the devil. She's evil. She's very powerful and her ways are evil, manipulative. I wouldn't be dragged within twenty miles of where she was, and nor will you, if you know what's good for you. She'll bring trouble. If you want to take your life in your own hands, that's up to you."

Despite this horrible scene, the violence that hung in the air, Rebecca could feel her stomach fluttering with excitement. Without a word, she turned on her heel and left for Lemellan. Megan watched the bright red blood spill in a single stream towards the plug hole, with a painfully slow motion that made her shiver with anticipation and dread of what was to come.

CHAPTER SEVEN

Rebecca found Lemellen along a wild track, banked high with cow parsley, protected by ancient oak and ash trees. Eventually, the ironstone gables stood proudly against the backdrop of the woodland beyond. The grandeur of the golden coloured house came as a bit of a surprise: she hadn't expected the old lady to have lived in such Elizabethan splendour. As she approached the great studded door with its strange carvings and stud work, a raven suddenly began circling around her head squawking noisily.

She stood there in utter fear, suddenly doubting her purpose, and questioning whether she really had a right to be there. What should she tell her? What was the point? To Lydia, she was a stranger. In those intervening fifty years she might have a family and husband of her own, she might not even remember her uncle. The situation suddenly seemed ridiculous.

As she stood agonising on the gravel, a large wolfhound sped past, running in through the massive door. *There must be somebody inside for it to be ajar,* she thought, pushing against the heavy oak. The door opened to reveal a great flag-stoned hallway, with rows of stag heads, all draped in ivy. The air was heavy with some kind of incense, heavier than church incense, and not as sweet. Her footsteps echoed on the flagstones as she quietly prayed that someone would come, so she wouldn't have to go further into the still, cold air of the gloomy passage.

She called out tentatively. "Hello!" Her voice was barely audible and broke off weakly with nerves. Further along the passage there appeared to be the library, a fire burning in an open hearth. The crackling of the flames drew her forward into a room hung with portraits and panelled with dark wood.

An elderly woman was seated at the window, facing out onto the gardens. Although she looked frail as she sat with her hands quietly folded in her lap, Rebecca stood entranced by her profile. Tresses of white-gold hair hung coiled loosely, over a beautiful black velvet bodice. Immediately she *knew* it was Lydia. Although she knew she would no longer be the young, beautiful girl she had seen in the photographs, there were still traces of the fine cheekbones and striking eyes.

The wolfhound snarled at the intrusion and Lydia finally turned her full gaze on the young girl standing before her. "Can I help you, my dear?"

There was no anger or even surprise at the intrusion. How could Megan have said those things about her, Rebecca mused?

"I ... I don't know what to say, really, only ... you don't know me, but I'm Jake Hammond's niece, Rebecca Pye. He's looked after me since my parents died. I've come here because I've done a wicked thing and I must put it right. You see, I read some letters I shouldn't have, including yours to my uncle and many others. I know everything, you see and I wanted to try and put it right, well, and to meet you. Uncle Jake seemed so different then, didn't he?" The words sounded foolish even as she spoke them.

There was a long silence. A flicker of anger perhaps, which quickly melted into a flicker of a smile, an understanding. "So he still has them, then?" she laughed ironically. "You're very lucky to have an uncle like Jake, he must be very kind to you, he always was to me. But I don't think you should tell him about meeting me though."

"Oh, but why not? I'm sure he would love to see you again. I wish you both could ..."

Lydia skilfully changed the subject. "I think I knew your mother years ago, Rebecca. You are very like her. You also remind me of how I was at your age. Inquisitive. Imaginative. Romantic."

Rebecca nodded, perplexed at this insight into her character. She glanced at a leather bound photograph album that lay by the carved chair with similar carvings to her uncle's oak *casonne*. Somehow the old lady knew. "He still has it then? I gave it to him many *many* years ago for safe keeping, and never asked for its return. He keeps the letters in it, doesn't he?"

Rebecca gulped.

"I hope that little fool Megan destroyed the book." She muttered darkly.

"What book?" *How did she know the name of their housekeeper?*

"It is of no matter to you" said Lydia sharply. Crossing the room she gently tilted Rebecca's chin toward the light. "You have nothing of him in you, that I can see. He was so blond. Have you seen many photographs of him when he was young?"

With a gracious incline of her hands, she gestured towards a book lying on the oak desk as if she had anticipated the visit. The first page was entitled 'Falklands', written in the same black flowery hand as the letters. It showed a large classical looking house with a portico and a great flight of steps disappearing under immense stone pillars. Under the shade of the portico sat Lydia, in a white shirt and jodhpurs. A dark-haired young man was placing daisies in her hair, shirtsleeves rolled up. They were both laughing and looked very much in love.

Rebecca was lost for words as she felt a great wave of sadness rise up in her chest. These people were so young and beautiful. It was hard to compare the glowing, taut skin of the young girl with the papery thin hands of the old lady opposite her. The hair had lost its thickness, but there were still traces of curls, and the eyes — they seemed to be the same, beautiful in their blackness. The man, laughing in the summer of his life, looked so strong and handsome as if he could combat the march of time with his perfection. She looked up at the old lady with tears in her eyes.

"Yes it's hard to believe I used to be beautiful once. That the woman in the photographs *is* me."

Rebecca started in surprise, ashamed that Lydia had read her thoughts.

"I always doubted my looks. And then, half of your life has gone before you realise that you do shine. *That's* when you realise that you have beauty ... when it is gone, when it is too late. Men will do many things for beauty, and there are only a few men that can see beyond it to the beauty of the soul. They are the only ones who will love you when all else is lost. That was my favourite picture of us." She added sadly, wistfully.

"The summer after the New Year's party?"

"Rebecca, how much has your uncle told you? You are an inquisitive little thing but sometimes it's best to let sleeping dogs lie."

Again, she registered no surprise at Rebecca's knowledge. The letters, after all contained so much, so many intimate details about their lives, that must have coloured her imagination and stayed with her. And so they talked about the smaller things in life and Rebecca came to many assumptions during their conversation. That Lydia was still married, or had married Niall Seligman, and so the chances of her original quest of Jake and Lydia reconciling themselves were very slim.

When the fire died low, Lydia took her for a walk in the garden, past the sunken lawns to the edge of the trees beyond. They sat on a rustic bench where the herbs ran wild, looking into the shadows. It was at this point that Rebecca began to feel let down. The glamour of the letters, the woman who had haunted her dreams and waking hours with her passion and beauty, was nothing more than a quiet old lady with apparently normal characteristics. It was as though the years had devoured her passion, as she listened to Lydia talk about the bees, the dogs and the garden. If she had once had a spirit, it must have died. Rebecca felt deflated by the conviction that age robbed people of their fire, leaving them dull shadows of what had been.

For her part, Lydia sensed that the girl was as insensitive as a cart horse, riding rough-shod over heavy clay. She had no intention of glamouring herself for the girl's benefit, or sharing any of the past with her. It was clear that Rebecca would never understand the hidden depths of the man she once knew, whom Rebecca called 'Uncle Jake'. She admired the girl's spirit, yet there was something about her Lydia couldn't warm to: a coldness about her that would be drawn towards, and foster jealousy throughout her life. And then it became clear. The similarity to Megan in her younger days was obvious. *What could she have thought to gain by allowing Rebecca to come all that way on her own?*

"Did Megan send you here?" she asked "You must know she hates me. What did she ask you to find out from me? What does she want?" Lydia's sudden fierceness, or perhaps the surge of power Rebecca felt her projecting, briefly restored the fires of youth.

Rebecca felt rooted to the spot as if paralysed. She couldn't think. "She didn't send me, honest. She didn't even want me to come because she said you were nothing but evil. I didn't believe her, that is why I came. She said you broke some oaths or something, and that you ruined my uncle's life. Why does she hate you?"

Lydia thought back to the strange, friendless young woman whom Nel had taken in. "Because the woman has no power of her own and jealousy consumes her."

A little power and knowledge had been used to wreak god knew what damage over the years, she thought ruefully. Lydia bitterly regretted not being with Nel at the end of her long illness, and still missed her guiding wisdom and strength. She often wondered what had happened to the things that were meant to have come down to her, the objects of such power that many feared. Megan had no right to them and could never understand their potency.

"I never broke any sacred oaths and I kept my honour with the people who mattered most. It broke my heart to leave, but I had no choice. That was many years ago. Be careful of Megan, Rebecca. She will try and control everything, and she is sly. She will watch you always. It would be best if you say nothing of your visit here."

Rebecca gulped and nodded, and as she did so, Lydia realised at once that the girl was fickle, and capable of a great ruthlessness, but how that would relate to her she was at a loss to imagine. She would probably never see the girl again but something in all of this was not right and filled her with apprehension.

Rebecca, however, was fired with a new excitement, a new hunger for knowledge. She returned to Martha's Cottage with a new purpose and, since it was past ten o'clock, the hour of her curfew, drove slowly down the drive, turning off the headlamps at the final bend. With dismay, she saw her uncle in the sitting room, with a scotch in one hand and something resembling a book or letter, in the other.

It seemed as if she had been staring at him for an age through the window but he seemed unaware of her presence, or her absence, for that matter. She felt rootless, as if she belonged nowhere. Uncle Jake only cared for her because he had to. If things had been different, she would have had her mother, even perhaps brothers and sisters to talk to. Her uncle seemed often so distracted. It was as if he was in his own world and she didn't exist.

The clock chimed above the soft music that had returned him to the past. It had been playing at New Year all those years ago when Lydia was only a little older than Rebecca. They had danced so closely that he could feel her body move under the silk of her dress and he had wanted to keep her close to him, forever. Never had she seemed so vulnerable and the only thing that had stopped him from carrying her off into the night was his great love for her. For he could see it was too late, that she loved somebody else and he could not change the way she felt. And so in spite of the shrivelling inside himself, he smiled down upon her as the clock chimed, kissing her cheek casually but with all the love he had, knowing it would be their last dance; loving her too much to want anything but her happiness. And despite everything she said, he knew that their time together would come, and that it was better to wait, for he was sure it would outlast this fleeting fascination she had for Niall.

But more than memories, he felt sick to think that Rebecca had just returned from seeing Lydia, when there hadn't been an hour every day of his life that he had not longed for her. Nel had tried to make him go to her years later, but he would not allow himself. She had sworn to give the word and he would come, and he had never heard. Megan told him of the other men in her life, and so the years had passed, with him finding other women casually as and when he felt like it. Some he remembered fondly, but he had never been as alive again as with her. Now nothing mattered, he had wasted his life. He should have forced her to see that she was making a mistake, he should have been stronger, but then the image of her in the wood, calling the moon always stopped him and awed him by the great respect he still had for her. And then there was his stupid pride always getting in the way.

So many nights she had come to him in a vision, and how he saw her most was in the circle at Midsummer, all powerful under the moon with her knife raised in the air, before she brought the power down into herself. It was unbearable, to think of how close he had been to becoming happy and now he couldn't bear to count the lost years in between.

The numbness affected the way he reacted with other people, even Rebecca. And now that she had betrayed him again, he felt the rage rising like bile. He heard an owl shriek and he knew he was no longer on his own. There was somebody watching.

Rebecca, crouching in the shadows, watched him pacing the room with the intense look of concentration on his face, as if he was solving some kind of riddle. Suddenly, he spun round and glared at the spot where she knelt, as if he knew exactly where she was in the darkness. The look on his face terrified her, he was livid. Despite her fear, it was unavoidable, she had to face him. Megan, the old trout, must have told him where she had been.

He opened the French doors and he beckoned her in. "Don't lie to me this time, Rebecca, I know where you've been. Just get in here. You might as well tell me what happened. I want to know everything, word for word. I want to understand why the hell you went. Lydia is a stranger to you, so why go to all that trouble to see her? What would she have to say to you of all people?"

He resented Rebecca for having been the one to see her, when all he had done was hide in the shadows waiting for her word to come. She had made him promise he wouldn't come until she sent for him, *and it had never happened*. What a fool he had been, so much for honour. What could he do now? Could he really bear to hear about how she looked, what she had said, how happy she was? It was too late but he couldn't resist not hearing something, sharing some part in the day, even though he knew it was childish to demand it.

Rebecca drew herself up as if she were an actress about to embark on a great speech, to tell him something of Lydia's words, to give his thoughts shape. Instead nothing would come, she could only stammer under his withering glare. But how to describe all that had happened? The house which seemed like a dead thing, shut up and barren, shrouded in the darkness of trees. Most of all how could *she* frame Lydia's own words of such eloquence and feeling. It had seemed more like a song. It was as if it had all welled up in her for so long, everything was showered so freely and openly on her, once she had told her the truth about the letters.

Jake loomed above her, pressurising her to parcel up the day and present him with it, like a bedtime novel. His unrelenting stare withered her words and suddenly she resented him again, his trying to bend her to his will. *What did she care for his curiosity?* Couldn't he have gone there himself? She had no time for his inaction, his self-inflicted grief complicating matters.

Then he was gazing out across the lawn and she wanted to be away from him, to be able to re-examine Lydia's words at her own leisure. The study stifled her with its heat and the animosity that sparked between them. Just when she felt that she must break the silence, he wordlessly opened the French windows and walked out across the lawn to the folly, staring right through her as if she were a ghost.

Glad for the opportunity to escape to the safety of her own room, Rebecca shivered under the blankets as she mouthed obscenities at her uncle. *Surely she deserved some thanks.* It hadn't been an easy task to drive all that way and find some god-forsaken house. Why could he not see that what she was doing was not only selfless, it was downright noble. All she was trying to do was bring two people together who obviously still cared about each other and if she were in their shoes she would have whooped for joy. Perhaps the older people got, the more selfish and obtuse they became.

The old lady had been ... not exactly unfriendly, but cold, distracted. She had offered Rebecca tea, and then wandered to her own devices in the garden. A short while later she returned, as if she had second thoughts about speaking about the past and the words came as a great release to her, as if she expected her life to end soon. Rebecca shivered as she recalled Lydia taking her face in her hands. Staring into her soul. These were not sad eyes. They were fierce, intense, *young!* Now she wondered if her uncle had seen the fire in them?

"When I was a girl," she had said, "I remember days of honey, magical times when everything stands still, untarnished forever. When you grow older and fall in love for the first time, you will remember it. Beauty will fade but nobody can take away the memory of love. I have been loved and I cherish it forever. I relive the memory to keep it fresh in my mind, because I will *never* relive that intensity ever again. It would probably kill me now!

"Most have no capacity for it, and you must avoid those. Never lose your spirit, because that is what sets you apart. If you are fine-tuned, if you crave sensitivity, cherish it if you are lucky enough to find a man who can feed your soul. My soul was lost and found that day. It was late summer, a Sunday, the birds were singing, nature was bursting with life, you could smell it in the air. I remember thinking it was strangely warm for the time of year.

"We journeyed to Thetford forest, deeper and deeper into shadow, the roof of the car was down so the smell of the trees filled the car. Great iron gates announced our arrival, and driving into the camp you could see scores of people. A few thousand maybe, clapping, all eyes on the ring. A perfect spring country day. Local people watching the officers on their horses. Glamorous, dangerous, modern day knights performing their tourneys. We walked to one of the tents, blue and white stripes, the colours of the Life Guards. A few of them graciously ushered us in. Manners shiny as a sword and hearts to match, lifeless. The tannoy suddenly grabbed my attention. Captain Seligman, who was your uncle's friend, was who we were here to see. I first noticed how small he looked perched astride that great horse, Fleetwood. He was beautiful, a true cavalry black, so polished, he shone in the sunlight ..."

LYDIA

I was remembering the intenseness of that day, while I skimmed the surface of it to the strange young girl before me. By midday, the heat had grown so intense that the faces in the crowd were shimmering like a mirage, distorting the distance on the other side. I glanced at Jake laughing with the men in the tent. He was so good-looking and glamorous, and I wanted it to be that we were about to embark on a great love affair. I had wanted him to come to me during the night, and he hadn't. Could it be that he didn't want me when I needed someone with passion, someone who wanted *me* above all else. But it left this lingering intense heat between us. At the back of my mind there was a vague impression that we *were* meant to be together, but that something had to take place before it could happen. I had no idea that fate was to sweep another path so dramatically in my way.

But then I grew transfixed by the men charging up and down the field on their horses. The noise in the tent behind had faded into nothing. Most of all, for some reason, I had been struck by a dark man on a horse called Fleetwood. The javelin he was holding seemed almost too big for his grasp, but then surging forward the throw was immaculate. With such grace as I had never seen before, they galloped in unison, speared the tent pegs effortlessly. He had won the first round. Before lining up with the others for the next round, the huge horse graciously came towards the tent, bringing the rider into my view.

He wore a blue polo shirt, a red sash, and he still held the great javelin. He had thick, wavy black hair, a small but powerful frame and dark china blue eyes. Still the horse kept coming forward to where I was standing. Steadily he came, his eyes on mine. In a moment we had understood the importance of this moment. Riding to an arm's length of where I was standing, that was to be *THE* moment, the most gallant gesture of my life. He nodded, as if to acknowledge some silent agreement, and galloped away.

In fifty years it had still been with me, the seconds, the ticking of the mini-seconds in which this had all taken place. And yet sometimes I had cursed this gesture, because it had set me on a course I could never have swerved from, even if I had wanted to. This was the moment in my life I would remember at the point of death. This was the epitome of my youth and my love for him. If there was one moment in my life the Grim Reaper could give back, to re-live for just a second, as he swung his scythe, *this would be it*. It had shaped my life and great sorrow. This was perfection, the prince of fairy tales, the saviour of my soul, the man destined to be mine. I remember gasping out loud, as if somebody had struck a blow to me.

Whenever I re-visit this day of the past, the reality of my withered hands and faded reflection strikes me with so much pain, taking me further and further away from the memory, from him and his love; until one day it would all be as if in another life. This always brings hot tears of regret, the slow and painful re-enactment of love. This was when I adored him, for no man could have been more perfect to me at that moment in time.

Wish me luck he seemed to say. Round after round, I watched him, transfixed. When he went up for the cup they had won, he held it up to me. He had won me over for life, without speaking a word; it was all bravery, steeliness. It was dynamism, pure energy and vitality. I had known he would come to me straight away although I could never recall what we had said to each other, only this otherworldly sense of elation, of coming home. The knowledge that this was *it*, the pivotal point on which my life would spin. Only that he had the noblest of features. This is purity I thought. *I will love this man.* He is brave. That was all to me then. He is my destiny. I will remember this day when I am old. Every time I summoned the memory, I felt I could almost reach out and touch it, it seemed so close. The smell of the horses, the grass under foot, the sweat on his brow, that second of humorous and questioning expression in his eyes. My empty mouth could still taste the champagne, the quail's eggs, and salmon. Hats and gloves everywhere. I could still feel his shaking hands.

The pain was never easier. It was as though my past, present and future were there in my hand: all I had to do was reach out for it, it was so close. *Where has the time gone?* I could hold them both there in their youth and perfection until I caught a passing reflection of myself in a mirror or window. A lifetime had come in between them now. I was different then. Beautiful, happy, carefree. I believed I was never going to get old and grey. In my youth I had imagined dying young and leading a fast glamorous life but that was before I knew how old people grasp at the last vestiges of life with a greedy tenacity.

And now it is impossible to let go.

CHAPTER EIGHT

Jake wanted to tell this clumsy, unfeeling child what Lydia had been like when they had both been young, but he knew no sense would come because words could not convey his true feelings. It was as if he were forcing her to materialise in the room again.

A great chasm had suddenly grown between him and Rebecca. She was a stranger now she had transformed into a young woman. Where had the years had flown? Where was the dark curly-headed baby, the joy she bought to the cottage, the gap she had filled as a child, when he knew that his hopes of having children of his own, were gone. Tonight he could have slapped her as she stood there with that smug expression; coming back to the cottage with a look of triumphal knowing. It was as if now he realised that the little girl he had put on a pedestal was, in fact, insensitive, all-seeing but knowing nothing. She was sly and he no longer trusted her, with her prying ways.

He stood alone in the folly, enveloped in the darkness, letting only the light of the moon illuminate his way. He went to his desk and unlocked the drawer that had long held the only jewels he treasured. The piles of letters, still trussed up in white ribbon. Letters Rebecca had not seen, old favourites he had kept close to hand over the years. The sheaves of paper felt stiff and cold in his hands; dead things that had lost their scent, like old oak leaves. He walked out into the night where he felt closest to her. By the lake he crouched by the reeds, barely visible beneath the pale moon, to remember ...

He had been so angry at the rejection, of being passed over for Niall; the talk of their marriage he had learnt second hand as he travelled relentlessly, pursuing his career. He heartlessly slept with women all over the world to forget who came to him in his dreams. He pretended to himself that he could ignore this haunting, but he knew she would be inescapable. He had ignored Nel when she begged him to go to her, when she had defended Lydia for the broken oaths the rest accused her of breaking.

That was why he had taken Megan with him, as if to spite Lydia when she left them all with no word. And with a sudden realisation he guessed that perhaps Megan had tried to steer him away from finding her again; perhaps he had been a fool to listen to her for all of these years. Who knows, her tittle-tattle was perhaps contrived to fuel his anger at Lydia; the many men, the lost baby ... she related all this to him during the intervening years, which drove him further away. When Nel had died, the speculation stopped and he missed listening to her prattle about Lydia, even if it had been not what he wanted to hear.

It was as if Nel had been orchestrating the strings that bound them all together and with searing perception, he saw how she had planned Megan's job so that *she* could keep tabs on *him*, in case Lydia had told him of the mysterious oaths they kept muttering about.

With a boyish gesture of anger, he threw a stone across the surface of the water. It skimmed right out into the blackness of the lake and as he watched the ripples shimmer out into stillness, he was startled by a sudden movement in the bushes to his left. As he spun round, he saw a large white horse disappear into the trees. He knew nobody nearby with a white horse, and anyway, it had a strange ethereal quality that suggested it may have been a trick of the light. And then, with a warm realisation he knew it was a sign and felt peace for the first time in years as he thought back to the animals Lydia talked about, marking mystical events.

He took out from his pocket the first of the cold lifeless letters and began reading it again by the light of the moon.

CHAPTER NINE

July 5th 1952

Dear Jake

Thank you for coming to Norfolk with me. It was nice that I could share it with you a little. I hope you didn't find it too strange. It was important to me that you understood what I believe in, *what I am*. That is why it is so difficult to be in London now when there is all that magic to leave behind. Do you remember how it was, falling asleep beneath the trees? Did you know there was a pair of barn owls watching us? Did you know they mate for life? How many humans like that? That's what I have always wanted - to be loved - *really loved* by one person. I think I have found him at last! Thank you for taking me to that day at Thetford, otherwise we probably never would have met. If you had predicted I would end up with a cavalry officer I would have laughed in your face.

The funny thing is, I can sense I never will be able to share with him what I shared with you. He doesn't have your sensitivity. It's strange because it's now becoming clearer to me that it is probably best not to be with someone who is like your own inner self. Otherwise the spirit becomes dulled ... perhaps. I can't explain to you why, but I do love him. I knew it from the day I saw him and I really think he loves me deeply, too. Perhaps I needed someone to ground my thoughts, and catch my soul from flying off all the time.

You will find your love, too. I live in a dreamworld, and yet you have become my soul-mate in that world, and if anybody knew how amazing my waking hours were in this life, it is you. You *know* I live half in that world and half in this. And you never criticised me for it. You have such a beautiful nature. I know that you had planned for us to be lovers, but it is not meant to be like that for us, at least in this lifetime.

But the fates don't like definites, for us to push the wheel. I am sorry if I hurt you but I could never lie to you. I have fallen in love with Niall. I know you will be happy for us. It is all due to you that we found each other. I never knew it was possible to love someone so completely, so quickly.

Be happy

With love *Lydia*

The searing pain of loss and jealousy scored him once again, just as keenly as it had the first time he had read those words, when he was forced to accept that his chance had ended before it had began.

As soon as he saw them together in the tent that day he knew that it was too late, that they were going to be lovers. He still felt the murderous rage. Why had he bought her here? The thought of Niall with her had made him feel sick. And so he watched her that day, her face close to his, her head thrown back in laughter, Niall not letting her go for one second. She had initiated him into the joys of childhood again, the thrill of life, and now she had left him in this dismal hole where there was no way out but through her. He had left her with Niall and driven back to London by himself. She had asked this of him. And now the wounds were still as painful as he re-lived the moment.

Hands shaking, he opened another letter. The postmark was Glenn Cannick. He caressed the folds of the paper, the familiar flowing writing and the smudges of ink that could have been made yesterday. He mused to himself that she must have run to the post box with it in the rain. A sharp memory of her face shining in the rain came to him. She had never minded the rain, or getting her long hair wet. The smudges were now as personal as fingerprints, they were direct evidence of what she had experienced and felt at that moment in time. Now he tried to imagine her as she sat on a hillside perhaps, writing this very page to him, amongst the heather. This one was written at Niall's family house in Scotland. Once Niall had taken her there, he had guessed she would marry him.

"Yesterday, we went out on the loch around Mucra in a small boat," it began. "The mist was descending thickly, swirling around our heads in great swathes, blocking out our features, as Donald, the ghillie sternly pushed the oars, casting great ripples in the stillness. It seemed to me that those watery depths held a thousand secrets. Its power and will to devour the lives of men came alive to me, Jake, and I suddenly grew very scared. We were so vulnerable in that tiny boat. I thought we would never make it to the other side. Niall's mother had told me a strange tale the night before, about men who had gone missing there without a trace.

"You could imagine it so easily beside the vaporous loch. The hills on the far side, shrouded in a purple mist, beckoned. It seemed as if treachery or tragedy would certainly call us to the murky depths before we reached the shore, as storm clouds lowered themselves on the murky slopes. Yet some part of me wanted to stay and be at peace, in limbo like that, between this world in our boat, the powers of the dreaded water, and the bank on the other side.

"When we climbed the hills, they were suddenly lit up by the returning sun, and then thrown into shadow just as suddenly by those dark storm clouds. The changes were constant as if nature were urging us to see her in all her beauty, as we came upon waterfalls, burbling streams and granite caves. When we had reached the top of one ridge overlooking the valley below it seemed as if I were in heaven. If you have ever felt so alive you will know what it is to sup life more greedily than you savour dreams. My life, if only for that moment was more rich than any dream I have ever had, more fantastic as I mused on the edge of the world. That is how the gods must feel up there amongst the rocky crags.

I was brought back to earth by a gunshot. Niall had killed his first stag that season. The stag had been running with the herd. King of the Hills. I scrambled over the brow to meet the kill. He was beautiful, this mighty beast that had stood so majestically and arrogantly facing the guns, and now his mighty antlers had come crashing to the ground like a twisted wreck. I marvelled at delicate hooves of such grace and fragility; at the great dark eyes, that now stared at us blankly. Had they seen what the fates were to bestow in that one final second? I wanted to cry and shout at the same time. This creature had been so beautiful. In the end my love for Niall overcame whatever my feelings about the stag. Who really was the King of the Hills that day?

Crossing the loch at nightfall, he gave me a stone from that spot. He told me he loved me, as we made love down in the valley, under the stars, while the stags chorused far off in the hills above. My veins raced with the stream and we were one with everything, the moon, the air was thick with love. We fell asleep there on the heather...."

Jake could read no more. About her growing love for Niall. It still pained him to read these changes in her. A photograph was the last thing in the pile: the three of them dressed for a ball. She was leaning on him, nestling in the crook of his arm (he could still smell her hair), while Niall stood stiffly in his Mess red. He was kissing her head protectively like a child, while Niall gazed out at the photographer.

She was like an angel that night; her eyes were shining with happiness. She had never looked lovelier. Yet she had seemed like a caged animal, edgy and nervous. It was early December and in the six months since she had been with Niall, he could see that her bubbling confidence had begun to erode. Her eyes shifted about the room. He couldn't hold a conversation with her.

Niall was his usual charming self. They had stood making small talk about something or other: he never could seem to remember the conversations he'd had with Niall. They all seemed so superficial, from hunting to the cavalry ... He often wondered how much of her Niall *really* knew, or whether she could truly immerse herself in the superficial threads of his world for long.

Three weeks later they had all stayed in Sussex for New Year's Eve. He watched her during dinner. She was straining like a nervous bird, willing Niall to look at her. It was clear from the pain in her eyes that he was hardly paying her any attention, having spent the whole evening chatting to the sister of a fellow officer. They were both slightly drunk and flirting openly with each other and he hadn't even noticed that Lydia had run upstairs in tears. It was clear to Jake what had gone wrong. The battle of winning Lydia was over for Niall, and he had now developed a cavalier attitude to her devotion.

When she came down again they were playing games in the drawing room. Some men had been blindfolded with the idea of having to identify cardboard shapes pinned on the girls and Niall could not have known she was in the room. Alex, an Australian friend of Niall's was straddling him provocatively on the floor – he had one hand on the inside of her thigh.

When Lydia heard their laughter, it felt like she had been kicked very hard in the stomach. The room was spinning, faces swimming before her, enjoying her humiliation. The cry was silent to her. She had to get out, out of this room, out of the house into the night, over the cattle grid into the darkness. In one small thoughtless action he had crushed her, in front of his friends. This was to be *their* night, the chance to show his friends that they loved each other.

She was a fool.

Jake remembered running after her. He could just about make out her pale dress under the moonlight, running to nowhere, chasing her sobs. He came at last to a barn where the hayricks scented the cold night air. She was sitting rigid with disbelief. The bubble had burst.

"Niall asked me to marry him tonight," she said simply.

He hadn't known what to say. It was all nonsense. He wanted to feel jubilant for her, but instead some of her great sadness lay manifest in him, in the pity he had for her.

"Lydia, don't you think you're over reacting?"

He knew he didn't believe the words, even as he said them. He knew that only the thrill of the chase had captivated Niall, and now she had capitulated so completely, the game, for him, was nearing to its end. Other girls, like those inside, knew the game: they were more sensible, keeping up their guard, until they were sure of the outcome.

"What was I supposed to do, Jake? You saw how he was all night with that girl beside him. I wouldn't have minded, but he never even looked up once, to look at *me*, the whole evening. I don't know what's wrong. My life's path had looked so set, so idyllic and now, I can see it's not as I thought it would be.

"*This isn't how it's meant to be.* And now I'm terrified that I love him more than myself; that he will never feel the same way. That he just isn't capable of feeling in the way that I am, in the way that I expect. If he can't love me, Jake, I don't know what I will do. I couldn't live like that. But if I couldn't have him at all, what then? I think I'd want to die. It's happening all over again, this dismal betrayal of what I believe to be normal. I only want a share of what I give out, no more. I really believed in the meeting of two souls, some sort of mystical union ... not that you would understand what I mean."

"I would give you an equal share, Lydia. I *know* what you feel."

Amazed, he listened her carry on as if she hadn't heard a word of his life shattering admission.

"If he even loved me to the height of my little finger I would be happy, because I know how filled with love I am. I have enough love for the both of us to last centuries. I just want a little from him, respect and love. Is that too much to ask?"

He felt cruel with rejection "Maybe you're asking too much from any man." he snapped at last.

She looked at him dumbstruck, at what she saw as a double betrayal. "What would *you* know about what I ask? What is fair? What I give? How I love? What do you know? Get out of here and leave me, Jake, you are just the same; the same as all those people. You introduced me to him for God's sake!" she yelled, crazed with anger and fear.

He started to walk out of the open barn to the house. He could hear laughter, far off on the lawn. And then it came, a strangulated cry he could never forget.

"It was my dream, you see, Jake. Gone, finished. I'm finished, there's nothing left in me. Even if I live for a hundred years I could never get back the love I felt for him. Now I have known him, this perfection he gave me, what it is to be happy, I can never be happy again without him. I don't want to live without him, it will be just an existence. *Please help me.* I don't trust myself."

The moon shone just enough that night through the gaps in the roof, to show the wild look of desperation in her eyes. She was terrified that she had been wrong all along in her life's quest for pure unblemished love. A love that she craved to give and receive, like a child. How could anyone stand up to that test? It was only then that he realised just how much she had changed from the strong vibrant girl he had first met.

He swept her up in his arms carried her weary body to the hay bales, cradling her like a baby. "Lydia ..."

"Everything good in my life I ruin, I have scared every single man away because I am so intense about life and when I tell them I love them, that they are everything to me, it scares them." She had begun to pull the small chiffon roses from her dress but she was more lucid than he thought.

"I know, I scare myself all the time, Jake, I sometimes think I really am mad. Niall has shattered my confidence, there's nothing left. At night I watch him dreaming, and I hate him because I fancy he is dreaming of other women, and when he says he loves me, I sometimes have to put it to the test because deep down, I know the love I am capable of will always be unrequited. I *feel* on a preternatural level; I hear every flutter of a butterfly's wing and I *hate* it because I am so alone in it all."

She was now sobbing uncontrollably and wandering about the barn like a demented thing. He knew her well enough to believe that her gifts of seeing and feeling were this strong, but now he was beginning to understand that such a gift could also threaten her mind and worsen her isolation.

"What did you say when he asked you to marry him?"

"Nothing. I knew he was drunk and would probably regret it in the morning, so I pretended not to hear him, so he could be let off the hook if he was too drunk to mean it. I think he knew, and didn't repeat it. He probably never will. Why are men so neurotic about marriage?"

Suddenly they heard Niall stumbling about in the darkness of the courtyard. "Lydia, *Lydia*, come out now! I know you're out here. Don't be ridiculous. Nothing happened. Unless you come out I'll spend the night looking for you. Please darling, come out, and talk to me."

Jake sensed that every fibre of her being yearned to reach out to him and forgive, despite what she had seen. She had whispered: "Quick, Jake do you mind leaving us? You know how he is with feelings, if he knows you're here, of all people he'll dry up. I need to know what's going on."

Crouching behind a hay bale, Jake watched as they just stood and looked at each other, as if neither dare speak or move. Then, a noise broke the deadlock, lifting the awful tension: the sound of pearls bouncing off the barn floor. Niall had grabbed her by the neck and broken the choker she was wearing. Her sob tore through the night as he kissed the tears from her cheeks. "It was nothing, Lydia, nothing at all. You've had too much to drink that's all, you're tired and over emotional. It's you I want. I'd be broken-hearted without you."

Jake slouched over to another bale, to try and get away from them. It was littered with the flowers from her dress. Placing his head in his hands, he moaned as Lydia raised her voice in the darkness. "You humiliated me in front of these people, *your* friends, on tonight of all nights. You ruined everything."

"I asked you what you thought to us becoming engaged next year, this year for God's sake. I love you, so don't do this, please."

The relief for her must have been immense because she literally fell on him. Taking her by the shoulders, Niall gently pushed her away and tucked back the loose strands of hair that had fallen out of place. Smoothing down her gown, he talked to her as if she were a child. "Let's go back to the party, show them nothing's wrong shall we?"

It had been brushed aside in order to keep up appearances. Niall had averted an embarrassing situation and for him it was already a distant memory.

CHAPTER TEN

The next morning Jake woke early, and from his bed he could see a small boat out on the lake. He could just about make out the two figures wrapped up against the January wind and recognised Lydia and Niall. He had hoped in vain that last night would have been the end of it all, for not only did he hate the sight of them together, Lydia's state of mind had disturbed him.

A great sense of foreboding permeated the room as he watched the skiff gracefully skirting about the lake. The water was still, cunningly concealing it's many secrets in the mud below. It was small relief how the morning brightened the horrors of the night. Lydia was laughing, trailing her hands through the reeds like a child, as if nothing had happened. Niall was making the boat spin round and round, creating circular ripples, that lasted long after they had sailed to the other side.

Jake found it hard to admit that even he could see they were so much in love, as much as it pained him. It was as if a ring of light encircled the boat, and the dull morning light had intensified around them. He sensed rather than heard their laughter, and yet he shivered with a sense that there was danger out there on the water. A fleeting glimpse into the future with a vague premonition of a small boat drawn into a treacherous undercurrent, drowning the occupants before his eyes.

As the vision in his mind's eye faded, Jake chided himself for drinking too much the night before and tore himself away from the window as the clear chime of church bells dispelled the sense of foreboding.

The pealing of the Sunday bells echoed Lydia's laughter as the boat spun around. She looked at the sky, and for a moment watched the rooks flying away to the north. Although there were no storm clouds, the sky was a hazy grey and a fret was gradually descending. Bad news would follow, she thought, but she forced herself back to the here and now to concentrate on the soft words her lover was speaking. She vowed to keep this man's love by living more in his world, for she was tired of being pulled away by visions and omens, doubts and worry.

She tried to ignore the swelling grey cloud formations by concentrating on his blue eyes boring into hers. He bent forwards and kissed her for what seemed like an age, until the coldness of the water numbed her hands. When he leant back up, with her face in his hands, he was stunned again by the sheer perfection of her beauty. The coldness had bought a flush to her cheeks and a realisation of just how he loved her caught his breath as if it pained him, it was so intense. Her reaction the previous night had alarmed him but now she looked so calm and reflective. Perhaps he *had* been insensitive, but her moods and passions were still a mystery to him.

The boat shuddered as it drifted into the bank, and they both listened to the sobering silence of the New Year's morning. Their future seemed settled but Lydia had a question to ask.

Trying to sound casual, she asked: "When you leave the army, will you go back to Wiltshire and manage the farm? Or will you stay on in London?" It took all of her will to hide the anguish in her voice, because she hated the thought of remaining in London.

"My uncle was telling me about this brewery in New York. He thinks it will be good thing if I go over to see how things are done over there. If I'm going to take over the brewery here, I'll need some kind of experience."

She realised he was deliberately evading the question but was anxious not to cause another scene. For his part, Niall wanted to marry her, to be with her, but he also realised she was trying to persuade him to leave London, and he suddenly bridled against being manipulated. He wasn't ready to retire to the country away from the thick of things as his parents had done. He wanted to succeed in business, not play the squire. He would ask her again, when the time was right. Last night he *had* made a hash of things, but now with her goading, he felt cornered. She would have to wait. They would stay in London together: they were too young to leave it all just yet, he decided.

Lydia could read his thoughts as if he'd spoken them aloud and inwardly she flinched, stung again with humiliation and hurt, but after last night she could hardly berate him again. She felt sick. Even though the boat had been bought to stillness, the water seemed to be spinning out of control, she wanted to get out. She felt dizzy and nauseous. How could she slow her restless mind?

"I'm not going anywhere without you," he said, sensing her withdrawal. "I promise, you are the most important thing in my life. Once we're engaged, we can live together. Wherever you want."

The words didn't register at first, but she was finally out of the agony of not knowing. He *had* meant it after all, the dreadful act of pretending she wasn't tortured by the possibility that he wouldn't ask her again, was over. And so the voyagers had avoided shipwreck and they had reached the bank safely.

Lydia knew she would savour these moments for the rest of her life. The way he looked down on her with complete love in his heart; these were the moments that reassured her she was right in handing over her will to him, and trusting him to steer their course. As they walked back to the house to say their goodbyes to their hosts, and to tell them of their news, she could not throw off an uneasy sense that her surrender would not bring her total the happiness she hoped for.

LYDIA

1999

There was nothing in Rebecca I felt I could positively dislike, but at the same time I couldn't trust her. I felt that there was cold calculation, despite her young age. Her determination to seek me out makes me wonder whether Megan has a part in all of this and I am not sure where it will all lead. On the other hand I pitied the child without a mother, and so I did oblige her with some memories. Her fascination with us unnerves me. I can only think of Megan at her age and it fills me with a sense of foreboding, yet something within me could not refuse, even if it is only to hear about Jake.

As I watched the girl leave, I felt the familiar prickling agony that I had learnt to live with all these years. As I turned the pages of the photograph album with Rebecca, I mourned the loss of my girlhood. It had all gone so quickly but it was too late to stop the rising sadness. Her questions had taken me back to that New Year, when I had felt the most intense agonies of pain and longing, and the perfection of love. I had never felt so alive.

The moment had come back to possess me, the image of how perfect he had been, of his fleeting expressions. It had been years since I had dared to look at the photographs because the ghosts it raised were so clear and the picture of Niall on New Year's Eve still had the power to make my legs buckle beneath me. And now, as I watched her car pull out of view, a dead weight settled on my chest until I could hardly breathe with the pain.

When the moment had passed, I walked out of the garden, beyond the hawthorn barrier towards the wildwood. I walked onwards as the sun began to set and the power grew. The dying light throwing dark shadows at my feet on an emerald carpet of grass. Already I can smell the scent of the fox and hear the screech of owl seeking its prey. The wood is coming alive in the darkness.

As in the old days, my dress trails over the daisies as I begin the ancient call before the dying of the light. Eagerly I gather the unseen about me, with guttural calls I muster their presence to me, while carefully selecting the correct wild herbs and flowers. I had a need to descend into the past, to relive it clearly in every detail. In desperation, as the tears fell, I collected the ingredients I would need to fill my need, to erase the pain which was sharper than ever.

As the darkness gathered, I walked quickly back into the cold empty house, to start my solitary ritual. Soon the moon would shine on the burner, where I had carefully placed the herbs. As the flame consumed them, I inhaled their familiar smell which was so acrid it stuck to the back of my throat, but I had to go onwards to forget the pain of loneliness and regret. I prayed that this time, they would show the way it would all end.

CHAPTER ELEVEN

It was the month after New Year. Niall had driven them to Falklands in the morning. Although it was very early, an almighty storm had gathered, buffeting the car. When they reached the brow of the hill that overlooked the house, they could hear the winds ripping across the park, shaking the ancient oaks. As they climbed the steps to the portico even the magnificent mahogany door creaked and moaned under the barrage of the wind whistling through the columns. The great serlian windows rattled loosely reflecting gathering clouds racing across the sky. It was electric.

They decided to go and run through the park and the energy of that day was like no other she had experienced since. Niall's mother, Lady Seligman, had shouted at them "You're mad, just like children. You'll be killed."

They giggled and ventured on, running on and on, arms outstretched as if the wind would buoy them up like birds. Horses cowered beneath an elm. Niall ran on ahead while she stood thinking to herself how strange the bird-less sky seemed. She was too absorbed to notice the creaking beech leaning beside her. A terrifying crack of wood rent the air in two. The massive tree had split. Its course was unstoppable, she could see it was going to kill her, yet it seemed in slow motion that the great branches fell above her head. Suddenly, from nowhere he had pushed her clear and she felt him sobbing, his body still protecting hers. The realisation that she had narrowly escaped death and yet felt so elated, so utterly caught up in love that she knew it would never end. It was more invincible than life, this moment proved it beyond doubt. She tried to quieten the voice inside her that said all this would one day be theirs, but now she knew it *was* meant to be. Niall was speaking to her, telling her how much he loved her, how scared he had been. It would have been to have lost everything; but amid the howling wind and the spattering wood, and more importantly the pounding of her heart, she couldn't hear the words. It didn't matter because, at that moment in time, she knew he would love her forever.

Laughing, it took them both to close the massive door against the storm. Entering the library, which was a world away with its roaring fire, safe and cosy with the dogs sprawled in the chairs, Sir Michael was peering across his fields, his face etched with sadness as if a tragedy had occurred. Their laughter stopped immediately as he slowly turned inwards with tears running down his face.

"Those beech trees were planted by my great-grand father. All that care and work gone in an instant. His life gone without a record."

Privately Lydia thought Sir Michael was being over dramatic, after all beech trees were notoriously short lived anyway. Perhaps he had seen more than an omen in the storm. It was the end of an era for him. It was at that moment that a roar hurtled down the chimney, partly extinguishing the fire. She remembered shivering just then, as if someone had walked over her grave, as if the tide had turned and something too oppressive to describe bore down on the three of them. They had all felt the same thing, but none dare acknowledge it, and so they looked down at the carpet until Lady Seligman broke the moment with a welcoming mundanity.

"Anyone for tea? There are some buns Niall, I bought them in for you." They decided to stay, the winds were too fierce to risk the drive back to London. And so they stayed at Falklands, safe in the warm library where the ticking of clocks was so slow and rhythmic like a heartbeat.

The vision was broken by the barking of the dogs, damn them. I had not gone deep enough, it was too soon to come out of it, and now my concentration is broken. I adjust myself on the chair, gripping the wooden carvings of the arms with steely determination. It might be the last time I go as close as this to the past. It was not a ritual to perform many times. I try with all my will power to crush the rising panic in me, the feeling that it is all slipping further away. I breathe in steady waves, inhaling more of the deadly concoction that had the power to kill twenty men at a stroke. Steadily the sickly incense begins to slow my heartbeat down and the rising smoke is hypnotic.

And then it came, unexpectedly. The memory was beautiful. It followed on a few weeks later from the first. It was as if spring had arrived early, only a few days after the storm. They were in Norfolk, at the farmhouse. The yellow aconites were out already and it was such an uncharacteristically balmy day for the time for the time of year that they had hoisted hammocks into the apple trees. She lay on him, rocking to the sound of the wind rustling through the branches.

Her hair tumbled out of one side of the hammock, above the grass. Niall had given her a chocolate coloured Labrador called Bertie, who pulled the hair as it trailed back and forth. It was blissful. Niall leant down and kissed her eyelids gently.

"Will you love me forever?" She asked, as young lovers do.

"I swear I will," he said. "Close your eyes."

He placed something on her belly. She remembered feeling how heavy and cold it was, as she traced the intricate carvings of dragons. It was a gold bracelet inset with one large amethyst. When she opened her eyes she could see an inscription in the gold. Their names were simply entwined. As they kissed, the sun filtered through the branches for what seemed an eternity. She could still feel the butterflies swarming in her stomach as he pressed himself into her thighs.

Finally, when he stood smiling with his lazy blue eyes full of love, he clasped the bracelet shut on her wrist. There was finality about it. It was as though she were now his, for always. This was the moment she had wanted, this subjugation of his soul to hers, yet she remembered shivering. It was as if a silent wind had come from nowhere. And then a chill. He hadn't noticed the shadow of a man standing over them.

A telephone rang from somewhere in the house and he had been called to answer it, and all the while this gloomy figure stood silently by the tree staring at her. Although she was used to seeing and sensing spirits, its power took her unawares and because she hadn't seen anything so clearly as this since she had been a child, it frightened her for its message was important. *Why come now? Like this?* And then, as he walked back towards the orchard, it suddenly vanished and she knew what the omen had been.

"Oh Lydia, he's dead". His voice in that one sentence betrayed everything. He had worshipped his father. Everything he had always done had been to win his approval. Now his voice sounded broken. "I've got to go to Falklands immediately. Please come with me. I need you there."

"Niall, I'm so sorry. Don't you think you're mother will want you there on your own?"

"No, you must come."

"Of course I will, if you're sure she won't mind."

"His heart gave out. There was nothing they could have done. Mother found him on the floor in the library facing out towards the park."

It was so strange to think that such a robust, powerfully raw man was suddenly dead, but then she remembered the storm and the coming of the Spring Equinox, where the balance was often reclaimed one way or another. It was a treacherous time of year.

The long journey was terrible. He didn't want to talk. His mood alternated between an eerie elation and complete depression. She could not penetrate his shock with words, they were unheard. There was a flower shop a mile from the house.

"Don't you think you should get my Mother some flowers?" he snapped unexpectedly.

"Oh, yes of course."

She made her selection and handed the florist the money shame-faced and wary. It had almost been an accusation that she had been unthinking. Flowers were the furthest things from her mind. She chose a bunch of white lilies. How futile the gesture seemed now. How would she give them to his mother? What could be said? It was all too late. As they neared the big black iron gates, her feeling of dread increased. Lady Seligman had never really approved of her and Lydia knew that she would resent her presence now. She needed some time to gather herself before facing the family.

"Do you mind if I get out here and walk the rest of the way? It will give you some time with your mother."

Niall shook his head with exasperation and without a word the car roared off down the drive. She watched him depart, slumped and exhausted. He seemed so small and vulnerable. She had wanted to protect him from the watershed that would rain down on him any moment, but she was helpless. Now, for the first time, when it was important, he was deaf to her. How to bring down the barrier he had bought up between them?

She walked away from the dark house and ventured to the 'Nut Ride' where they had so often walked together. A small Victorian iron gate opened grudgingly. The path was overgrown with trees and rhododendrons. How could his father have left all this beauty? Far off into the woods the bird song drifted down through the breaking leaves. Primroses lined the passageway, which drew her further and further along. Kissing branches overhead soon blocked out any sun there had been, until she was soon in deep shadow. In the half-light rabbits ran ahead, darting in and out of the bushes.

Here late snowdrops had burst through the hard ground and it made the death of a man more tragic still, when the year had so much life. She came upon the central clearing where the first in a line of sculptures faced her. Imposing classical figures looking out blankly, passed the sundial, where the path swept around the trunk of a massive oak to the folly. This small, thatched hut, with its wattle and daub walls had been half devoured by time and seasons.

The hut looked out over the fields at the edge of the wood, and she could see that the sky had very suddenly grown black. A mighty crack of thunder boomed overhead. It was quite different from the last storm; there was no energy in the air. Instead, it seemed to suck the energy from her, so she began to feel quite listless and dizzy. The air was still and oppressive. A great torrent of rain poured down as she sat crouched in what remaining shelter the folly could offer. Lightning danced across the dark fields beyond.

Under the rotting roof she began to say her good-byes to Sir Michael. She reasoned that if his soul were anywhere it would be in his beloved woods. It was a fitting place to say farewell. She summoned his spirit to listen as she vowed to love Niall and his beloved Falklands, if she ended up here. A blackbird swooped down on the bench beside her. He sang his tiny heart out as if in final lament. A hare darted out and paused on his hind legs. From the way he stopped, looked straight at her and away again, she sensed a warning.

"What is it you old wise thing?" she asked. He looked toward the path and took off.

It was then that the children – Victorian children - came. There were shouts, singsong rhymes, taunts, giggling. When the silence came again she strained to hear them. There were whispers all around her. Stones fell from the sky and were thrown up at the folly. She got up and ran to find them. The blackbird flew up and led her closer. The noise was growing all the time until she could hear four or five of them. They were luring her to the sundial. She stood frozen as they weaved in and out of the statues, sometimes showing themselves, children with malevolent eyes, venomous hearts. They didn't want her there in their wood. A larger stone hurtled through the air and landed at her feet. The hare leapt from the undergrowth and bounded away. The blackbird was chatting madly, circling above. The voices were getting louder. Taunting, laughing, chanting.

Filled with fear she wanted to run with the hare and bird but her feet were somehow rooted to the spot as she felt them close in around her. With her heart racing, she summoned a golden light of protection and tried to mutter a rudimentary spell. The words failed her in her haste to get away. She had to remember. Something terrible was about to happen if she stayed in wood any longer. Her heart pounded as she tried madly to settle her breathing. At last, managing to weave a web between the malevolent spirits and her, she was given a silent reprieve. In the quiet, she ran, on and on, with weak jelly legs, led by the blackbird flying overhead, she crashed through the dark tunnel in search of the light at the end. Their evil eyes were on her back; they were running behind until she eventually saw the clearing and the rusty gate. Still she ran on soaked from the storm.

It was only when she had arrived under the portico of the house that she saw her dress was ripped and dirty. Catching sight of her mad, breathless reflection in the window, she saw there was blood smeared on her face from the brambles, her hair wild and loose. Beginning to doubt her own sanity, she tried desperately to instil some calm and reason. As a child she always felt in control of these ghosts and now she was terrified of them for the first time.

Suddenly the door opened and Lady Seligman looked at her coldly, with undisguised loathing as she steadily surveyed Lydia's appearance. In one split second Lydia read her unspoken thoughts. She was outraged that the girl could go prancing about in the woods, having fun on her own like a child without any respect for the dead, no love for her son. *You have no place here*, she was thinking, and there would never be an opportunity to put things right, to explain, because their worlds were so different. There was now a stubborn determination on the older woman's face never to let her son marry this mad creature.

"I'm so sorry," she muttered. They were the only words she could muster because she knew whatever she had said to Lady Seligman, she could never make amends.

All the years of quiet resentment Lady Seligman had felt about Sir Michael's drinking and 'playing the field' were somehow channelled into these few seconds of burning hatred for this girl. If Niall hadn't been standing in the hallway she might not have let her in. In her eyes, Lydia was a little money grabber, who wouldn't wait two minutes before she would get her out of the house once they were married and now, technically, the house *was* Niall's. It had to be prevented somehow. Strangely the death of her husband had bought her sudden relief and happiness. She would have power for once and, most importantly, she and Niall could remain there at Falklands, just the two of them. Possessively she wanted to keep her hold over him forever.

Coldly she opened the door wide enough to let the girl in and led her to the morning room. Lydia knew now how it was to be. This is what she had feared by coming here. She suddenly felt humbled, and out of place. Why had Niall insisted on her coming with him? Even she could understand that his mother came first on the day of her husband's death. She sat on the edge of a chair, desperately trying to think of something to say that wouldn't be mis-interpreted.

"It must have been a terrible shock for you, Lady Seligman."

The other woman, lighting a cigarette, looked at her coolly, with open hostility beaming radiating at her through narrowed eyes. Lydia could hear Niall outside, talking to the gamekeeper. *Please come now,* she prayed, willing this torture to end. It was as if she was being made scapegoat for all the Seligman's troubles. Lady Seligman was also willing her son to come in and divert her welling feelings of hatred towards this girl, who now represented her husband's infidelities throughout their long marriage. If she'd had some of this girl's beauty, perhaps he might have loved her faithfully and not subjected her to all those years of humiliation.

A car rolled up on the gravel outside. "The Empsons are here," she announced with relief, her voice as clipped as crystal.

It really was unbelievable, Lydia thought, this stupid pretence that everything was all right, this resolute love of socialising even in death. It was sickening to her. Where were their priorities? What to do now? There had been nothing in her upbringing to equip her to deal with the formality of death. All she could feel was the hatred bearing down on her, willing her to go away. If she had a car, she would have escaped.

"I think it would be best if I went to my room. I'm sure you don't want to have to make small talk with a stranger," she said when Niall came into the room.

"Yes, all right," came the reply. To her surprise, he sounded relieved.

Lydia plodded slowly up the grand staircase, tracing the polished mahogany rail with her fingers. She had dreamt of this very staircase over and over as a small girl, when she had tumbled down its graceful curve many times. Seeing it for real for the first time, it was as if destiny had meant her to come here. Now it led her away from the very people with whom she needed to belong, the sound of their voices fading in the distance.

Finally she reached the safety of a bedroom, and on opening the door she discovered that it had been Sir Michael's. Already it was as cold as a tomb. The air was still and charged. *He was here.* There was nowhere else for her to go, since she could hardly wander around as a stranger in this great house. She could sense Niall's father over by the window, looking out into the courtyard as the stable yard clock suddenly struck the hour but his shade paid her no heed.

Lydia didn't want to sleep, but there was nothing else for her to do, since there were no books. The room was freezing and every time she tried to close her eyes under the heavy coverlet on the bed, it was as if she were being watched. Images of clocks circled her mind, everywhere, there were thousands of them, ticking, chiming, tormenting her sleep. Whispers and laughter wafted out of each corner. The courtyard clock struck once, twice, three times, as she drifted in and out of sleep. She turned in the bed fitfully, hot and cold, waiting for Niall to come and fetch her. Four hours passed by.

In desperation, she crept out onto the landing, cold and hungry, to be greeted by peals of laughter from below. Fury welled. Why had he insisted she accompany him, when he was now choosing to ignore her presence in the house? Retiring upstairs had been the decent thing to do while those who had been the closest to him, remembered Sir Michael. She didn't mean for them to leave her there for so long   Pride stopped her from going into the drawing room, and if it hadn't been raining, she would have escaped back into the grounds. Why had he insisted on dragging her here? What purpose did it serve? All she had wanted to do was to offer comfort and companionship to the man she loved but it was clear she wasn't even being given a chance to do that. She felt used and useless. There was no use in waiting to be rescued like a Princess in the tower. He had forgotten she was there.

The long case clock ticked away more minutes. How could she go back to that room, or tell anyone about the voices she had heard? Slowly she edged down the stairs and saw Niall crossing the hall from the library. She ran down and trapped him before he could return to his guests.

"Give me your car keys. I need to get out of here. I've been shut up in that room for over four hours. I thought you might have come and got me." Even to herself, her voice sounded petulant and whining.

"You only think of yourself, Lydia. *My* father isn't even cold in the grave and *you're* upset." He threw the keys at her with venom. "Damn you and your feelings. Get out."

It was too late, the words had been said on both sides. Lydia wanted to go after him and make it right but there were the Empsoms to think of. She wanted to be part of his grief, to help him, not shut away in a kind of limbo. Did death give him the right to be so cruel?

"Do you want me to go back to London?" she said sadly, in an attempt to win back some kind of warmth.

"It's up to you," he snapped. She could see by his eyes that he meant it, that he really didn't care anymore. How could he have changed in the space of a few hours? The words cut into her, this cold indifference.

"You knew I would have been waiting for you to ask me back down. I couldn't just wander about your Mother's house."

"It's *my* house now."

The inference made her sick. The corners of his mouth were twisted in a half smile. A stranger might have thought this was a statement made in shock, but she knew him better. The realisation was growing that he was *excited* by it all, at what he had become in one day. *Sir Niall Seligman.*

Without another word she ran out into the rain, to the safety of the waiting car. Driving aimlessly through the country lanes to while away time, she finally accepted that there could be no rest in her until she had gone back to him and made her peace. There were some early spring flowers on one of the banks and so she stopped and picked some for him.

By the time she returned to the house, the Empsons were gone. There was silence. She walked into the drawing room, where Lady Seligman sat with her youngest son, Angus. "I went for a walk," she stammered as they caught sight of the posy. Further proof of her frivolity, they seemed to imply. "Where is Niall?"

The look said it all but Lydia stood her ground. She wanted to tell Lady Seligman that she had it all wrong, that she wasn't a selfish brat. Words on either side were pointless now and it was Angus who took pity on her and broke the silence.

"He's gone for a walk in the park."

It was still raining but she ran as fast as she could. This was to be the final chance of putting things right, to reverse whatever evil thoughts his mother had put in his mind, poisoning whatever he wanted to believe.

"Niall, I'm sorry. I am only frustrated because I can't help you. I want you to turn to me for comfort. I would die for you. Please don't do this." She proffered the posy with an outstretched arm across a great puddle that stood between them.

Slowly, he took the flowers and tearing them one by one, he cast them into the muddy water in an expression of pure malice. The yellows and pinks of the delicate petals were drowned in the mud. He gave her the look of disgust. Her outburst of feeling, her lack of control and self-respect, had revolted him. To him, she was just a selfish girl, and no matter what she said it was clear that something had changed in him forever.

Lydia felt it all slipping from her grasp and would have rather died just then, than lose his regard and love. She was scrambling madly to restore herself in his eyes and offered him her hand. He flinched as if her touch had scorched him, and walked away across the park to where he had saved her from the falling tree only weeks before. And, like a faithful dog, she stayed - still determined that he should love her again.

Later, that evening, she walked into the library and found Lady Seligman seated by the dying fire, with her arms wrapped around herself, and rocking in disbelief, as the loss of old familiarity was sinking in. Her eyes were fixed ahead, utterly bereft and untouchable in the rawest of grief. Lydia had stolen in on this moment and seen this woman's soul, her vulnerability and felt humbled by the capacity of the human body to keep breathing with such a loss.

Locked away in her own world, Lady Seligman was listening as the wind whistled down the chimney. It was where she and Sir Michael used to sit in the evenings when they were first married. Niall was the spitting image of him and for her it was as if all those years, *her* reality, was now a fantasy. She was back then, remembering how they had been in their happiest moments together before she'd discovered his infidelity.

All those years had gone in an instant. And then it slowly hit her again, that *he was gone*. Now this stupid girl had all the best in her son, that she had loved in his father. Lydia still had her looks, her youth and *his* love. She wanted to jump into the girl's body and experience it all over again.

The cold must have bought me back, my bones are aching and the fire has died low. It must be late. The moon is now high in the sky, and it shines through the casement window illuminating my aged hands. The sudden sight of them is shocking after re-inhabiting the body of a young girl. I must have been dreaming for hours, and it pleases me to know that the magic had been so powerful.

Wherever Niall was now, he will have sensed it and longed for me once more. There is some satisfaction at least in that. I would have pulled him under with me to share the dreaming of the same memories so that we walked together once more. No matter who he was with now, there is always that claim on him. For nothing that is so powerful can simply dissolve into nothing and the intensity of our past is etched over us both.

CHAPTER TWELVE

1953 April

Niall and a group of friends had rented the Chalet Malaise in Val D'Isere, and among them was Jake Hammond. Although Niall was still seeing Lydia, his anger with her over not attending his father's funeral, had not burned itself out. Her behaviour had merely served to endorse his mother's opinion that she was not the sort of girl someone in his position should marry. To teach her a lesson, it was decided she should not be allowed to sit in the family pew with its carved griffins: the family crest having been carved into the ancient oak in 1843 when the brewery had made plain old Mr Seligman rich enough to attract patronage for a small title.

Niall was enjoying the attention his newly-found status had brought him, although he was still cold and unforgiving towards Lydia. How could she have said she cared about him and then deserted him at the funeral, and behaved so badly on the very day his father died? The longer he was in the company of the other girlfriends, the more his doubts about Lydia set in, especially after his mother had voiced her doubts about the girl's suitability. Perhaps she *was* unstable: she would never be biddable, that was for sure. Neither had she anything in common with his social set. The only person she made any effort with during the holiday was Jake, who was far too patient with her in Niall's opinion, but then he, too, was one of those bloody sensitive types. Jake was far too good looking and too popular with the girls for his liking, but they had been good friends over the years and he had a grudging respect for the way he was carving out a career writing exploration and travel books. Given Lydia's black moods, he was a welcome and amusing addition to the skiing party.

Niall was finding that every time he caught sight of Lydia, there was an overwhelming sense of betrayal and remorseless anger directed towards her. Why couldn't she just do what was expected of her, like the other girlfriends. Why couldn't she accept that she had ruined their romance for him with her bloody intensity? And now she wouldn't let it drop. She was coming across the bedroom towards him, pathetically holding her ski goggles before her.

"Niall, I know your father has died, and I've told you a million times how sorry I am but it's as if you have blamed me personally for what happened. I don't mind being on my own in the day but can't we have lunch or dinner on our own? We never get any time together, without your friends, and you're always surrounded by people. It's not a holiday, it's just like it was in London. I want some time alone with you," she stammered.

There it was again, the whining, demanding attempts at manipulation that grated on his nerves. "Keep your voice down, Lydia. They can all hear us down there and you've embarrassed me enough already."

He looked down on her wide-eyed expression, her lips slightly parted in shock. The more he wanted her, the more he hated her, it seemed. The more beautiful she became for him, the more he pushed her away. It was this overwhelming desire for control, and the knowledge that he would never be able to.

"Are you now saying there's something wrong with my friends? Sorry to disappoint you, Lydia, but life's not some fairy tale as you seem to think."

"What's happened to us, tell me!" she shrieked.

"Just grow up Lydia, and lower your voice. How dare you need to ask, you should have been at the funeral."

"You told me I couldn't sit with you, so I thought I wasn't wanted there."

"You're not officially family", he roared. "How could you ever think you could be? You're certainly no lady" His voice venomous, he lunged, forcing her legs apart with his knee. The strength of his anger, and now his perverse excitement, surprised even him.

She struggled frantically, managing to connect a blow to his face. "You asked me to marry you, you bastard. What has happened to you?" His eyes were bleak and expressionless, his mind numb with desire and anger. She thought he had been the one. "I wanted children with you, everything. You weren't the one, you let *me* down, and now it's all ruined."

He now had her hands behind her head and was forcing himself on her as she wept silently. During the terrible act, she escaped her body like a bird, watching as the thread of love between them was slowly being retracted by his anger, as though he had blocked every emotion from her and was taking back everything he had once given. She watched the grisly reversal of everything that had gone between them, this hatred in slow motion as if it were happening to someone else. Finally, shocked and degraded, she sank to the floor.

He towered above her. "Name *one* thing you've ever done for me. Make a list. What? You say you love me. How? Prove it"

It was like asking her to drag out her soul and lay it there at his feet. *Can't you feel my heart, my darling, swimming at your feet amongst all of this filth on the floor?* It was a double blow, this denigration of love and now this doubt. Her mind worked desperately for ways of proving it to him. She was at a loss to respond to his ridiculous demands. And then it came, the sharpest blow.

"I wish you weren't here," he said quietly, sadly.

"I thought ..." She had to catch her breath as it teetered on choking her. "... you loved me." He had to. It was her one saving grace. Her whole life pivoted upon the answer. Love knew no barriers, it could conquer anything.

"I don't know if I do anymore," came the matter of fact reply, as if she were suddenly a stranger.

"*Niall, do you still love me?*" she cried hysterically.

"No!" came his reply, although he wouldn't meet her eyes as he said it.

She heard him leave the room and walk down the stairs, even as the last of him trickled out of her. Ashamed and feeling dirty she listened as he became cheerful again. "I'm going out. I don't want her to follow." His voice floated up from outside, as if she were some dirty piece of his past he was trying to obliterate.

Lydia dragged herself to the balcony and, like someone condemned to madness, she watched them file out dutifully behind him, like nursery children in pairs, throwing embarrassed looks back at the small figure crouched on the upstairs balcony.

She felt winded and lay on the floor trying to catch her breath. The shock was spreading slowly, like poison from her heart into other parts of her body. Everything had been staked on him. Powerless to breathe or blink, she stared at the closed door for what seemed like an eternity. Surely he would come back, and say it had all been a terrible mistake.

The door opened but it was one of the girlfriends who had come back to gloat. "You really are so selfish Lydia. Niall's father has just died and you are causing scenes like this, you're ruining our holiday."

Lydia didn't know how much more could she take. It was like a dream, this second cruelty coupled with wild untruths. Was she going mad? Were they right in what they said about her, behind her back? Perhaps she *was* a monster without any feeling. The trouble was, she felt *too much*. And now, this sheep of a girl was seeing fit to berate her. How dare she judge? They were strangers but she was the one who'd been flirting outrageously with Niall since they arrived. Now, obviously aware that Niall had just ended his affair with Lydia - (for hadn't he responded to her cooing sympathy and her lifted leg?) - she couldn't resist finishing off her rival. Lydia ruined the balance of their social circle, and yet again she was an outcast, an outsider, not belonging.

A vase of flowers narrowly missed the girl's head. "Get out before I kill you, you stupid little bitch," spat Lydia.

The girl fled, no doubt armed with the view that Lydia was indeed raving mad, ignoring Jake in her hurry to tell the others what had happened. Entering Lydia's room, he heard her muttering to herself, senseless words repeated over and over again. *For hadn't love been to the death?* That was what love meant to her.

"Leave him. He'll be back," he said reassuringly.

But they both knew it was the end. Jake had thought this would be his most victorious moment over her, a moment he had secretly wanted in recompense for the hurt she'd caused him. But this was worse than he had expected. He watched the vital life-spark drain from her second by second.

He tried to lead her inside and close the windows, but she had to stay out there on the balcony, as if to watch Niall's last moments without her trail across the night air. The snow looked so warm and peaceful, like a soft gentle release. Perhaps this was the only way to prove her feelings to him. Anything to claw her way back to his heart.

The words were slow and dead when they came. "I don't know how to pick myself up Jake, I honestly feel like dying." Finally, the acceptance had come that even if she could win him back, she would never fit in his world. "I don't want to go on. Please let me jump. I love him. You know I love him. Tell him. Why won't he listen? Do you think I was wrong to not go to the funeral? I thought I had done the right thing. What do you think?"

It was gibberish, a frenzy of words to pull the fragments of her mind back together. Over and over she sat blaming herself, if she had done this or that, things would have been different.

"Lydia ..."

"Oh Jake, I have nothing left, no strength to go on. Please. Help me, I will die without him, I swear it."

The realisation that Niall could produce such an emotional outburst, even to herself, was an additional shock. As Jake left to fetch her a brandy, she stood looking out over the valley as if to project this immense love to wherever he was now. Like an animal sniffing the wind, she willed him back with all her heart over the freezing space below.

In her mind's eye, she neatly cut away at the skin with a small knife. From both wrists, there poured the brightest of red love, spilling like a beacon on the fairy white and virginal snow. This was the sacrifice she would have made for him, cutting out her own heart. She was triumphant in the knowledge that she was not mad, her love was strong and true. He would know that, one day. She would not have to live without him forever but for now, she stood there with the life-light going out of her.

When Jake returned, there was a disturbing peace about her. She said with a smile. "Jake, I don't want life without him, but I swear he will pay for this. May he have a lonely life, a loveless and childless marriage, and may he never rest, may he be haunted by me as long as he lives."

Jake held her cold hands and saw how right she had been about the soul and the body being connected. He knew she would never be the same again, that she would never get over what had happened, and even if she ever did come to love him, he would never have all of her.

CHAPTER THIRTEEN

1999

Since returning from Lemellen, Rebecca's hunger to know more about the past intensified. Triumphantly she stroked the photographs that Lydia had given her to show her uncle. By not giving them to him had made her feel as though she had regained control. Studying the well worn images, she looked at each in turn for the hundredth time, as if to discover some clue behind events. There was a group shot of about a dozen people on the ski slopes. Her uncle stood at the back looking strikingly handsome, like a film star. His presence seemed to dominate the others, and he stood a head and shoulders above the rest. Niall was in the middle, at the front of the group looking serious and seemed to be staring at something beyond the camera. It was curious that Lydia was not included.

The next was of her uncle with Lydia. They were part of the same group, having lunch or dinner somewhere during the holiday. Lydia looked detached, stunningly beautiful, but lost and sad. Niall sat next to her but his head was averted as if he were talking to someone off camera. with his thoughts turned elsewhere. While Lydia seemed unaware that somebody was taking their picture, Uncle Jake was staring at her with a look of complete devotion and love on his face.

It was curious. Perhaps they were lovers behind Niall's back, and that was what went wrong. But then *that* didn't make sense either, because Lydia had been so in love with Niall from the way she spoke, and from the letters Rebecca had read.

She wished desperately that someone would adore her one day, especially someone as good looking as her uncle had once been. With a sigh, she turned to the mirror and gazed at her reflection. To her, there was nothing unusual or remarkable about her looks, and it was obvious she would never possess great beauty. She wondered whether her mother had been beautiful. Her hair seemed to hang lankly and her complexion was too pale for her liking. When would she fall in love and have the adventure she craved?

Putting on a CD she wistfully daydreamed up her perfect man, the romance she would have one day. University seemed so far off, but everybody said that was the place to fall in love. To end up alone like Lydia, must be terrible; worse still to never have loved and still be a spinster like poor old plain Megan. Megan was a bit dotty, as her friends said, but Uncle Jake ... how could such a good looking man end up on his own?

Idly she took up the tongs on the dressing table and began curling her hair. Maybe that would make her feel better, more 'girly'. She must have sat for ages, staring at her reflection whilst humming to the tunes in the background, when suddenly the looking glass seemed to cloud over. With a terrified yelp, she started with the shock before realising it was just Megan, standing at the door to her bedroom and staring back at her reflection.

"Shit, I've just burned myself. Shouldn't you have knocked, you gave me a fright."

"I've been calling you for ages, lunch is ready, but as your were playing your stereo at full blast, you wouldn't have heard much would you?"

Sucking her burnt finger, she noticed Megan advance towards her. Although she bent over the dressing table protectively and scrabbled to put away the photographs before the housekeeper saw them, it was too late. Megan snatched the one that had intrigued Rebecca most.

"Ah yes. This must have been taken on that trip to Val D'Isere. Look at your uncle, staring at her like that, poor man. He never got over her."

"Didn't he have loads of girlfriends though, over the years? That's what he told me?"

"Oh yes, but he never loved any of them. They were just to pass the time. She broke his heart, and Niall's too. I told you, she's a dangerous woman. And not a day goes by where I don't pity your poor uncle for the life he could have lived. He could have found a wife, had a family, but no, even though she didn't want him for herself she couldn't have had that, she would have been jealous.

"Every year I watched him get older and lonelier. His dearest wish was for a family - not that he doesn't love you - but he would have had so much love to give. It is said that she cursed every man she was with. Both of them came to no good, no happiness. I bet he would rue the day he met her, if he could only see it for himself, instead of carrying on with this stupid adoration. But he was bewitched, glamoured, in any case."

"What do you mean? Look, I know for whatever reason you've never liked Lydia, but maybe we should be thinking about poor Uncle Jake rather than her. He isn't getting any younger, and I'll be off soon, and then he'll really be lonely. Would it do any harm to bring them together?"

It was true, Uncle Jake *had* suddenly seemed to age, as if a great tiredness had come over him. Sometimes she had found him late in the evenings, sitting on his own, too heavy with drink and his memories of the past to speak to her.

"If you don't heed my words evil will come of it, now stop before it goes too far. I know what's best. I've known him a good many years more than you have lived, young lady. And I've known her, too. Don't forget we come from the same blood in a manner of speaking."

God this woman is mad, Rebecca thought. Megan had a look of malevolence in her eyes that was beginning to scare her. She wanted her out of her bedroom but her curiosity was roused. "What do you mean?"

"Never you mind, but remember this, we did grow up together, I knew her."

"In Norfolk you mean?"

Before she could answer, Megan grabbed Rebecca's hand and turned her palm upwards. "Take my warning for the last time, before it's too late. Leave this whole thing alone, or you will be tainted by it too. Rebecca, there is danger ahead for you if you carry on this course."

When she had left the room, Rebecca was stunned with shock for a few moments, but on reflection old Megan had always been a bit loopy. It was obvious, she had been jealous of Lydia. Whatever Megan felt she had no time for her, it was her uncle who was the priority, and it was time to be practical now she'd had the facts re-confirmed. Adults were so complicated. The whole thing was unnecessary: the stupidity of it all was that this suffering was self-inflicted. It was a clear-cut matter, pure and simple, and the quicker somebody sorted it out, as far as she was concerned, the better.

She understood everything now.

Whatever had happened between them, however pride or hatred had overtaken their love for each other, neither deserved such great unhappiness. It was like a great canker, eating them away. It had to be made all right.

She would just check on a few more facts, and thanks to Megan she knew just where to find them. She would find Nel, the lady mentioned in the letters. The gods made it easy once again to uncover another chapter. From one of Lydia's letters she found the address of the Norfolk farmhouse, and of Nel's nearby. She would go directly there the next morning and see the old lady for herself, if she were still alive.

Giddy with excitement, she planned the next stage of her adventure meticulously. She would soon re-organise this mess and bring some order, some sense into everything. These old people really did know how to get themselves in a pickle. Why did it have to be so complicated?

Rebecca left soon after breakfast the following morning. Summer was humming into life, and the cow parsley obscured every corner. Every space, every corner was filled with emerald green, the richness of new life was breathtaking. Following the narrow lanes until she reached Eadenhoe, she quickly found the little cottage, hidden by a thicket of honeysuckle. Cats peered from the clematis around the entrance.

Her heart lurched with excitement. It was like a fairy tale, now that she had found the Nel of the letters. A cuckoo called in the distance, adding to the mysterious ambience she was expecting. Opening a smart glossy green gate, the garden was marshalled in rows of colour, fuchsias intermingled with neat little pansies and marigolds, all planted in lines. The cottage was newly whitewashed. This *wasn't* what she had anticipated, and her heart sunk to see a portly man with an apron strapped around his girth, whispering pleading words to a gas barbecue. He hadn't even noticed her intrusion into his world.

A woman came out from around the side of the cottage, bearing a basket on her arm, and buoyed up by startlingly white trainers. Rebecca curbed her gaping expression.

"Hullo, can we help you?" mouthed the red lips.

"I ... I don't think you can actually." Surely Nel couldn't have had such normal and disappointing relations?

"I'm looking for a Mrs Nelson, I thought she still lived here."

The woman brayed like a hyena. "Oh Gerald, did you hear that? How amusing! The old lady would be about 150 years old by now, dear. No, no, you'll find her in the churchyard at I'm afraid."

She was still laughing as Rebecca eyed them with disgust. They had shattered her day, her whole perspective. An important figure from the game had been taken out. And these impostors, what were they? Day-trippers playing at living in the country, weekenders from suburbia. They had no doubt bought Nel's romantic cottage for a disgustingly small sum and had ruined it with the tidy new extensions and gleaming conservatory. It wasn't at all the atmospheric place of Lydia's history that Rebecca had been wistfully re-creating in her mind's eye.

Well, at least they could give her directions for Elmere? Hopefully Lydia's farmhouse would still be intact. They had to get a map, but they got there in the end.

On the way, she stopped at the graveyard where black sheep grazed among the gravestones. Most of the graves had dissolved into grassy hillocks that protruded softly through the earth. It seemed as though burials were not all that common here. The new incumbents probably waited until they got back to London to be cremated, she thought sadly. The names on some of the old tombs were beautiful. Maud, Alicia, Octavia. She wished she had been named something a little more imaginative than Rebecca. The round flint tower struck an ominous dark shadow across the grass which seemed to sever the graveyard in two.

She started to look in earnest for Nel.

After she had circumnavigated it twice, she gave up. There was nothing. Could she have been called something else? There wasn't even a single headstone in that timescale. As she neared the perimeter for the last time, she noticed a crooked wooden cross under a gnarled oak tree. Under the green mildew the rotten wood bore the faint name of Morgan and what looked to be two triangles on each end. Strange, she thought. Maybe it was an animal's grave, oddly placed between the edge of the graveyard and the field. Never mind, onwards and upwards. She strode purposely towards the rusty gate, never noticing the small markings on a similar wooden cross in the field behind the old oak where the girl's mother had finally been laid to rest.

She found the farmhouse in a valley, on the other side of the hill. The sun was almost setting and the red glow, threw the Norfolk brick house into surrealism, with the whole landscape projecting out fantastically from spinning hedgerows. At the end of a long row of horse chestnut trees she drove past the sign. 'Hall Farm Cattery'. There was a cartoon type billboard painted with the faces of a lassie dog and a cat licking each other. It felt more like Hollywood than rural Norfolk.

The drive was smooth and led to the house. The nearest end looked as if it had been rebuilt fairly recently, it was modern with neat pink frilly curtains. She could see that the other side of the house was still intact, as she had imagined it would be. The grand red chimney pots rose majestically clear of the modern extension. It was strange to think that Lydia had grown up here, all those years ago. She wondered who had done this monstrous thing to the wing at the back.

Just then, a man in a lime green tracksuit appeared from the back door. The stable yard suddenly came alive with cats and dogs and she saw that all the old stables had been encased in wire cages filled with 'Hotel Guests'. To talk to the 'lime' man would have made matters even worse. Her dream of finding it all as it had been were dispelled. She left him in a cloud of smoke, flapping like a frenzied budgie.

It was with great sadness that she drove back. Her hopes had been so high. The excitement over the prospect of meeting Nel and seeing the house as it had been, was replaced by depression. She felt even further removed from the events of the past, and the romance of the fruitless journey made her reflect that the modern world seemed so reassuringly predictable and safe. Their homes were now so false, so ugly, encased in 'rural picturesque'. How could those dull people from Ruislip have the same passions as the ones she was so desperate to find?

On the outskirts of Norwich, she found a MacDonalds and tucked into a cheeseburger. She decided to go back and take control of the situation. These old people couldn't possibly be left to wander through life demented, or broken hearted, or shrivelled up. The idea was empowering. She, Rebecca, had to make things happen and that was what she had to do without delay.

CHAPTER FOURTEEN
1953

It was May when Jake bought Lydia home to Norfolk, back to Nel's cottage. She couldn't have gone to London and risk bumping into Niall on every street corner. She hadn't thought for a second that she would never return to his house, or to her own flat, where they had spent so much time together. She had left behind all those trinkets, the things he had given her.

The nights and mornings were the worst, when she would dream of him and wake bereft, rocking senselessly like a baby, back and forth, unable to come to terms with what she had lost. She was without a voice for a whole week with the shock of losing him, simply because she didn't dare to open the floodgates lest the pain was too great, and so she drifted about the cottage voicelessly, without expression or spirit.

It was always her way to dive in and out of her own dream world, and so her aloofness was part of her nature but even to those closest to her, she was closed and lost. It was disarming even to Nel how she would drift in and out of the room, seeing beyond them all with haunting lost eyes.

Jake and Nel sat facing each other one morning at the cluttered kitchen table. Silently drinking coffee as the sun streamed in the open door, they both thought about the approach of summer.

"I expect you'll have to go and earn a living sooner or later, my boy. You can't stay here and hope for a miracle, wasting your life away. She'll come right when she's ready, but you've done all you can."

She felt so much for the young man who was obviously heartbroken to watch Lydia's gradual decline and saw how each day his love grew for her. "I feel like I am to blame in some way. I introduced them together. God knows I wish I hadn't. Why does she feel everything so bloody acutely? Why can't she be like the rest of us? What the hell she saw in him anyway baffles me, and it makes me so angry to see her wasting her life on him now. Why can't she just pull herself out of it?"

He slammed down his mug and began pacing the room in agitation. "I'm scared Nel. It's like being around a child, when she looks at you with those great big eyes. It's as if she is a simpleton, a complete innocent and she's silently asking *Why me? What have I done?* I can't stand to see her like this, I don't know how to help her and every day she is further from the girl I ... knew..." He struggled to finish the sentence but he was overcome with emotion.

"You mean loved. She's made of stronger stuff than you think. She's still the same girl and you will always love her, I can see that. Now is not your time though, you will have to be patient and follow the flow. This has happened for a reason. It will all become clear, soon enough.

"I blame myself too, in many ways. You see, she has been like a daughter to me and I have always taught her to see the best in things, to love like there's no tomorrow. To live, and never close your heart. To feel your way through life with your heart, to seek a sacred and mystic union with one love of your life. Look where it's got her. I know you think she's just in shock, but it's as if she's dead inside, there's nothing left. She gave it all to him. How could she tell us about all that grief? What words could start to explain her pain? The poor, *poor* girl."

Jake saw Nel was crying and stretched out a hand to her. She was an amazing woman. No more did he belong here than Lydia, really. But she had made him feel like family.

"Maybe I *should* go back to London. You can't put me up forever and I'm probably the last person she wants to be with. I just don't know. I just felt I couldn't just leave her there in that flat alone."

"Now you listen to me, boy," Nel said, fixing her fierce green eyes on him. "You don't go far and don't give up on her, because when she comes out of this, and she will in time, she'll want you around. Trust me."

"I don't know ..."

"It takes time, you know, women of our mettle can be funny things. Just be patient. She is in a bad way. Did you know that she sometimes creeps in to my bed? She chatters to me all night long about imagining him with some beautiful girl, the way he had been with her in the beginning, all that courtesy. She chatters like a baby to keep the silence of the night at bay.

"Nel, she says to me. It's worse than him being dead, because I know he chose not to be with me. The world is too small to contain the two of us to live in parallel times and for him to choose not to have me. He did love me, didn't he? she asks over and over."

"Do you think he'll regret it?"

"She was so sure of him," Nel responded.

They looked at each other over the expanse of the table, aware that the only thing keeping her alive was the thought of Niall finally recovering his senses, and his love for her. His rejection was still a dark dream to her, and to speak of it would have given shape to the reality. And while they talked on and on, Lydia watched time trickling out of her hands, distancing her further and further away from him, until the days would turn into weeks since he left.

Her great dilemma was that despite all her arts, and with all the magic she knew she could conjure, she was loathe to craft a spell to win him back. For if she had, she knew that she would never know his true will. To do nothing was perhaps worse, and here was the torture, the great irony. She was moribund. There was no balance left to formulate a sentence let alone a spell.

And so great was the old lady's love for her – for Nel did love her as she might have loved the lost child – at night time, when the chill of the room threw up its shadows, she might have formulated a great spell on her behalf. But when the morning came, something told her to hang back, for to tie Lydia to this man forever was not right. Besides, the coming of the Solstice gave her great faith that everything would be re-balanced. Lydia would then see she was best without him, *she would see.* He had been a foreigner to her ways. A more selfish part of her welcomed Lydia's return to Norfolk, where she could resume with more serious business, the work of the coven, and in her own mind she looked forward to sharing ancient secrets once more with her favourite protégé.

Jake, however, had begun to feel like a prisoner in the small cottage, he needed to breathe again, to escape from Lydia's grief. In the beginning, he had been so sure that he could bring her out of it, but for all his kind, patient love, he failed to bring her up to the surface. He heard her mad mutterings which always began with "Do you think he'll be sorry ... did he love me Jake?" until one day he had heard enough and left.

He could do no more.

The morning of his departure, he watched her sleep, grey faced and ashen under the great yew in the garden. It was hard to remember the bright being who had cast beauty around everything. She was so different from the girl who had captivated him, the one who had lain with him in that very spot a just over year ago. He should have ravaged her then and there, and things would have been so different. In many ways he cursed the day he ever met her, but since then she had changed his life, his perspective. He was empty without her, and just being close to her had bought him happiness. With great sadness he kissed her cold cheek as she slept and left for London.

As she slept, Lydia dreamt of bright seashore of jewel-like images. The beach ran for miles, further than the eye could see. It was only a little way before she knew there were golden dunes before the sea. It was there that the light glowed red. This was her heaven, the mysterious place she knew she had come from, and would return to one day. She had only dreamt of it a few times before, but it always left her marked and she remembered the importance of it always. There was never anyone else but her and the great white horse. He came into view, just on the horizon, as the sun set. The sun's last rays turning his huge haunches and his long white mane to shimmering gold. They galloped for miles and the wind lapped her face the sea re-vitalising her senses before they came before the great tower on the horizon.

Lydia knew in her subconscious that she would only reach the tower as her life was ending: that she wasn't meant to go there yet. She could have cried with happiness, with the freedom and elation of it all. She cried out to be taken onwards to the tower, it was so breathtakingly beautiful. She wanted to stay here, where she felt so free and happy. Instead, the stallion stopped so abruptly that she slid from his back and was caught by Daniel, her lost childhood friend.

They were children once more, as they had been when he died. Children have no need for words. They had the favour of angels. Her heart was warmed by old simplicities, the eternal source of joy was returning to the cold body she inhabited. They ran and ran inland, until they found a beautiful meadow where a blue dragonfly skimmed her face for a second. As it rested on the field of orchids, she noticed its brilliant azure body which matched her memory of his beautiful child' eyes.

After a time, the boy pointed to the tower by the sea, shimmering on the water. She understood that when the sun finally set it, everything would fade into nothing. Following his pointing finger out across the ocean, she closed her eyes and smiled, because the loss no longer mattered. Everything would be all right, in the end. She had broken free, credulous that she had forgotten that her end and beginning was in nature, the eternal source which gave her more than love.

When the cool shiver wind of the afternoon awoke her, she ran laughing out of the shadow of the house to catch the sun around the other side of the garden.

She was free.

JAKE

When the letter from Nel arrived I was in the middle of preparing for a trip to South America. I had submitted a proposal to the publisher some months ago, and the day before I'd received news that my book – a study of a lost Peruvian city – had been accepted. Under the circumstance, the letter seemed to have come from another time and place, since several months had passed since my last visit to Norfolk. Although I had returned to London with a heavy heart, I had single-mindedly re-assumed my career and was surprised just how effortlessly things had gone for me. Nel had always assured me that this would happen when I had found the right path, and it did indeed seem to be signalling me that I had chosen the right thing to do. More importantly it made *me* happy and I was proud of my writing.

Now, sitting on the bed among half packed suitcases and maps, I hesitated for several minutes before opening the letter, having recognised the post mark and the writing, immediately. How many days I had longed for a letter, some news from Lydia or even some gossip from Nel, but nothing had come. I had worried myself long into the night about how I had left Lydia, and whether she would ever be the same again. There were even times when I had started to drive there, only to turn back having convincing myself that she needed time to recuperate, to get over Niall. And now, this letter made my stomach churn with dread.

I could bear to read the news it contained. There was also an underlying resentment that it should arrive at this time, because it rocked the calmness I had found again in my work. Lydia could only bring more hurt, simply because the unexpected and unpredictable occurred whenever she made her presence felt. More to the point, I feared the inevitable pull she still had over me and I knew that ultimately I had no power to resist. The other, inner part of me, shook with excitement and finally my hands trembled to open the envelope.

I was both relieved and intrigued because it was an invitation to Nel's cottage for Midsummer Eve, for the Solstice. I recalled my first visit but it seemed an age away. I was young then. Since then, my life had changed so much, and my steel has been tempered to razor sharpness

The thought of seeing her again in two days sent out conflicting emotions. There was no news of Lydia in the letter, which could be either good or bad. Although I could hardly bear to think of her pining over Niall, I also bitterly resented the fact that I couldn't express my love for her because of it. Besides, there was no time to become embroiled in any more histrionics because I was due to leave in a week's time.

I surprised even myself over just how quickly I made my decision. Whatever came of this visit, I had to either leave her now, or risk losing everything. I couldn't go on living on a knife edge and allowing her to cloud every thing I did, in the hope that she might call. I resolved to grab life with both hands and risk everything on the outcome of the Solstice. I had been passive for far too long, often feeling *her* emotion, *her* pain, more than my own.

When I arrived at Edenbridge they had set fire to a great pyre just outside the village, on top of a small hill. There were countless faces all laughing and in good cheer, but none I recognised. This was always a time for rejoicing but the heaviness had settled back in my heart as I walked up the slope towards the heat of the flames. I remembered being told that today the year is in balance, poised for the next turn of the wheel, when day and night were of equal length and the fleeting moment everything stands still, before darkness overpowers light. In a strange way it mirrored the crossroads I now faced: whether to stay, or to leave unmarked by yet another rejection.

Standing on the perimeter of the merry-making, I was distracted by a movement in the trees below, at the base of the hill. A small roe deer darts in and out of the thicket, and then comes to rest at the edge of the copse. Our gaze meets momentarily and then I am surprised by its sudden gallop towards the fire, unafraid and drawn like a moth to the flame. Its sudden leap through the flames was met by a brief moment of stunned silence, followed by a loud cheer from the crowd, as it disappeared into the shadows on the other side of the hill. I remembered something Lydia once said about watching the signs and for the first time I think I understand what she meant.

The intense heat scorched my senses as the evening tide came nearer, and with it the darkness, slowly descending around the circle cast by the Bel-Fire. The golden flames transfixed me, the scents of the wood strangely powerful and making the air thick with anticipation and power. By now I was weary of searching her out; my eyes were becoming sore from the smoke. Even Nel was too busy to talk as she was orchestrating some winding dance as the music began. My resentment turned to anger, which has always fuelled a thirst for wine, and as the deep rhythmic call of the drums closed in, I couldn't resist the call join the dance.

A troupe of young girls in long white dresses shimmered in the firelight as the music pulsated. Hair woven with holly and ivy leaves, these nubile beauties circled the fire, pulling the men into the dance as the sound of laughter mingled with the crackling flames. The night was imbued with a strange power that was being summoned by the music and the dance.

I sat through the rest of the night fuelled by the power of the Solstice and when dawn came, I had one of the young girls on my knee. We were kissing when suddenly and without warning, the first rays of the sun burst over the tops of the trees to the east, filling the world with its rosy glow.

It was at that very moment that I saw Lydia for the first time, and in spite of her recent tragedy, I had never seen her look so lovely. She was as new to me as this new dawn, and as she smiled in the half-light, I gently pushed the young girl aside and walked to where she stood, marvelling at the change in her. She was serene, the old fight had been restored in her; all that mad intensity had gone. And yet there was a womanly beauty about her now; the girlish innocence was gone. Her hair was longer, twisted with oak leaves and passion flowers and without speaking, she led me to the wild wood. Loving me without words as my heart sang for the first and last time, along with the birds stirring with the light.

CHAPTER FIFTEEN

Lydia had not seen Jake for so long, that he seemed taller, more broad-shouldered than she had remembered. All the girls were taken with him, he looked so handsome. Why had she never noticed it before? She had watched him for what had seemed like hours from the other side of the fire, her heart racing that he had come, yet she was ashamed at how he had last seen her, weakened by grief. She had watched in the shadows, frozen to the spot as he began to take an interest in one of the younger girls, with her long brown hair gleaming in the fire.

Just as Lydia was about to go to him, the girl began dancing around him, lifting up her skirts teasingly. On her way round again he grabbed her until she fell on his knee and he began kissing her. Lydia could hear laughter all around, but she was not part of it all. Why was this starting to bother her? It wasn't as if she had a claim on him, yet her jealousy made her indignant.

Nel caught sight of Lydia staring in disbelief at Jake and his companion. She had been spoilt until now with Jake's constant devotion and Nel watched with drawn breath. *Which way will you go my beauty?* It looked as if Lydia would turn away and leave, but then she drew herself up and began shining from within, as if she had turned on the power, as she used to do. Only Nel witnessed the rising of her inner energy with its characteristic flickering blue flame. Even against the Bel-Fire it was breathtaking. Her eyes were huge black almonds, her hair hung in waves, the colour of golden wheat. Her lips were sensuously parted in concentration.

As if she had willed it, Jake suddenly looked up, breaking away from his clinch with the girl, and saw her there. She walked a little way towards him with a half-beckoning smile - he rose to meet her, as if he had no power in him to do otherwise.

Nel watched as they walked towards the dark shade of the wood. At the edge of the trees Lydia took off her garlands and placed them on his shoulders lovingly. In response, he swept her up into his arms and carried her into the wood. From her vantage point, Nel saw the majestic flight of the heron over their path, the strange pattern of the clouds as the sun broke through, the beginning of the rain and she knew with certainty that this 'marriage' had been pre-ordained for years.

Their coupling beneath the lights of the Bel-Fire was as natural as the dawn and it had a great meaning, echoing the age-old, primitive rites. This joining was sacred and there *would* be a child conceived this night, she was sure of it. Whether it was a boy or girl, it would have bestowed upon it the power of the sun rising above them, with the moon still shining in the half light.

CHAPTER SIXTEEN

Jake and Lydia returned to Nel's cottage at midday, walking idly through the sun drenched lanes as if in a dream, drowsy from lovemaking and relief that everything had come full circle. They had found each other again. There was a sense of calm, of homecoming between them. Lydia looked as young as a virgin bride with the pink flush of happiness on her cheeks and laughing like children, they entered the cottage.

Nel was chatting to others of the group but they all turned abruptly and stopped their conversation. Lydia laughed nervously, holding her lover's hand, as they waited uneasy in the protracted silence with all eyes on them.

"Why are you all so serious, has something happened?"

"A great thing has happened and you were the instruments through which it could take place. Your joining at such an auspicious time and place will bring us a magical addition to the family," Nel answered cryptically.

"What do you mean?" Jake demanded, gathering Lydia closer to him.

"Come on Lydia, don't act the fool. You've used Jake as much as Nel used you both, hissed Megan's voice. "Haven't you told him? Surely even you, Jake can see that coupling under the Bel-Fire would have repercussions!"

Suddenly the realisation of what Megan was saying dawned on

Lydia. It now seemed so obvious. The rite on the top of the hill for fertility would ensure that a magical child would be conceived with all the power of the high summer. She had heard it said that Nel was conceived that way, and others of the group, but now she felt dirty, as if they ruined what had passed between herself and Jake.

"Nel, you wouldn't ... I mean, you gave me no warning. Why didn't you say something?"

Nel looked uncharacteristically closed. "You of all people Lydia must have known."

Jake spun her round, holding her face in his hands. "Lydia, did you use me? What is going on?" He felt the sickness rise within him.

"Jake, I would never have done that to you."

"What are they meaning Lydia? What have we done? What have they done to us?" he pleaded.

"I don't know ... Nel, tell him, it will be all right. You didn't mean it, I mean there must be such a small chance, it would be ridiculous to think ... it was our *first* time."

She broke off, recoiling at the way they were all solemnly looking at her belly. "You set us up! You actually engineered the whole thing, didn't you? Well you can't come in between us, and you can't stop me from going, and then you will never see the outcome will you? What will that benefit you all? You will have lost me and with what power I have in me, I vow that you will never have the benefit of my presence here, ever again."

"You can never break the ancient ways, Lydia and we will never let you betray your oath." Nel spoke to her like a child.

"We will follow you, you will never leave us." They echoed

Their words chorused around her head until she felt dizzy with revulsion and confusion.

As if from a distance, she heard Jake's voice. "You're all sick! I'll make sure you never see Lydia again, try and follow us and you'll have me to answer to. You can't behave like this, terrorising people. You're bullies with empty words. You can't touch us anymore. Lydia get your things, we're going." Jake said, turning to her.

They left the cottage and the silent, malevolent stares, hurrying away from Eadenhoe as fast as they could through the lanes. They had only driven a few miles when Lydia asked him to stop.

"Jake, please, I need to go to the tower to think what to do next. You know the place I told you about? It has great power and I need to be there with you to find a way, to think what we should do."

"Has all this taught you *nothing*? Leave the old ghosts. We're young, life's too short to get bogged down in all this. Let's enjoy living life as it comes, don't seek to control it all anymore."

"That's just it, I can't move on. They *will* come after me, after us, they will never leave us alone. I know too much and you shouldn't underestimate their power. I just want to go to the tower one last time, because I'll never be able to come back, not once I've broken away."

The tower, all that was left of the lost village. Those families who had survived the Black Death, were cleared out hundreds of years later to make way for the big house to have its uninterrupted views of parkland. The tower of the church had been left as a folly, rather than a reminder that it had been built by the Normans on the site of an ancient pagan temple.

They parked the car hidden in the trees at the edge of the estate and picked their way carefully up the back drive of Eddleton Hall, lest they were seen. Lydia guided him silently through the densely planted rhododendron bushes until they came to the clearing where the brooding flint tower stood, its reflection captured in the lake.

Quickly they made their way to the shadows of the ruins, where Lydia pulled Jake down onto the grass beneath the tower. They lay looking up at the jagged stonework jutting up into the clear blue sky. The sun was hot. He looked at her lying in the crook of his arm. She still wore the white dress and the sun shone through the cotton outlining her breasts. He stirred with longing and they made love again under the shadow of the tower.

When it was over, they lay silently for a while, drowsy from the sleepless night and the hazy sunshine. "Jake I'm scared," she said finally. "Maybe I can never escape them. I will be pregnant, that's for sure, I don't doubt their power there, I've seen it all too often before with others."

"Shh, don't ruin it. How can they have done that to us? It's preposterous, and even if it were true, I'd look after you. We'd be together. You could come with me to Peru, wherever you want to be. It will be all right little one."

She lay his hand on her belly, and he felt her breathing rise and fall slow until they succumbed to heavy sleep.

Before she fell asleep, their words circled around in Lydia's head. She was not sure which scared her most, the consequences of leaving them; the dangers her knowledge carried with it; or the prospect of a baby. Would Jake really stand by her. So much had happened so quickly, but she was sure that the forces had been potent enough. She felt them within her.

Lydia silently called the spirits around the tower to assist her, to make her invisible at whatever cost, wherever she went. Before the ghosts of the ancient dead appeared in her mind's eye, before she bid her old friends farewell in this sanctuary where she had often been guided by their wisdom, her grandmother appeared reminding her that there were other ways, other ancient places to find the Mysteries. The thought of her grandmother weaving her simple magics alone, comforted Lydia and showed the way of her future.

Her visions followed thick and heavy and whatever message they contained would shape the course of her life, as the tower itself had done on occasions ...

... the car was racing on. The speedometer rose, hovered then fell again. She'd have to go quicker than this to get there in time. She knew what was going to happen scene-by-scene as exactly as in a well-rehearsed play. Norfolk went on and on. Blind panic willed the car to go faster. She willed herself to embrace a new landscape of sweeping hills and valleys, to fly out of all this beautiful blue azure sky engulfing them. Oh, to replace warm red brick cottages for grey slate and mellow Wiltshire stone that she had grown to love.

In another forty-five minutes, if she could keep up this speed, she would find Niall and save everything. It might just be all right. She tried to temper the passion and hope with the cold fear welling up through her belly. Nausea leapt up in waves for the first time since that night in Val D'Isere. It had been so long since she had seen him. Imagining the face she had known so well strained all of her will, for it would fade on the slightest lapse of concentration ...

The fumes were noxious, pure evil sweeping though the rooms at Falklands one by one, the explosion ripping through the house. Niall couldn't be sure where it had come from; his ears were still ringing, his head dancing form the shock. It must have been the boiler in the poolroom he reasoned. Making his way down to the cellar he cautiously peered around. He had calculated wrongly. In the distance there was another deafening blow. The main bedrooms were now engulfed in flames, furiously devouring tapestries, carpets, lace covered dressing tables, embossed silver mirrors and brushes, ancient wedding gowns, family portraits. It devoured with meticulous hunger.

On and on it tore, running out across the landing. Ancient oak beams were toppled like cocktail sticks, crashing and heaving apart from the roof after all those centuries, obliterating the beautiful rooms below. One by one the ballroom windows blackened with smoke, witnessing great chandeliers torn from moulded ceilings, the gilded mirrors and grand piano feeding it's course. On to obliterate volume upon volume of books in the library, collected over five centuries. All that loving care, all the history and delicacy gone in minutes.

Niall had been caught by the end of a beam crashing through the ceiling. By the time he came round, the cellar had filled with rubble and a thick, choking smoke. At the far end of the room he could just make out that another larger beam was blocking the only exit. Slumped against the wall, he wept silently and waited for the inevitable ...

There was only four miles to go.

She had seen Niall shoot across most of this land, jump his horses over the stone walls. They had made love in the remains of the Roman villa. The wrought iron gates of Falklands were a mile away and for the first time since then she felt a host of butterflies rise upwards with the thought of seeing him again. The car seemed airless as the heat of the summer's day became more stifling.

The farm worker put the tractor on full throttle. He had started his shift at five that morning. He was tired, wanted to get the job done and now he had been called back to Home Farm. If he hurried he reckoned he could make it in fifteen minutes there and back. The crash happened 200 yards from the drive. The car had spun on a bend, out of control, smashing head on into the tractor, The tractor driver couldn't have braked in time and the car hadn't stood a chance. In a minute it had caught fire, followed by an almighty explosion.

"If there are any remains of the body after that, it'll be a miracle," the farm worker said to the policeman at the house ...

They had come in the nick of time to rescue him, and now amid the hum of people, the roar of flames and wailing sirens, Niall hardly noticed the glum-looking police officer approach.

"Today is a sad one for Falklands, sir. Looks like it's all cursed around these parts today. In all my twenty years, never have I seen a crash like it. Terrible. I believe it were on your land sir, the Nut Ride. One of your workers hit her head on."

Lydia, he was thinking always had peculiar feelings about the Nut Ride. "Oh dear, was she badly hurt?"

" 'twould have been a miracle to have survived that."

She looked down from above, her spirit-form sobbing to return to reality, where she could be with him. As the terrible news sunk in he sank down to his knees on the gravel, calling her name and then leapt up to find the wreckage of the car. She wanted so desperately to comfort him. He was so vulnerable and alone. There was a peculiar mixture of elation in her: she knew now that she was an integral part of his own being and yet there was such an overwhelming sadness within her because she was now dead. It had all been in vain. How could she share and bask in this love. She cried out to be flung back to the flames and in to her body, and when she realised her own screams were fading to nothing, that her lifeless body was drifting further and further upwards, she awoke in the plush grass, safe in Jake's arms crying ...

The shadows of the late afternoon had gathered and now Lydia shivered in the chill of the north wind. Jake woke, murmuring softly to her, nestling her with kisses. "Hush my love, what is it?"

Without thinking, for she was still half asleep, she said: "It is hard to tell you, but they were so terrible I felt that I was really there. It was Niall, he was in great danger and I had to go to him. It was the Nut Ride, the house was burning. I had to be with him ..."

"What are you talking about?" And then it registered with a thud. She could no more detach herself from her dreams as she could from Niall. "*After everything between us!* Megan was right, I *was* used, except *you* used me for different ends, to feel wanted again. You'll never love me in the same way will you?"

She kept on looking at the ground and he wanted to hit her with fury. "I was prepared to give up my life to you, to have this baby – if there is one – in spite of my career, everything. Why do you destroy everything and everyone who loves you? I loved you beyond anything, but I can't be with some one who is so obsessed by the bloody past. I need your love too, and if you can't let go of Niall, how are we ever going to be together. You have hurt me too many times, and I can't take any more."

Something caught his attention, above the lake a sudden mist had gathered, hovering between the earth and sky, mirroring his confusion. He wanted to hurt her in his desperation. "Niall never loved you Lydia. Face up to it. It was me who introduced you, remember? You weren't meant to fall in love with him ... he's a bastard, always has been, but that's just his way. He doesn't have any feelings, and even *you* couldn't change that. Did I tell you I saw him again last week? He's in love with another girl already, Lydia, they are going to be married. Ask anybody. I bet he doesn't even remember who you are."

Eyes wild, she unleashed a torrent of force on him with her nails, fists and legs. "What do you know about anything Jake?" she spat. "What do you *really* know? Don't ever belittle my feelings. I know he loved me and he still does. *How dare you?* You knew nothing about what went on between us. It was a dream, but you can't take the fact I dreamt about Niall. I couldn't help it, any more than I can help my feelings. If you can't stand them, then go, leave me here."

When he got to his feet, she was dumbstruck with the realisation that he was actually going. It was too late, the words were out. But surely he wouldn't go now that they had found each other again. She couldn't bear it and her hurt rose up drowning her senses. She slapped him, and saw in an instant by the sorrow in his eyes, that she had lost him as surely as the moment she had lost Niall.

He walked briskly away from the tower, and for a while she tried to catch up until he finally pushed her away. "Just go home Lydia. Leave me."

"I hope you mean that Jake, because you'll never see me again until I'm either old and decrepit, or dead. I vow it, and you'll be sorry. Go on, leave and don't you ever try to find me." Still she ran to catch up with him, desperate to make him stop but unable to keep the malice from her mouth. "Did you think that what happened last night was special? It meant nothing to me; it's where I sleep with all my men."

Hoarse from screaming, she watched him disappear among the rhododendron bushes. With a heavy heart, Lydia left the tower for the last time, too exhausted with sorrow to weep. Was it Nel and the others, had they done this in anger? Or was the magic at the tower too powerful to trifle with? Had she awoken something too powerful for even her to control? Whatever the tides of fate were doing with her, she was certain that she had to leave Norfolk for good. She loved Nel, but how could she forgive them after what they'd done to spoil things with Jake? If there was a baby, she would never be free if she stayed.

CHAPTER SEVENTEEN

Two hundred miles away, Falklands sat gracefully in the soft Wiltshire countryside. The stable clock chimed sweetly, marking the hour. The Midsummer sun shone gently over the level parkland, and though the glorious yellow silk curtains in the drawing room. This scene never failed to please Niall. All was harmony and elegance. Yes, he had done rather well, or had been given rather a lot for a man of his age.

Sometimes, first thing in the morning, before the duties of the estate called him away, he would think of Lydia. He briefly felt the sadness in losing her, but all of this was such a consuming novelty. He paused to admire family portraits which hung in gilded Rococo panels. He had never been told they were merely depictions of other ancestral lines, picked up as a collection of instant ancestors by his own family, who were keen to disassociate themselves as far as they could from the brewery that had made them their money.

The mahogany library table gleamed impressively in the reflected sunlight and he felt drowsy. He rarely dreamed but he was pulled into a deep, lucid dream where the images ran so vividly ... Mrs Bryant, the housekeeper, was summoning him for his bath.

"Good morning Mrs Bryant. What's for breakfast this morning? I fancy something different"

"I could arrange for a nice kedgeree, Sir Niall."

"That would be fine. Thank you."

"The gas man from the village was here at eight, Sir Niall, so I took the liberty of showing him into the bedrooms and drawing room as you instructed. He said he'd be done in an hour."

"Jolly good"

It had been a wonderful idea of Sofia's, to have those modern gas fires fitted throughout the house. She was such a clever little thing, and had been *so* keen to redecorate the house with the aid of Colefax and Fowler, where she worked. All those pretty chintzes. Even though her nose was on the large side, she was a good egg, ... even if she did want to nail him into marriage. He chuckled to himself, he did love new gadgets. He daydreamed about the balls he would have, to show off the splendours of Falklands with all the fierce pride of the parvenu. He was so happy in his little kingdom, so safe in this world. It was all perfection. The clock tower in the courtyard struck the half hour and everything was in its place, all as it should be. Lydia ... Lydia ...

The man from the Gas Board leapt into his cab, having doffed his cap to Niall in servitude. He didn't mind the early hour, he'd doubled the fee after he'd set his gimlet eyes on this stately pile.

Niall was still deep in thought. Maybe a swimming party would be better: it would certainly please his friends. It would be like reliving the Cresta. Yes, they must do that every year, no matter what. Some things in life were that important. His secretary bustled into the library momentarily disturbing his morning's business, namely the reading of letters at his late-father's davenport. The rows of musty books hadn't been read for decades, they were bought for their bindings, rather than their content.

"Will that be all, Sir Niall? Only I have to take my son to the dentist this afternoon."

"Yes, thank you, Susi."

All this magnificence was affecting him. He decided to take a stroll before taking out his new hunter.

Suddenly a huge explosion ripped through the house.

Once the initial shock had subsided, his army training automatically took over and his first thought was to get to safety. There was an ornamental skylight in what was left of the roof and there wasn't much time before the whole thing caved in. It felt as if there was no air left in this living tomb and should the chemicals by the pool go up, there would be another explosion worse perhaps than first. Mentally fighting for survival, realisation had come to him like a vision. Falklands meant nothing to him now. Life was the essence. Love was the stuff of life, of real dreams. He could have rotted away in this house losing sight of what mattered. The one thing that had given him the most joy and pain was *her*. Sod the house, he would get out and make it right. He had to get out, not to save his own life, but to make it right with *her*, as a matter of honour.

Her ideas, the logic she applied to everything came together in blinding colours: was this revelation dished out by the gods to jolt him out of his dream. What had he been thinking of to lose her like that? She was the only one who had ever cared for him. It all made perfect sense. Life with her was a necessity. He loved her beyond and above his own life. Shards of glass rained down over his face as the skylight gave way, and all he saw was a vision of her in that white dress.

In two seconds he was out, gasping for air and running to safety. From across the lawn, he surveyed the surreal image of Falklands burning. Strange to think that the bees were still going about their business as if nothing dramatic was happening within yards of the immaculately tended beds. It was ridiculous to think that only an hour or two ago, he was so smug about all of this. The wheel of fate could bring you up and smash you down in an instant. *Darling Lydia, heart of hearts. She always knew.* In his dreams, she had come to him, driving all that way to warn him and then there had been a terrible accident. She was dead.

Once he had cut himself on the arm with a razor. Even though the blade had gone in quite deep, the flesh just blanched, the blood came later. Now it was like being many fathoms below the sea, suspended with no light or air; like the time he had stared incredulously as a boy at a dead baby shark on the bottom of the seabed. It drew fascination before feelings of sadness. He didn't feel his legs go until he tried to pick himself up. There was no feeling anywhere as he came to terms with the great loss of her. He drew in breath at the pain. It was all too much for the mind to register ...

When he awoke, he saw that he had only slept for half an hour, because the dream had seemed so crammed with events and have coverer a greater passage of time. As he shook off the drowsiness, he went to the great library desk and pulled open a drawer. Gingerly, he held the photograph. It had been taken only at the beginning of the year, when there was so much promise in the world. He studied the delicate face, the small rosebud mouth and searing black eyes which looked out lovingly at the camera.

Once the pain had subsided in his chest he shoved the silver frame back in the drawer, out of sight. It still couldn't block out his dream that kept surfacing in fragments to trouble him. He hoped she was all right. What a mess he had made of everything. With his head in his hands, he allowed himself to re-live his nightmare; for she had been so close he could have sworn she really had been with him. Perhaps she had been in love with him after all, despite the doubts he'd had after the way she had acted when his father died. Perhaps he should have never listened to Jake who had told him she'd been seeing other men. He was tired of playing events over and over in his mind and now it was only his pride that stopped him from telephoning her.

His mother's brisk footsteps finally pulled him from his daydreams. Registering the look on his face she snapped like a terrier.

"Niall, for God's sake, you're not still moping about that silly girl are you? She never cared for you. She wanted your money. Even when your poor father died, all she could think of was herself, the selfish little hussy. I hope you never bring any one like that here again."

He didn't have the strength to argue with her, not today. The dream was unlike any other; it had pulled him down so heavily and unexpectedly, and now he felt disorientated, as if she had been there with him and he missed her desperately.

Lady Seligman eyed her son speculatively. What she had meant to say to him, was that now Michael was gone, there was no excuse for him not marrying. She had to remind him that there was the family name to perpetuate, shoots and lunches to organise. No doubt both she and his friends would make sure he chose a manageable girl, so that their weekend parties could carry on undisturbed. Belinda Hargreaves for instance, she was in most of the papers and magazines that week. He only needed a little encouragement. Belinda had everything one could desire: experience as a chalet girl, a spell at cookery college, secretarial school, her love of children, her lack of O-levels and sex appeal were an asset.

LYDIA

1999

When you had gone I was numb with shock. If only I had gone after you to explain but I have never stopped thinking about us at the Solstice. That night it had come to me so suddenly - looking at you through the flames - that unlike Niall *you* were my soul-mate and I wanted *you*. I implored you with child's eyes to leave the other girl and come into the dark of the wild wood with me and I led you like a precious prize to the spot under the rowan tree. While the birds strutted to life, bristling deep in the branches I laid down with you under the red berries of poison and love. There were no words between us now that the moon had just gone and the sun was warming the night. You cupped my face, and made me feel beautiful, crowning my hair with oak leaves.

I felt drowsy with intoxication. Rocking under the stirring nature bed we welcomed the summer with love, *hail met, hail met, hail met, hail met, hail met,* hails merging into one long stream of starry magic, carrying us on this boat, this tide of longing. And when it was over I nestled like a chick into your protective arms, surrendering to this homecoming, a total capitulation, a religious union. That ... Oh! *that* was the best and worst day of my youth.

A baby had been conceived that night and I gave birth to a baby girl who looked just like you. Nel had been right, she *was* special and knowing. I saw in her eyes that she would have great power from the start but I only had my poor Ellie for such a short time. She died just short of her third birthday. After years of trying to resist, (for you must have known my love, and still you made no effort to find me), I had to try and contact you again to share the pain, for it was unbearable. You were gone for years, where no-one knew, exploring and forgetting, I don't doubt. Sometimes I still blame myself, perhaps when I said that they would never use a baby of mine, I had got what I asked for and my wish was granted with terrible consequences.

Although they knew – in the end – where I ended up, they never tried to bring me back. Too much had happened. But I always thought kindly of Nel and missed her, although my last memories of her that day were so uncharacteristic. Years later, she wrote me a last letter before she died, to tell me that Megan had gone to live with you. I wondered if you knew that they were just making sure that you never betrayed their secrets, and I pitied you for having to suffer the old snake ...

... As I drew back from the smoke of the incense, I felt repulsed as I realised I was talking to myself in the cloudy mirror, a lonely old hag with just a pile of memories that were so beautiful in comparison with my reflection.

CHAPTER EIGHTEEN

Rebecca arrived back from Norfolk late that night. The curtains were drawn and she breathed a sigh of relief: Uncle Jake would be asleep. She just had to make one more trip into the folly, in case there was something she had missed. It had been raining, and she picked her way across the sodden grass. There was no moon but there was a chill in the air, ushering in the autumn breeze.

Inhaling the musty air as the door creaked open, she felt her way to the desk. After the key clicked, the drawer slid out smoothly on dusty runners. She moved indiscriminately like a jackdaw, too intent on finding anything else of interest to bother thinking about the consequences.

Sifting through the mountain, she found more letters from Lydia, and two addressed to her with Uncle Jake's writing. She took out the first. It was dated 23 June 1953. There was no address on the front, just *'LYDIA, By Hand'*. She had obviously never received it ...

Angel,
Whatever you decide to do as regards him and me I will never regret or forget anything about last night. The way you won me over with such a simple breeze over my neck. It sent goose pimples all over me, shocking and exciting me rigid. Like a young bull to the slaughter I followed you to the near blackness of the wood until we

found a bed of leaves and a young thrush above us chatted whilst we made love as the sun came up.

I drew my breath with the sound of your hair fluttering softly in the breeze as I tried to reason why the gods had made you so beautiful, never more so than this morning. Through you, I tasted the essence of life, pared down to the simplest form. I made you mine over and over in our mystical marriage bed. I crowned you my angel, my midsummer queen, my heart of all hearts now and forever.

You said this was the day of madness, of fairies, of wild magic. You said there would be a child conceived on this day. And then you looked away and laughed. Knowing you, you planned it all. *Did you use me?* I will never know now, because I have had enough of all of this intrigue and heartbreak. You are not the only one who has suffered agonies. I have no choice but to go because it will lead to nothing but an endless stalemate for me here, with you undecided. And how can I ask you to forget him?

Perhaps when we are both old and wrinkled, you will remember me. And yet, I fear that even age will bring no solace in me. How can I truly love twice? In that respect my life is probably over. In some ways, I hope that what magic passed between us at Midsummer does result in something but I doubt you will ever let anyone as close to you as you did Niall, and I am sure he will never come back to you, despite your dreams ...

The room had grown dreadfully silent so that when Rebecca had finished reading she could hear her own heartbeat. *Poor wretched man*, she thought. She motioned to put the letter back on the pile. The others – for she had checked - were recent bills and things. And then, it caught her eye, that photograph of the three of them her uncle must have recently laid on the blotter.

She could have cried thinking of her uncle, broken hearted like this. She had never realised just how much he had loved Lydia, and her regard of the older woman began to slide to somewhere between jealousy (hadn't she always striven for his attention?) and hatred.

Lydia had obviously been too selfish and morose about Niall to care about Jake. She had ruined his life: he had never married nor found anybody else to her knowledge. And now he would die a lonely old man in years to come, once she had left the cottage. With a terrible rage Rebecca thought of all the wasted years when he could have found someone, the lonely years he had spent in the cottage. Fate hadn't led her to any old pile of letters for no reason.

Suddenly she noticed a beam of light. *Shit, she'd been caught out.* Hoping that somehow she hadn't been seen, she crouched down between the drawers and the desk. The light had gone out but she sat still, hardly daring to breathe. In the darkness she heard the door creak. It was so sinister, this presence that couldn't be seen and she thought she would explode with nerves.

"Rebecca I have been watching you. Come out."

The torchlight shone again and there was Megan's face, creepy in the darkness, with a mad look in her eyes. Rebecca didn't know which was worse, the fury of Megan or that of her uncle, but right now something in the old woman's face scared her. She shone the torch full in Rebecca's face and began interrogating her.

"I want to know what you have found. Which drawers have you been in?" she hissed.

"It's none of your damn business, and what right have you to be in here? Even less than me I would think, you're not even family, you're just hired help."

Megan surprised her by laughing and then she stopped as abruptly as she had started. "That's where you are so wrong my girl. I have a vested interest in these things, to see that they don't get into the wrong hands ... such as yours. I think I have found most of the important documents that could have posed a danger, but you unearthing things and I won't stand by and let you meddle into that which doesn't concern you."

What was the old woman going on about?

Reaching forward, she grabbed Rebecca's wrist and twisted it painfully. "Tell me what you have just read, show me!" she demanded.

Rebecca now felt very afraid, she had never seen Megan like

this and meekly handed her the letter she had just read. As Megan perused its content she asked her, "Was there a baby born to Lydia and Uncle Jake?"

"Oh yes, there was, a little girl, but that evil bitch never even told him. He still has no clue it was his, poor daft thing. Do you know that your wonderful Lydia killed the baby purposely before its third birthday? What do you make of the harmless old lady now? I told you she was pure evil. She ruined the life of your uncle and he never got over it. She could glamour herself all right, there was no-one better at catching the men in her web. She was a mistress of manipulation and still is. She even has you deceived."

Rebecca's fascination with Lydia was now rapidly turning into a burning, irrational hatred. The thought of a mother killing her own baby repulsed her. She thought of herself losing her parents and all of her old resentment quickly shaped into a loathing for Lydia, just as Megan intended. She felt so stupid for idolising her, had she but known. *Poor, poor Uncle Jake.* She had to take revenge for his sake.

Rebecca and Megan came to an uneasy truce. In return for keeping silent about what Megan had told her, Rebecca vowed not to go back into her uncle's study. Unbeknown to the housekeeper, however, the girl had kept some of the letters in her bedroom. Sitting in the darkness under the covers of her duvet, she formulated a plan for revenge, and also to bring a conclusion to the open-ended story she had uncovered. Intently, she studied each of the letters until she knew the handwriting of each of them and felt confident enough to write the invitations that gave form to her machinations.

CHAPTER NINETEEN

Far away, under the dark of the moon, Lydia stood in her kitchen, stirring the dark mixture on the stove. The wind was blowing gently thought the wisteria so that she could smell the peaty earth, a sure sign of the rain to come tomorrow. It was a recipe for blackberry and apple jam her mother had given her, not that Isobel had ever cooked it herself.

Memories of Isobel flooded into the confines of the kitchen: her laughter, her own ambitions for her daughter. Where had they all gone? She never quite forgave Lydia for letting Niall go. She had already told her friends about the wedding and had even planned an apartment for herself in the west wing. And then Lydia had shamed her. The phone calls grew less frequent, the visits stopped. Isobel had always led her to expect a charmed life for herself and they both believed Lydia would be rich, and beautiful, and loved. It was funny how the fates could punish you.

Stirring the years before her, Lydia reflected on the great passage of time that had swept her here, finally alone. Where had the time gone? The time that had changed so much, that had wrested her hopes and dreams, and *him*, away?

After leaving Norfolk, she had moved to deepest Somerset, where the winters were gentler and the ghosts were less intrusive. Away from the Wild Wood. Everything had changed. She no longer had ambitions to write or to paint. Survival demanded that sacrifice from her. And so there were the long years – she had no idea of how many – that she foraged for money, doing the odd tarot reading, candle making and part time labouring jobs that had made her hands so weathered.

It was not often that she dared to think about the beautiful baby girl that she had lost, but now the memory of the day she was killed bubbled up with the other remembrances of things past. It was late in July, just before Ellie's third birthday. The village made the same observances to the Old Ways, just as she had known in Norfolk and so she had taken her daughter to take part in her first Harvest Home.

As the carts rolled in with the first sheaves of golden wheat, the crowds were exuberant. It was hot, even though it was late in the afternoon and as the shiny red carts appeared along the dusty tracks, there was an infectious atmosphere of excitement and joy. As they came into the village, the carts rumbled under their heavy loads. So transfixed had everyone been that nobody had noticed Ellie dart out from the crowd until it was too late, and she was lost under the heavy wheels. Only after that did Lydia truly understand Nel's long grief at losing her own daughter in similar circumstances.

After that there were men who came and went, shapeless clouds now. What were their names? One had left her this house. He was married, and it was not her place to tell his wife of their affair.

Her penance was that every day, every long hour that had spread itself out over time, she had thought of *him*, although the razored grief had long since stopped. Only with time, had she come to accept that she had been so distraught at Niall departure because she had felt a sense of guilt that she had not done the 'right thing'. Age had bestowed on her the wisdom to see at least that she had done the best she could.

The blame was his.

This daily wrestle between Craft and good sense became, if anything, stronger. It would have been so easy, so satisfying to craft a spell. It would have bought her some small satisfaction but then she still wanted him to remember her as she had been, and so she preferred to come to him in her dreams.

Every so often, there would be dream-time that would blast the senses, challenge reality until she was never sure whether they really had been together. These she kept close to her heart, and so now, scrying on the surface of the deep red mixture, she could see the pony and trap. It was beautifully painted in red and gold, the pony, a piebald mare had cowslips woven in her mane.

It was Midsummer's Eve, 1955. Two years after Jake had gone. The fair had come to the local market town and it was going to be a full moon eclipse that night. The rarity of the eclipse and the fair would help combine ancient traditions. There were flame-throwers, circus acts, gypsies, and stalls and Lydia was going to earn a month's money in tarot readings.

Images began to pour through her, intoxicating her like wine. She could smell the dusk in the air, the candy floss, the horses, the fires, the excitement, the midsummer grass under her bare feet, the calls of the stall owners, the laughter of the crowds, her own baby crying on the sheepskin bed on the trap, the red striped tent and the hand-painted sign. She remembered the red dress and the pretty lace shirt she wore.

So many people milling in and out made her dizzy. The fairground mirrors reflected the lights and moving images all around her. There seemed to be no way out. There were so many people that she retreated running to her tent. There were two or three people waiting. There was a man inside already.

As she lifted the flap the oppressive heat inside the tent hit her. The man was wearing a soft creamy shirt, she noticed as she came in from behind. The scarf was pulled around his jet-black wavy hair and the sound of his breathing resounded in the silence that was growing between them.

With the thud of recognition her heart screamed out that this wasn't how it was supposed to be. She had rehearsed this moment a thousand times. She was going to be beautiful, wrapped in a silk dress under the moon, all alluring and mysterious. Very slowly she edged her way around the table in the knowledge that to see his face might cast a thousand arrows in her heart. Breathing steadily to control the tears she sidled around the table. They were as close as lovers. She could hear his breath and could even reach out to hold his warm hands in hers after all the long years of waiting.

All the bitter recriminations, all the anger at his betrayal faded in a moment and all she saw was that handsome rider on the black horse, on that shimmering day when his gallantry swept her off her feet. It would have been as natural as the rising sun to throw herself into his arms and be cradled against his chest, safe in his love. *His lips, what mysteries can they spill now the deed is done?* With all the love she had ever felt in her heart and more, the love of forgiveness, she picked up those beloved hands in her own. For she was sure he knew as he grappled with his own emotions.

CHAPTER TWENTY

Across the hills and far off in the starry night, Niall stirred. Under the moonless skies, he left his cold sleeping wife and threw open the casement window, needing air to breathe in the stifling room. Something wouldn't let him sleep and he feared the usual onset of emotion when he allowed himself to think of the descent into dream-time. So often, especially of late, Lydia had come to him like the breath of wind on the lake. His love for her had grown over the years since his marriage, like a steady wave, secret and unbidden. It was unstoppable now but at least the years had taught him to accept that. And now he was able to allow the familiar ebb begin, relishing the meeting with her, stepping in waking hours through the walkways of old dreams. For some reason, as he craned his neck to find the moon, it was the memory of the fairground his brain chose to select ...

Niall picked his way through the crowds, wearing a soft linen shirt. It was a stiflingly hot day. The heat and the crowds were oppressive, and he screwed up his eyes against the hot glare of the sun. Belinda was by his side, and her constant conversation about nothing and everything, grated on his nerves for the twentieth time that day.

"Oh darling, these people are so common. Look at them with their great bundles of candyfloss and hot-dogs. How disgusting.

Look at that fat man, how revolting!"

Their life consisted of constant dinner parties and social engagements that, even for him, were too frequent. Life wasn't the fun it had been, and he was increasingly irritated by her social ambition. And then, of course, she had omitted to tell him until after they were married, that children were impossible with her. Adoption wasn't the same. All after his mother had chosen so carefully. He couldn't afford a divorce with the roof of the house needing replacing and so he would have to settle for mediocrity.

"Niall, look, what fun, I haven't seen one of these since I was a little girl. Oh, go on, please have your fortune read. I'll go after you. Don't be shy, go on."

He hated such things and didn't want to go, but now she was pushing him into the little red striped tent. "Look, leave me alone will you, you know I hate these things."

Before he could stop her, Belinda had paid the money. Wearily he stepped forward into the darkness, if only to get away from her for a few moments. Going through the charade of asking the question his wife wanted him to ask about their future plans, he felt so shrivelled and blanched with the futility of it all.

"Thank you sir, go inside and she'll be with you in a minute."

The tent was dark and oppressively hot and outside he could hear his wife croon. "Oh, what a lovely baby."

The flap of the tent closed, muffling the sounds outside. The old lady had placed a black silk scarf around his eyes. It was curious he thought, but she said it would help him to concentrate, to channel his mind for the fortune teller. He just wanted it over and done with, yet as he waited, he felt as if his spine had currents of electricity running along it. Eventually he was aware of another's presence in the tent. It was the younger woman who had come to tell him his future. She started to speak to him but he couldn't concentrate on the words, because the voice sounded so familiar. He couldn't quite place it ... a well-educated gypsy woman, was all he could think.

Lydia was so close to him that he could hear the breathlessness in her voice. Then she was silent for a long time before taking up both of his hands in hers. He noticed that boldly she stroked his signet ring with old familiarity and that the bustle outside seemed to have melted away in the intensity of the moment.

Lydia was struggling to force away the sickness of loss that had lain buried for so long, but it all came back to her so powerfully that she couldn't catch her breath. The tent began to sway and summoning all her courage and also restraint (for wasn't it natural to want to kiss those lips and hold him, *I am coming home, coming home my love!*), she reached for the hands that had held her so often.

The woman's touch was so soothing, so gentle, it was like the touch of a lover. The long strokes of her fingers he found erotic and yet at the same time filled with the pure unconditional love of a child. They were young hands. He strained to see her face.

For Lydia's part, there was so much to tell him but her tears would fill a lake, and suddenly there was a reprieve jerking her back to reality. Her fingers found his wedding ring.

So grief *had* had short shrift. This was the proof that his love had been as shallow as a saucer. For she remembered it had only been two year's to the day that she had gone to him in her dream after Midsummer. He must belong to that flimsy woman outside, hollow as a piece of rotten wood. What to do? If she were to get up she might fall, all feeling had gone in her legs, she was all numb. How many times could you die?

After this silence the oppressiveness of the tent bore down on them.

After a while he asked. "Are you still there? What is my future then?"

It was to have been hers, his future, all hers, and her's in him. Now there was no future, just a vacuum. She had loved him into the grave in her dreams, and now this realisation, this dreadful gift of recollection was given back to her so she could say to herself, there is no future for either of us now. *It is all over.*

Niall couldn't stand it the silence any longer. Something so wonderful was happening that filled him with terror. He adjusted the scarf by surreptitiously scratching the back of his head. He first caught a glimpse of beautiful hands, so slender and brown. There were no rings ... but then he saw it. There could be no other like it. *This* woman was wearing the bracelet he had given Lydia, its centrepiece cut from a single amethyst, carved with dragons embossed in gold.

For the first time he wondered if a man can choke on his own heart? What if the dead do come back to haunt the living? He peeped again, too scared to tear the blindfold off completely lest it wasn't her, lest his rising hope in seeing her face was dashed. If those *were* her hands, what recompense could he made to express their love and his sorrow? The hands *were* hers. And they had been his: her lips, her hair, her eyes, had all been his once. He had possessed them all.

Lydia saw the tears roll down his cheeks. *He knew.*

Neither of them could speak.

With a cry she tried to stop him taking off the blindfold, for the years had left her tired and weathered. Her life had changed so much. How could she look into his eyes? Blinking, he saw that she was even lovelier than his memories.

What had he done? She heard his heart breaking in the silence and with a kiss to end all others, she met his mouth as to a homecoming. He reached out to hold her but she stepped away; he was not free to give anything to her anymore. Choice had been granted to him and it was too late. There was this hollow twig outside. His hands loosened the knot. The moment was thick as treacle. *My love my love, come to me forever.*

A voice pierced the silence. "Niall darling, it's the Empsons. Do hurry up, I thought we might take tea with them." The past and present had joined full circle and he could have willingly murdered his wife with bare hands.

"My darling Lydia ..."

It shattered. Lydia bolted from the tent but in that second he had seen her once again, her face looked younger. More beautiful and childlike than the one he remembered and it would haunt him until he died the last - physical - death. He tore at the canvas but there were too many people outside and she had disappeared.

And he died once more, only to rise again at the sound of Belinda's voice, which he cursed. All he could see in the myriad of mirrored images was the huge Ferris wheel rising up out of the crowds like a gargantuan monster. Its passengers swung in ignorance, loving the ride that ferried them up and down, reflected as giants and pygmies in the moving mirrors, round and round, powerless as fleas.

CHAPTER TWENTY-ONE

The room had grown menacingly cold. Through the reflection in the glass Lydia caught sight of her own image. Scowling she turned away from the aged, papery face, finally acknowledging and accepting the loss of beauty after all these years, and she drew on all of her indomitable courage to finish it all. The flowers of the wisteria hammered impatiently on the window pane to be let in, or to lure her outside.

Fingering the worn pack of cards, she drew in her breath to choose one. It fluttered down onto the table. It was a second or two before she could bear to lift it, because she knew that this is the card of all cards, the conclusion, the shape of the words to come. The Tower. Old familiarity: the lightning bolt, the figures tumbling from the crumbling tower amid the rain of fire and sparks. Now she saw her old lover with new eyes, the falling emperor's crown, the background of deepest black bore a new realism. The years of silence, of carrying around so much that has been left unsaid was now unbearable. Lydia felt burdened by all those unspoken emotions that should have been jettisoned long ago. All those things in her life that had been left unfinished would have to be concluded before her own life ebbed away.

She chose a thick oyster coloured paper, the kind a magician would choose to record the finest of his discoveries. Settling against the hearth, and gazing into the flames for a few moments, she let them lap up her senses, stir the passions that were still ever present but now tempered, bridled. Perhaps it was the thrusting, fearless curiosity of Rebecca, who had reminded her of her own candid way as a girl before the trials of life that had turned her focus inwards.

But then she had been so restless since Jake's visit.

It was time to close the chapter. Lifting the silver pen into the scented ink, she began to write to him for the first time in forty years.

My darling Niall, it began ...

CHAPTER TWENTY-TWO

The letter arrived at Falklands by the early morning post. Niall and Belinda were hosting their first shoot of the season and their houseguests were still finishing breakfast. The gamekeeper came in to the breakfast room, and for some reason – whilst trying to listen to the man as he discussed the pegs - Niall winced in pain at a memory of Lydia, sitting there in that room as a young girl, surfaced without warning. They had forced her to shoot that day, to test her mettle. His father, and this man's predecessor had decided it over breakfast, at this very table forty years earlier. And now he was asked to discuss pegs.

"Oh, let Belinda decide " he said impatiently.

He glanced at his wife with a measure of disinterest. She had aged well, he thought dryly, but then there had never been any beauty to wither in the first place. No magic to fire him up. They had had an unremarkable life together and he bitterly resented there had been no children. It had once been his dearest wish, to leave all this to a child, but now there was such despondency over everything. All these years they had wasted time, diverting attention from their loveless marriage with inconsequential house parties. They had achieved very little together, apart from a reputation as a decent couple and generous hosts.

He heard the words issue from her mouth as you might watch an old film. "There's this rather interesting chap coming down today. Jake is one of Niall's oldest chums. A gifted writer I think. Niall hasn't seen him for a few years, have you darling?"

It was perverse, that despite all the hatred that had passed between them, Lydia was the link that forced them to persist in this 'friendship', that had become a necessary horror for both of them.

"How did you meet him darling?"

"Army," he barked.

His regret at letting Lydia go had mellowed into the acceptance that he was now old, and could never recapture all that was firmly rooted in the past. Just recently, however, it was this 'acceptance' that was driving him into a morbid realisation that time was running out. Oblivious to her husband's ill-temper, Belinda sorted through the morning post, flapping an envelope for him in the air.

"Darling, this came for you just now." The postman was crunching his way off on the gravel drive as she spoke.

He looked at the old-fashioned, oyster writing paper for a long time, as if it reminded him of something he couldn't quite place. He looked up and realised resentfully that they were all staring at him in his own house, like a pack of dogs waiting for him to move. Then he knew. It was *her* writing, even after all those years, it pricked his senses until he felt alive in every cell, alert to every pin drop. His heart was pounding to open it. At last, it had come, this contact with her. Ignoring to their curiosity, walked out of the room with a mumbled excuse about checking the shooting ground, only pausing briefly to collect his dog and his gun.

Niall walked straight to the Nut Ride where he could be alone, where they had walked together on countless occasions. Autumn had descended and all around was the scent of the thick damp earth. The harvest had been dismal year, rolls of hay lay in the fields, sodden after the heavy rains. Even the land itself seemed to have given up. A mighty wind tunnelled down the canopied walkway, whistling up moans of the old woodland and he reflected that it might be too windy to shoot, which would mean having the house full all day with people he didn't want to see. The row of statues and the ruined folly were in view, and there in the half-light, partially sheltered from the rain, he read.

My darling Niall,
I have been pouring over pictures of you and I when we were young ... reminded of those days of early summer because a young girl has been asking questions about us. I think of a gesture, a sigh, a saying, a dress, the movement of the birds in the trees, the moon, a balmy night and I feel I could still reach out and touch you. I am old now and still you make me sigh when I think of you. Sometimes I just think of the years that you laid waste. Do you remember how I loved you? Still I flinch when I am reminded of you and I, walking, holding hands, laughing like children.

It took me years to get over the guilt you inflicted on me, for not caring enough, when *all* I had ever cared about up to then was you, *only* you, my darling. At some ill-defined moment, you chose to listen to all the others, and shut your heart to me. I knew you still loved me, but you were just a snob. Your lifestyle was always so precious to you and I wouldn't have been rich enough to have made a good catch.

In Val D'Isere you began to hate me and you didn't know why, but it was because you could never quash my spirit. I wasn't like one of your poor horses you could train to do the things you wanted. You realised we would have always been locked in a battle like that and your manly pride couldn't allow you to have a spirited wife. I couldn't be what you wanted me to be.

But you also ruined *my* dream. I truly believed that lovers, real lovers, went to the grave touched forever by their closeness, immortalised by the heavens; that real lovers would fight to the death for each other. I never really had communion with your soul, and you settled for a trophy wife, whom everyone knows you have merely abided for all these years.

Do you ever consider that my love for you would have lit up the world? That I would have risked everything for you? Do you know that I still dream of you after all these years? In one dream, I came to save you from a fire at Falklands. God, how I hated waking up to find you not there.

When I saw you in my dreams, at the fair ground, I felt as if my life had been given back to me, because you were dreaming and feeling the same things. It was more than a dream, and I know we have met like that a hundred times over the years. It gave me some solace at least to know that you too, would wake lost and empty. I loved your eyes, they sparkled like a little boy's, the green in them was so beautiful, I can picture the way you looked at me now. I was made beautiful by the look on your face. I knew your love for me had been real, that you were as incredulous as I and that in other lives we had been lovers before.

Yet, the realisation has come to me too late, and with some surprise that it was Jake who was the love of my life. All the times I was crying for you, he came and understood. It is only now with great age and weariness that I have realised I have been free of you all these years, because it was *him* that I loved. I see that now, and that thinking it was you all these years, drove him away from me.

The one and only time we made love was as the sun came out at Summer Solstice. It was a magical rite of union, such that men and women dream of, a total union of the soul, the mind and body that had never before happened to me, or since. It is time I told him the truth after all these years, because he still believes it is you I have loved. I must close this tragedy of wasted years, once and for all.

He never married, and it is all *our* fault. I hate you when I think of all that love wasted. You deserved mediocrity, the relentless round of the season. At least I was spared that. As you finish reading this letter, what is the *real* tragedy to you now? The loss of children? The loss of happiness? The loss of love? I hope it will now be the realisation that you could have had me, and that I would have gone on forgiving you anything, loving you, if only you had been as courageous as I believed you to be that day I first saw you. You have destroyed all of our lives, but most of all your own, my love ...

In the great hallway, they were all waiting for him. An unbearable tension had been building, throwing all its occupants into an uneasy sense of foreboding. Niall was missing, which was unheard of, at the first shoot of the season. Jake was crossing the hall carrying a tray of glasses for Belinda when he noticed the look of peevishness on her face as she studied an envelope in her hand.

"He's probably gone off to read that other letter. I know it's a woman's hand. I just know it. This one, too ... what do you think Jake? If he's starting an affair now, I would have said he's a bit past the male menopause for all of that. You would have thought the shoot would have occupied his mind, you know how he loves it."

Jake recognised the flowery old fashioned hand writing instantly and felt the tray slip from his fingers as his legs turned to jelly. *It was from Lydia.* In the split second that the tray hit the floor, the guests heard a single gun shot, far off in the woods. As they stood in shocked silence, it was obvious there was a general gut feeling that the shot had come from Niall.

Jake raced instinctively for the Nut Ride. It conjured a thousand words in his mind, stories Lydia used to tell him about the restless spirits there. '*Picking my way though the tunnel of death*', she had described it. In the clearing he found a chocolate-coloured Labrador lying motionless in the undergrowth. Hot blood oozing from the dog's mouth and its eyes still staring sadly at something in the distance. Niall was sitting in the folly, coming to terms with the greatest tragedy of his life: that he could have had her, that he *could* have changed things. The years had gone so swiftly and only now he was forced to come to terms with the fact that he had wasted them. In his youth he had been so proud, so arrogant, to think that it would be all right without her.

Thinking of her with Jake made his blood boil, and the irony was that the passing of the years made his rage no less potent. He had wanted to rush straight to the house and grab his old friend by the throat. Why had Jake not told him about their brief affair? Niall had wanted to kill him, when he finished reading the letter and in that second, the only thing he could do with all of this agony was to turn his gun on poor, innocent Bertie, before rage took hold of him completely.

Now, staring out over the flooded fields, he felt numb with shame at the futile gesture and as he sat there, unable to move, the letter caught flight in the wind.

It was with something of a surprise that the second letter from Lydia came immediately after the first, which had filled him with such shock and great sadness. Now she was urging this meeting at the tower, in Norfolk. The place he remembered her speaking of. This was the reprieve he had waited for, for forty years. He would let life take him full circle.

On reflection, Niall had almost wished he had turned the gun on Jake. *Why had he never said that he loved her?* Niall was taken by surprise with this murderous jealousy. What to do with it? It was a bit late to challenge Jake now and this was the reason that the old dog had taken the brunt of his rage, a ghastly reminder of what he now saw as a betrayal by his old friend.

The second letter from Lydia had shocked him almost as much as the first. An invitation was the last thing he had expected, but on reflection it all made sense. She had probably been filled with anger for so long, that she had tried to merely hurt him after all these years by stinging him into action. The tower, being so dear to her, was a fitting meeting place for a final chance to put things right. Yes, this time he *would* let life take him full circle and put *everything* right.

CHAPTER TWENTY-THREE

With growing hatred in her heart, Rebecca had written fervently to perfect a plan that had been so coldly conceived and carried out. Convinced that she has misjudged Megan, and that Lydia had ruined everything for everybody for purely selfish-reasons, Rebecca saw herself as a self-appointed judge, jury ... and executioner.

They were all too obsessed by the past, she thought as she'd posted off the last of the letters. *Where had it got them all, Lydia, Jake and Niall?* As Megan said, they were all childless because of her and her vicious curses.

The beauty she had first seen in the romance surrounding the three of them had now been completely dispelled. Megan's words came back to taunt her for being fooled by Lydia'a seemingly ladylike exterior. *"Nothing but evil, that woman, pure evil."* Now blind hatred drove her on. Lydia had had the undying love of two men, while she, Rebecca, had never had the love of anyone.

Niall would have received the invitation to the tower by now, she mused, with a secret, satisfied smile. She had copied Lydia's hand-writing so many times, she was confident that nobody would suspect a thing. It was ingenious, the idea that they *all* meet at the tower, each in ignorance that the other had been invited. She knew that even now they would be powerless to resist Lydia's call, and the tower had been spoken about so many times in the letters, it seemed like an obvious place for the final act of the story to be played out. What she had planned for them was a master stroke of genius, a piece of theatrical mastery. It would be the final act bringing justice at last.

The next morning Rebecca glanced disinterestedly at the news paper as she waited for the postman. With a smile of delicious anticipation, she relished the fact that all three would have received their invitations by now. Things were shaping up nicely, after all.

Minutes later Megan came into the breakfast room bearing a tray of post. She wondered if the letter would be on the tray, or whether Megan had intercepted it, if she had believed it to be from Lydia. Surely she knew the hand writing as well as Rebecca did? Her stomach was reeling in knots. Would he see through it? Over the top of the newspaper she watched with pleasure as Jake turned ashen at the sight of the hand written envelope. All of a sudden he slurped his coffee and sloped off like an animal with its prey, to the folly. She could hardly believe it was so easy. It all seemed to be working like a dream.

When he read the letter, Jake was so overcome with excitement that he did not stop to look at the invitation with suspicion. The tower had always been so special to her, after all these years it was fitting that they meet there rather than anywhere else. It had seemed like yesterday sometimes when he thought back to the day of the Solstice when they had made love in its shadow. While they had aged and weathered he wondered if it still stood unmarked by time. It would probably see a thousand more lovers.

He had never been able to go back there, not even when Nel had asked him to visit her on her deathbed. As she lay dying she had implored him to swallow his pride and go to Lydia, but he had never been able to follow her wishes. Perhaps he had not been foolish to venture to Lemellen after all, for it surely prompted the letter.

Rebecca paced the garden willing her ruse to pass undetected. Her uncle was all distracted, she observed with satisfaction and the thought of Niall and Lydia in the same state filled her with warmth.

She now viewed her uncle with pity, seeing his obsession with Lydia as stupid and weak. It even made her dislike him but she couldn't wait to see his face when his darling met her end in front of his eyes.

When Jake left the cottage after lunch, Rebecca ran to the folly to double check that the stack of morning post really did contain the invitation she has so carefully penned with so much thought. The desk was piled high with papers. On the top of them, she was proud to see her own handy work, asking him to go to the tower on 21st September, the Autumn Equinox, three days away. *Any fool could pick up Lydia's ways. And what an end to the year this would be!* What a harvest she would inflict according to her judgement, just like the Grim Reaper. Flouncing out into the daylight with a wide grin, she missed the second letter, still tucked in its oyster coloured envelope, also sent the day before by Lydia herself.

My dearest Jake
I still dream of the Midsummer fire, and the glade in the wood where we lay all those years ago. Those memories, and many others of you have lost none of their power. They can still whirl up out of nowhere and move me for days on end. I hanker for that moment in my life, when all was so fleeting, because the days were so honeyed. I look at the old photographs of you and I, and Niall, especially the one taken of the three of us that summer. I try and trace out the beauty I once had on my face. I try to etch it back with my hands.

I knew you came to see me that day as I sat reading in the summerhouse. It was after Rebecca's first visit here. I suppose her tale stirred you and, ever-brave, you came to me after all these years. I would not look up and I willed you not to come to me because I was scared. I wanted you to keep the memories of me in the golden years of our life, untarnished. I wanted to die all beauty to you. Vanity stopped me from meeting you that day, even though I have dreamt of nothing else for so many years.

My great confession is this: that I have been too vain, I should have come to you. I was too proud, and so hurt when you left, that was all I could think of. When I wanted to come to you, I was scared that you would no longer love me if you saw me changed. So it was better for me to leave things in a way as they were where the love we felt for each other at the Solstice could never be touched. I can die a happy old woman content in the knowledge I have had my one love. *It is you.*

Time and wisdom has shown me the depth of your love for me and mine for you. I was wrong to think it would fade, that to leave you alone would be best for both us. I never forgave you for going away, the second betrayal of my life, I felt, but you never came to find me because you thought it was Niall I was in love with. Most of all, I can never forgive myself. Only in old age, to have come to this realisation about the nature of love, is such a waste and I hope you can forgive me.

Like fools we have let time ride over us, ride over all this love a hurricane couldn't destroy after all these years. I am tired of the life left to me without you. I am exhausted as nightly I dream of you and I in the moonlight, together. I do not want to die without you, or my life will have no meaning. Nothing else matters.

Can we meet at the Tower once more? Can we lay the old ghosts to rest? I will wait for you at there the next full moon, in three day's time hoping that you join me. If you don't come I shall say goodbye now and hope we will meet in Summerlands, and that you always know how my soul is yours alone.

Lydia

When Lydia opened the invitation to the tower from Jake, she was so moved, she didn't stop to question its authenticity. As far as she was concerned, he had remembered the Equinox, her favourite time of year, and how special the tower was to her. She hoped that over the years he had remembered all the times that were sacred to her. She thought it odd that his letter mirrored her own, but then she had never believed in coincidence. It merely fuelled her hope that he *would* be there to meet her.

As if to bridge the time, Lydia sniffed the paper for the slightest scent of him, and then tried to absorb some of his essence, but strangely perhaps, there was none. She shut the casement window on the night air, which sent a chill through her old bones and dulled her senses.

Hadn't fate always been like that with her, she reflected, *and hadn't they always been in tune with each other?* It was all as it should be. He had even remembered the small boat she used as a girl. It was still there apparently, and she was to journey across the lake to the tower where he would be waiting.

JAKE

There are so many questions I have longed to ask you, so many lost opportunities. I keep the letter you have written as if it is a holy relic, and I look out in my mind's eye, at two young figures at the Chinese Temple where it all began. *He studies her face for the first time, when she comes to life during her description of the tower. It is then he falls in love with her.*

Those were still my feelings at Midsummer all those years ago. I thought such feelings could never be eclipsed, but they have intensified over the years, and nothing, least of all the distance I have tried to put between us, has dimmed them.

As the blue heron skims the small lake near the folly, I cry out silently, asking for the strength to withstand this great relief of emotion I feel, and the excitement of what is to come. I try to imagine how I will pass the three days in a state of fevered anticipation.

I scan through in my heart, the great jewels and treasures of my memories of you, our time together and my great happiness in life. The two are inseparable. I feel as bright as the autumn sunshine glinting on the lake and as young as the coming day.

I will find peace again.

CHAPTER TWENTY-FOUR

It was almost the appointed hour. Rebecca had searched out the boat her uncle had told her about and, surprisingly, after all these years, and despite its age, it had been re-painted and lovingly restored. She severed the tether and rowed to the other side of the lake. In the moonlight, the great house came into view across the water, and the miles of undulating land that once belonged to a friend of Lydia's mother are now owned by the National Trust. Everything was immaculate, even the old boathouse she had read about in the letters. As the boat skimmed silently over the blackened reeds glistening in the moonlight, a breeze whipped the black hair from her eyes so she could clearly see the ruins of the tower against the luminescent harvest moon. This, she knew, was Lydia's focus of her childhood, central to her romantic memories and worship of the old gods.

From her rucksack, Rebecca extracted the saw. Its shiny surface glimmering, and capturing a maniac's reflection in the new steel blade. Slow methodical strokes punctured the bough, the splintering wood adding to her elation in the invisible night. So fixated with what she must do, she even overlooked the nick of the blade on her foot as it tore through her canvas shoe. Through the small hole, a murmur of black water gurgled upward, mingling with a pool of blood at the bottom of the boat. Quickly, covering the evidence with a bucket, she withdrew to watch the drama unfold from her pre-chosen vantage point, a clump of willows between the lake and the tower. From here Rebecca knew she would see her plans unfold and the slow, cold end to a life. She had meticulously planned to put an end to the romance, to the love she could not comprehend. Unhinged by Megan's shy whispers, she relished the thought of both lovers watching Lydia's slow death, as she rowed across the lake to reach them. *She will never see their faces again, despite being so close for the first time in years.* And they will be powerless to help as the reeds drag her lifeless body down into the mud and slime of the lake bottom.

While Rebecca was putting the finishing touches to her plan, Niall was nearing their rendezvous. With every twist of the road, his memory was sparked by those brief honeyed days in Norfolk. He fleetingly thought of Belinda left behind at Falklands as the narrow lanes came back to him with loving familiarity, even after all the years in between. Now that his heart was about to be united with his soul, he knew could never return to that loveless house for which he had sacrificed so much.

He tried to imagine Lydia aged but the image wouldn't come and the realisation struck him – too late – that her beauty didn't matter. Once he had explained, and sought her forgiveness for all the wasted years, they could live out their lives like young lovers. He would put everything right. She would see that he had aged a lifetime without his life-light? Nothing mattered to him now but the grace of love. It was timeless as was her wisdom in the Old Ways, which now came back to haunt him in the form of the great stag he shot at Loch Ranoch nearly fifty years ago. He recalled Lydia's words of warning about the sacrifice that the animal's death would surely bring on them.

It was dark but the moon shone on the water, making everything appear serene and peaceful. His years of stalking had honed his senses to a razor-sharpness and he caught the sound of twigs breaking underfoot. Scrambling through the wet grass, trying to see through the darkness, his vision was suddenly obscured by swift moving clouds covering the moon. The darkness was impenetrable, and even the reflection on the water was lost for a moment.

LYDIA

The dew on the grass pulls my cloak heavier with each step as I approach the lake. The air is thick with memories. It has been so long, yet nothing has changed and I feel as though I am a young girl again. The wild folk, the spirits in the trees are watching and their power is nothing if not stronger. *The magic has not faded.*

The outline of the ruined tower pinpoints the lost village, and adjusting my eyes as the darkness falls, I can hear the ghosts of the villagers gathering, chattering excitedly. They are here to witness my homecoming and also something more. I crane to hear their words but the more I strain to catch them, their meaning dissolves on the wind disturbing the willow's branches.

The boathouse is illuminated under the moon when it appears again from the cloud and with amazement I notice that it still shelters the boat that was always here. Now its purpose seems clear, to ferry me to my fate on the other side of the lake where the tower stands. Its ruined shape is monstrously elongated on the water's surface now the moon is released from the clouds. I sense the silence of even the ghosts and the wild folk, and realise that never before has the moment seemed so charged with significance. It is as if my life has come full circle to this point, and every moment I have lived has bought me to this place.

At first I think nothing of the ropes still being wet as I untie the stern. I am aware of the willow's eyes that are watching as I try to steady the boat with one hand so that I might climb in. As ever the water spirits lure me seductively into the water with their treacherous song and I remember the depth of the lake. I concentrate on blotting out their presence, and ask the sylphs dancing above the water to blow me over the freezing surface quickly. In the silence, when nothing answers, a movement suddenly catches my gaze.

A magnificent hare has come to stand on his hind legs at my feet, still rooted on the dry land. His body extends to the whole height of the boat. Although I feel that my destiny is pinned to this journey, I instinctively take my hand off the side of the boat as if it were scorched. *What is it my beauty?* An old memory of an unheeded reminder in the Nut Ride comes sharply to mind. And by the grave sadness in the hare's eyes, I understand. To ignore the call of nature is to abrogate my being. There is method in this madness. He has come to warn me of great danger, and I shiver in the realisation that some evil has been here to this beloved place.

I am still determined, however, and sure that the ghosts of ancient lovers will let me have my one moment. I invite them to escort me safely to their wedding tower, where the thousands of ceremonies, weddings, christenings and burials were celebrated. The listening trees and I are one, and they cloak me in invisibility as I make my way around the water's edge to the majestic remains of the tower.

Towards to my great purpose.

CHAPTER TWENTY-FIVE

Niall shakes like a young boy as he fondles the assignation note. Something catches his imagination as he thinks of his approach to her in the tower. With the romance of a young lover, his thoughts give shape to a plan. She will watch him come to her across the lake. He feels a sickness in the pit of his stomach at the closeness of her after all this time and hopes his journey to her will remind her of the New Year's Day when they sailed aimlessly and in love around the lake, just weeks before they were due to be married.

A little stiffly, he casts off in the little boat which is propelled onto the water by his enthusiasm for the adventure. The chill of the night air adds to his exhilaration.

The willow's gasp is too late. Rebecca cannot reveal herself and risk being found out so she remains hidden, trapped amongst the trees as the horror registers that she is about to witness his death. Niall has rowed out to the deepest part of the lake, and it is all too late to do anything to stop him, she realises with a moan. Watching the story unfold, she is powerless to change her malicious plan.

With a smile breaking into the blissful laughter, Niall can just make out Lydia's form up there on the windy battlements, waiting for him. He can see her long tresses being caught by the wind, the way they always used to be. She is dressed in white beneath the moon, his beautiful bride. Even from that distance, the fabric seems as light as gossamer, revealing the dark outline of Lydia's body. He had forgotten the great power she emits, but now it all comes back to him until she grows in stature like a medieval enchantress, willing him to come closer as she cups her hands up to the moon. Even the soft breeze blows him in the right direction, to his fate.

Niall has been so captivated by this vision of her, that he is oblivious to the water filling the boat. When it reaches the deepest part of the lake, when he is furthest from the land, the water overwhelms the boat. It tips him back into the icy depths, until he can feel nothing of his legs in the cold. Struggling to the surface, he tries to swim but the water is too cold and his breath will not come, his legs are entwined in the reeds below that have him like a vice.

When he feels the hand of death caress his heart, it is as if he has fallen back and landed in the dream. He and his young bride are drifting, aimlessly on the lake, letting love steer their boat as they lie in raptures with the sky above them. It is New Year. They have everything ahead of them. He closes his hand on hers. She will soon be his wife.

LYDIA

I hear the waters swirl beneath me, but the cloud has obscured the moon again and it makes me shudder. The lake seems so black now, and so treacherous that the thought of the boat fills me with horror. I wonder if the old coven has been here to settle old scores. Something is amiss, and I know this from the silence of the spirits that gather below in the remains of the chapel. I wonder if he will come. I am reminded that the tide of Lammas always brings with it some kind of sacrifice. The moon is still behind the cloud, and I can see nothing below.

When it appears again, it is honeyed with the thinnest of gossamer clouds skimming the surface. I shiver in my thin dress as the autumn breeze brushes my hair. Age seems to bring with it a greater sense of the wonderment at each tide and now, this harvest has more meaning to it than ever.

Although the gods can be cruel, and they have been, I feel that they must grant me this last wish. He will surely come. For if he does not, my heart will break. I listen with my whole being for my lover's approach through the ruined church below. For an age there has been nothing but the call of the wind circling the tower. I had determined, like a gambler, to rest everything on this night, sick of four decades of impasse. I know with dreaded certainty, that if he doesn't come, my faith in the mystical power of love, in the memories of my life would be shattered.

Now the shadows of the dead are everywhere, they have come to line the ruined village to watch. The immense stillness is suffocating as I stand in the battlements, poised for this final skirmish, my crusade of the heart. When I have nearly given up all hope, I hear something in the wind. He calls out for me from below as the tears of joy course down my weathered cheeks, and in my mind I see the two young lovers embrace in the grass below at Midsummer.

I hear you Jake, race up what is left of the turret steps. Your shirt and hair are wet, from the rain that has come. It outlines your body well, and you still seem as strong as I remember. When you finally reach the top step, you come over to me as I stand on the battlements of the flint. You have found me again as real lovers do.

The moon pales into the sky as you sweep me off the ground and we meet in a thousand kisses, sanctioning all the years of sorrow and pain. I am made young and beautiful by your great love, if only for this moment.

Through my tears I can see that the white stallion has come for me. He stands proudly in the wind, his withers quiver with impatience. His hooves stamp the earth sending an echo which resounds upwards through the tower to my feet. He is pure white and fearless, as I had always imagined he would be, to carry me home. He is here to carry me to the Summerlands, beyond the wild seas to the castle I have dreamed of, but never visited. I realise with painful irony that this may be the sacrifice that has to be given, my life. How cruel the gods could be at this moment.

I look at you and hang on for dear life, desperate not to let go, for I am not ready. I choose to remain here and close my eyes to erase the horse's image. You whisper to me, calling me by the old names you had for me. You tell me that we have years ahead of us still and I feel as if I can hear the bells of the lost church in the ringing on the wind.

When I dare to open my eyes, the stallion has gone, it is not my time. And when the screech of the barn owl resonates across the lake I understand, that it is not our sacrifice to make this time.

Lammastide

209

Lammastide

210

Lammastide

Fiction and Humour from ignotus press

Whittlewood
Suzanne Ruthven

The Wild Horseman
Harri Slaymaker

Coarse Witchcraft 1
Craft Working

Coarse Witchcraft 2
Carry On Crafting
Rupert & Gabrielle Percy

See the website for full details of all our titles or send SAE for a current catalogue to ignotus press, BCM-Writer, London WC1N 3XX

www.ignotuspress.com

MOONRAKER